Plane Death

Plane Death

Anne M. Dooley

NeWest Press

Edmonton

Canadian Cataloguing in Publication Data

Dooley, Anne M. (Anne Moore), 1937-
  Plane Death

  ISBN 0-896300-14-6

  I. Title.
PS8557.O64P62 1996   C813'.54   C96-910476-6
PR9199.3.D5565P62 1996

Editor for the Press: Diane Bessai
Editorial Coordinator: Eva Radford
Cover design: Diane Jensen
Interior design: Bob Young / BOOKENDS DESIGNWORKS

NeWest Press gratefully acknowledges the support received for
its publishing program from The Canada Council's Block Grants
program, The Alberta Foundation for the Arts, and The NeWest
Institute for Western Canadian Studies.

Printed and bound in Canada
by Printcrafters

NeWest Publishers Limited
Suite 310, 10359 - 82 Avenue
Edmonton, Alberta T6E 1Z9

For Peter

ACKNOWLEDGEMENTS

The following friends and kind souls did their utmost
to keep my imagination within bounds and the details accurate:
Deputy Police Chief of Operations Norm Doell of the Saskatoon
Police Service; Clyde Johnson, Transportation Safety Board of
Canada, Edmonton; James K. Wood, M.D., Saskatoon; and a
working geologist who wishes to remain anonymous. Authors
Suzanne North of Saskatoon and Professor Bill Sarjeant, (a.k.a.
Antony Swithin) of the Geological Sciences Department,
University of Saskatchewan, provided helpful suggestions and
welcome encouragement. My editor, Dianne Bessai, provided
wisdom and expertise. Also, thanks to each member of my
family for never (audibly) impuning my sanity when I sat
down to write. My heartfelt thanks to you all.

A.M.D.
Saskatoon
March 12, 1996

1. Sunday Morning, October 10

Out where the lake was deepest a few tendrils of fog hung just above the surface, barely visible in the first cold moments of dawn. A flock of geese cruised slowly past a small brush-covered island. On the shore a solitary magpie picked at the remains of a fish, then spread its wings and took off into the brightening sky with a raucous call. It flew first over the water and then over the rising sea of spruce and pine, as if surveying its domain. It ignored an unoccupied log cabin nestled into the trees and continued along the water's edge until it finally fluttered down to perch proprietorily at the top of a tall white spruce on the edge of a little clearing.

Beneath the tree stood a large and comfortable grey-stained cabin that blended almost invisibly with the surrounding forest. The big windows that rimmed the wooden deck were securely shuttered, but the door stood open. In the growing brightness the man inside checked two more items off his list: water lines—drain; generator—off. They were the last major jobs. Now, his coffee pot and a blue enamel cup were the only things left to tidy up. With the shirt-tail of his red plaid flannel shirt wrapped around the handle, he took the pot from the small butane burner and poured the last of the contents into his cup. Always a neat man, Walter carefully tucked his shirt back into his trousers before taking apart the burner and stowing it into the duffel bag that lay next to the door. He looked around satisfied that everything that needed doing to close up for the winter had been done. The drive back to the city would take six hours, maybe longer, but there was time enough to sit and enjoy his coffee.

With cane in one hand and over-full mug in the other, he limped onto the porch. Awkwardly, he went halfway down the steps, his cup in his right hand held wide against spills, his cane in his left to take his weight, and carefully lowered himself with a grunt and a thud. The morning air was fresh and cold and he wrapped both hands around the hot cup to warm them. The sharp, crisp odor of pine combined with the smell of strong, black coffee to produce a heady aroma. He closed his eyes and sniffed with pleasure. From high in the spruce the magpie scolded. He saw it up there, black and white, bold and sassy. With wings assisting, it balanced precariously on the end of a slender branch which bowed from the weight and swayed in the light breeze. Walter thought it was probably laying claim to the property for the winter, telling him to hurry up and leave.

While he sipped from his steaming cup, he surveyed the orderly clearing. Tarp-covered logs lay neatly stacked between two trees; his rowboat lay inverted across two logs. A narrow path snaked through the woods and down to the water, and from the path a track led to his parked and loaded van. He looked down the path to the lake which was deathly still and grey. And that, he thought, was not a good sign. The weather was going to change for the worse. He looked up. Sure enough, the clouds were thickening and turning darker. It would probably rain, and it might even snow. It was a good thing he had decided to get moving early. The few little tracks that passed for roads up here on the Canadian Shield would not take much moisture before they turned to a thick grey slurry.

His cup was almost empty when the magpie gave a final strident call and swooped from the treetop almost to the ground before soaring up and over the cabin roof in a skillful display of flight and feathers. In the relative silence that followed he became aware of a faint new noise. It was a peculiar, mechanical kind of sound that grew louder.

Chain saw? Someone logging? They better not be cutting on his land! He cocked his head and strained to hear but the sound seemed to have stopped. He sipped and continued to listen. When he heard it again it was more distinct. Outboard? He searched the water for signs of disturbance, did not see any, and decided it did not really sound like an outboard anyway. Whatever it was, it got louder. It sounded laboured, began cutting in and out, and then all was still. The last of his coffee spilled as he struggled to his feet and stood straining to hear. The crackling and snapping that came next raised the hair on his scalp and sent a shiver through him. He felt almost more than he heard the *whump* that followed. In that instant, if his old brain was not playing tricks on him, he knew exactly what he had heard.

With all the speed he could muster he hurried into the cabin, grabbed the empty coffee pot and tossed it and his cup, unwashed, into the canvas bag. With a worried frown, he slammed the door and hobbled down the steps and along the path, dragging the bag behind him.

The road was dusty and rutted, merely a cut through the trees. He drove as rapidly as he dared, hunched over the steering wheel in a futile attempt to spot and avoid the worst of the potholes. Any speed at all caused the bottom of the van to scrape the uneven surface. It was slow going when what he needed was speed. He had to find a phone. The closest one he could think of was at the gas station about ten or so miles south as the crow flies, but he was not a crow and by road it was twice the distance.

Who should he call? RCMP? Probably. They could handle it or relay the message. Or would they? It was a small detachment and if they were out patrolling this sparsely settled region of northern Saskatchewan there might be no one in the office. So, who else could he call? An airport, yes, but which one? Who should he ask for? Of course, he could always call Flannigan's Flying Service in Saskatoon and ask for Elie. The advantage of that was that she would not think he had lost his mind. What he was going to say was going to sound pretty crazy. But, if she was flying? Anyway, he reminded himself, this was the Thanksgiving weekend and she was probably with her family. He would not disturb her unless he had to. Family was important to her. No. He would try the RCMP.

It began to rain, a steady rain that reduced visibility and quickly formed puddles in all the low spots. He strained to see between the slaps of the wipers while the van splashed along. Finally he reached a crossroad and pulled into the sodden forecourt of the filling station, bypassed the pumps, and parked as close as he could to the phone booth that stood at the corner of the white, shingle-covered building. He opened the car door and with the help of his cane and the frame of the door he levered himself to his feet.

It was only two steps, but they were two steps through a puddle, two steps through driving rain, to the phone. He stood, soggy footed and damp shirted and, with his hands feeling empty pockets, he realized that he had no change. With a sigh he stepped back into the rain, and through the puddle, on his way to the office. A bell on a spring tinkled as he opened the door.

"Help'ya any? Looks like it's goin' to last awhile, don't it?" The voice came from behind the cash register.

"It does at that. Look, I need to use the phone and. . . ."

"Phone's outside beside the building." The man slowly rose and leaned against the counter.

"Yes, I know that." Walter painfully shifted his weight which caused his shoes to make sucking sounds. "Can you change a five?" He fished his wallet out of his rear pocket and took out a bill.

The man squinted at him. "Ya going' to buy somethin'?"

He glanced at the half-empty shelves displaying dusty cans and bags of chips and said, "I can stand to top up the tank. I'll pull up to the pumps after I call."

"That your van beside the phone? You'll have to pull up to the pumps. Hose ain't that long." He grinned hugely at his little joke.

Walter realized that appealing for speed would likely require a lengthy explanation for which he had neither the time nor the patience. He had to get help. In uncharacteristic meekness he stepped back outside into the rain. He positioned his car in front of the pumps, unlocked the tank cover, and returned to the office wetter than ever. Impatiently he watched the man take a black raincoat off a hook, put it on, and button every button. The man added a big-brimmed hat and stuffed his feet into black rubber boots before going out to brave the elements and pump a little gas.

When the transaction was finally complete, Walter returned to the phone. The RCMP officer he talked to sounded as if he wanted to be helpful but he could not seem to understand. He politely suggested the twenty-minute trip to the detachment office so an explanation could be made with the aid of a map. He gave directions.

The road the officer directed him to take was narrow but hard surfaced, a veritable highway compared to the other. Walter pulled onto it with the van's heater blowing full blast. His plaid flannel shirt was soaked and he was chilled to the bone. He sneezed. This was taking too long. He knew what he had heard. He was sure about it. Someone, maybe more than one someone, was in big trouble and time was important. If help arrived soon enough there might be a chance. He had seen it happen. He knew first hand it could happen. He and his shattered leg had been pulled from a Lancaster turret that had barely made it back. He had seen a Spitfire pilot pulled from a flaming cockpit. But help had to be there. He drove on through the rain in a black and anxious mood.

At last he turned onto the gravel in front of the Hacker Lake RCMP Detachment. As he maneuvered himself out of the van he decided that, as buildings went, this one was a pretty poor excuse. It was a prefab wooden construction and ugly as sin. Given the same materials, Walter, a retired architect, knew he could have done a better job. He hobbled through the wet, up the wooden stairs, and opened the door.

The constable was young and like all policemen everywhere he greeted his visitor with a certain wary scepticism. In spite of that, he did make an effort, for which Walter was grateful. A cup of scalding, brackish coffee was provided to warm him up, and his wet shirt was hung steaming on the back of a chair near the space heater.

The officer listened and wrote, asking the occasional question, while the old man described what he had heard. It had been a single-engine aircraft with engine trouble, and it had crashed into the woods. He was absolutely certain that was what he had heard. The officer wanted to know how he could be so sure. Walter testily replied that it was because he had served in the RCAF in the Second World War. He had heard such sounds before. When the constable heard that, he stopped writing and gave his visitor a hard look.

Walter pointed out the location of his cabin on the wall map and gave the time he had heard the crash. His finger traced a circle around what he thought was the approximate location of the accident site. The officer took it all down, slowly writing until the report form was filled. Only then, with a smile only slightly too broad, did he say he would look into the matter. He returned the shirt, warm but still damp, and wished Walter a safe journey home.

2. Late Afternoon, Sunday, October 10

She did not have to strain to hear it because it was a muscle-bound, look out, ready-or-not-here-I-come kind of sound. But it had been rumbling and flashing now for quite a while and the ground was still dry. Lovely theatrics, thought Elie, now just get on with it and rain! The flashes came intermittently, almost nervously, like a fluorescent ceiling fixture on the fritz. They came from cumulonimbus imbedded in the grey stratus overcast, enormous, nasty, anvil-shaped thunderclouds that rose well above the path of airliners. The kind of cloud that turns seasoned pilots into white-knuckle flyers. Mother nature was in a snit.

Elie Meade, rubber-gloved hands covered in hot suds, scrubbed the gunk from the bottom of the ham pan while she watched the display. It certainly was not normal Saskatchewan weather on that mid-October Thanksgiving weekend. But it fit right in there with the cold, windy, miserable excuse for a summer they had endured. Carried by a sudden gust of wind, the first few rain drops smacked against the window. They had celebrated Thanksgiving with a Sunday afternoon dinner instead of on the more traditional Monday. Sons Brad and Grant had brought their girlfriends, and dinner went off without a hitch. She was pleased about that. Even her husband Don, subdued, tense, and preoccupied for weeks, relaxed and enjoyed himself. It had been a good day.

But now the way the weather was brewing up she was glad that the family had dispersed early. The boys had gone back to their apartment—to study, they said—and Don had caught a flight to attend a ten-day conference in California. He was told, almost ordered, to represent his company, even though the company was only picking up part of the cost. With two kids still in university they could not afford the added expense. On the other hand, they had to afford it. His company had downsized, a word Elie hated, and was considering even more cuts. Morale was down, remaining staff was working ten-hour days, and like everyone else Don was running scared. She worried about it and about him. It was impossible not to.

She set the pan in the drainer, brushed a strand of chestnut hair off her forehead with the back of a wet glove and began to scrub out the sink. Don's job was not the only thing troubling her. After dinner she had been in the kitchen packing up the leftover ham and apple pie for the boys to take with them when Brad asked, "Mom, do you happen to remember what I did with my rocks?"

The items in question were the result of a young life-time of compulsive rock collecting. While some kids were attracted to bugs, snakes, or stray dogs, Brad had always filled his pockets with stones. When he was just five he had offered one of his rocky treasures as a Mother's Day gift, carefully pointed out the pretty colours, anxiously watched her face to see if she liked it, was so pleased when she did. It was still on a bookshelf in the living room, still had MOM in wiggly red tempera paint letters on the bottom. At one time or another everyone in the family received gift-wrapped stones for a birthday or Christmas. Brad's geological acquisitions became a family joke.

"You took the ones you wanted and I put the others in the garden. When everything was in bloom they looked really nice around the plants. Do you need more to keep those mounds of paper from sliding off your desk?"

"No, some of mine just went missing, that's all."

"In your room, how can you tell?"

"I'm glad you're finally telling your mom about it, Brad." The comment had come from his girlfriend, Samantha.

"Tell me what?"

"Promise you won't get excited, okay?"

"What a marvellous beginning. Should I sit down first?"

"See, a while ago we had a little break-in." Her sons shared a two-bedroom apartment in a slightly run down building several blocks from the university.

Grant spoke up. "Nothing to worry about, Mom. It was a month ago and the weird thing is that only Brad's rocks went missing."

A break-in? Nothing to worry about? It made no difference to her that only rocks had been taken. Her boys' small place in the world had been violated, their safety challenged. Just thinking about it sent a prickle up her spine. Perhaps they should still be living at home, a common enough arrangement for university students. Family finances had forced Sean and Liz, the two oldest Meade children, to do that. Elie still felt bad about the necessity, too. Learning self-management, self-discipline, and how to budget was to Elie as necessary a part of attending university as listening to lectures. When she was their age she could have used such weaning. Instead she had found herself suddenly hurled into adulthood to fend for herself. Still it was possible that the apartment, intended as a recognition and encouragement of their growing independence, had been a mistake. She hoped not.

"Did you tell the police?"

"Yep. We were good little citizens but they didn't seem very interested."

Motherly prodding had produced protestations and assurances but no more information, and Grant, Sarah, Brad, and Sammy rode off on their bikes, armed against starvation and burglars with leftover ham and the remainder of the pie. Hardly suitable weapons for protection unless, of course, a burglar could be felled by a ham bone or

PLANE DEATH 9

downed by flying pastry.

She finished wiping the counter of the big, old, friendly kitchen and retreated into the family room to kick off her shoes and collapse into the soft, flowered cushions of the couch. She zapped the TV to life, turning up the volume to compete with the rain which gusts of wind hurled against the picture window. Moving along the bottom of the screen was a weather warning for severe thunderstorms with the possibility of heavy rain, large hail, intense lightning, and dangerous winds. Terrific. She got up to check the house.

It had grown quite dark and she switched on lights as she moved barefoot towards the oak staircase. She padded along the upstairs hall and in and out of rooms. In the master bedroom she found the window open a crack and a puddle on the sill. With the window closed and the water mopped, she paused long enough to watch the long drooping branches of the weeping birch in the front yard whip around in the wind. A brilliant flash of lightning showed water overflowing onto the sidewalk with rain that fell too hard for the storm drains to handle. It was the kind of night for building a fire and snuggling up with Don, not rattling around the house all alone.

Back downstairs she made the rounds, checking that the doors were locked and the alarms set. She poured herself a glass of the leftover wine and returned to the couch where she toasted Angela Lansbury, as Jessica Fletcher began to unravel another tangled skein of deceit and murder. Too bad Fletcher did not make house calls to solve cases of rock theft.

A streak of lightning and a nearly simultaneous boom of thunder made her jump. Instantly, the TV picture disappeared and the lights flickered and dimmed. Then she was sitting in the dark hearing the violence of the storm as the rain pelted the house and gurgled rapidly down the drainpipes. Outside everything was isolating black. It was so dark that she thought the whole city could be affected. It was definitely not a night to be caught outside. She hoped the kids were warm and dry. She got up and felt her way to a built-in cabinet, opened a drawer, and gingerly felt around for the flashlight that she knew—well she was almost sure—was in there.

In a red brick, four-storey apartment building near the university, thirty-four assorted CD players, tape decks, radios, and TVs simultaneously lapsed into silence in thirty-four small apartments. In one of them Grant called out, "Brad, where's the flashlight?"

"It's here somewhere . . . just a second, I'll find it. . . ."

Sounds of vigorous rummaging came from Brad's bedroom and a moment later a ring of light slid around their living room walls. "Where are you?"

"In the kitchen. I was making a sandwich when the lights went out. Damn near cut off my finger." From the doorway of the tiny kitchen Brad swung the beam onto his older brother who stood at the sink running cold water over his hand.

"I sure hope you didn't bleed on the ham. . . . Here, let's have a look. Oh, yes . . . a candidate for transfusion."

"Very funny, mouse brain. Give me the light so I can go find a bandage."

When first aid was complete, they sat opposite each other at their dinette table and ate sandwiches and apple pie. The flashlight lying between them cast elliptical shapes on the wall.

Between bites, Brad said, "Looks like this whole area of the city is dark. You think we'll get power anytime soon?"

"How do I know? I just wish we had some candles. One flashlight doesn't help much."

"We can always make scary shadows on the wall and

tell ghost stories. WOOOOoooo. . . ."

"Droll. Very droll. When are you going to grow up?"

"Do I have to? Tell me, oh great and wise old bro', how come you're so grumpy?"

"Because," said Grant, "this weekend was the only time I had to work on that midterm paper for the Wart. I was just about done. With my luck, when the power went, the computer ate it."

"Not if you saved along the way."

"Yeah, well, I think I did but I know the last couple of pages are gone for sure. It's due in on Wednesday and old Wart-head docks fifty percent for late papers. I've got to get it done. I think I'll go to bed now and get up early."

"Sounds reasonable. Me too. How about I set the alarm for six?"

"Brad, the clock's electric."

Elie had assembled every candle in the house, stubs included. They flamed and flickered merrily in the family room, creating deep, dancing shadows in the corners. Outside the downpour continued; inside the sharp odor of ozone permeated the air.

The weekend had been so hectic that she still had not read Saturday's paper. She pulled it off the coffee table and, holding it up to catch the flickering glow, skimmed the front page. Furious home owners had confronted city council over a rezoning decision. The city was cutting back on services but property taxes were going up anyway. Goodness gracious, what a surprise.

Near the bottom of the page she saw "Diamond Strike" and read that diamonds, the largest a gem quality stone 0.54 millimetres in size, had been found in till samples taken by Ev-Met Mining from a site in northcentral Saskatchewan. The price of Ev-Met stock was reported to have jumped dramatically.

How big was 0.54 millimetres? She tried to visualize it. Something smaller than a pin head? You would have to find bucketfuls to make it worthwhile. How on earth did they even know where to look? She conjured up the picture of a grizzled old prospector panning for diamonds in a gravel pit. If she remembered, she could ask about it the next day when she flew a charter up north. Her passenger would be Maurice Benoit, who was the chief engineer for a uranium mine, but he would probably know something about diamond mining too. The trip on Thanksgiving was a usual thing for him. Maurice always flew up on holidays. If his men were away from home he would be also. She reflected that it would be nice if Flannigan's new manager was even halfway as thoughtful. If Joe Flannigan knew what was happening to his beloved company, he would come back from the dead.

Joe Flannigan, who was always a meticulous planner, was known to have consulted a lawyer about updating his will not long before his death. The lawyer read the old will which had been languishing in Joe's bank vault for decades. He asked numerous questions, took copious notes, and after Flannigan's death reported that Joe had clearly intended to have a new will drawn up. The problem was that not even the original will could be found. A thorough search of law office, bank vault, and Joe's filing cabinet failed to produce anything but dust. The result was that the court appointed a manager for Flannigan's Flying Service until the will was found or the matter could be sorted out. The appointee was a young man not long out of an MBA program. Nobody had expected another Joe Flannigan, but they certainly had not expected someone like James Campbell either.

On his first day Campbell marched into Joe's old office, took down Flannigan's original, sunfaded, forty-five-year-old, four-by-six-foot framed logo that had occupied the place of honour on the wall behind Joe's desk, and hung his MBA diploma on the nail. To the staff the removal of the prized symbol had seemed almost a death in itself. John Gardner, the chief mechanic, requested permission to hang the logo in his office. The request was denied and tensions increased.

After that episode nothing much had happened for the next few days and everybody let out a sigh of relief. Collective wisdom said to let Campbell hole up in his office and draw his pay. The staff did not care. They would look after Flannigan's for Joe. Business continued as usual. Company policy was followed as always and everybody had been confident that they could handle whatever came along. Besides, Joe, the great planner, had included a variety of contingency plans in the company operations manual. Everything had run smoothly, everyone had done their jobs, and, except for missing Joe, everyone had been relatively happy. Until the end of the first week.

That was when a series of notices appeared on the bulletin board in the staff room. One stated in part: "I am quite prepared to make the necessary tough decisions to improve the bottom line." A chill ran through the hangar, and later the same day five people—two pilots, two mechanics, and the night dispatcher—found pink slips in their message boxes. Morale instantly went up in smoke.

Another notice started with "henceforth" and set about to change fees. Within days this caused the flying school to lose some students and several charter contracts were cancelled. With fewer engineers, aircraft maintenance backed up. This, along with the fact that there were fewer pilots, played havoc with flight scheduling. When the notice labeled "Mission Statement" went up, nobody had the heart even to read the thing. Now, nobody was happy, everyone was under pressure, and nobody knew what to do about it.

Elie shook her head and focused on the window which still streamed with water. She yawned and looked at her watch. It was ten-thirty. She gave up, blew out the candles, and went to bed.

Grant lay on his back in his small, dark bedroom listening to the rain and the hiss of tires on wet pavement from the occasional passing car. Under the circumstances going to bed early made sense, but logic had nothing to do with actually falling asleep. He rolled over on his side, pulled the covers over his shoulder, and finally began to drift off.

Not quite asleep he became aware of mouse-like noises and wondered vaguely if they had remembered to put the ham back in the fridge. He came more fully awake and wondered if Brad was stirring around in his bedroom. Suddenly he heard two small, sharp knocks on the wall separating their rooms and he reached out and rapped once in return. Whatever he thought he heard, Brad heard it too.

Quietly he turned back the covers and got out of bed. He reached his bedroom door without stubbing his toes and met his brother coming out of his room holding the flashlight like a club.

Without a sound they moved across the cramped space of the living room to the door and listened. They heard metal on metal. Someone was messing with the lock. Brad moved a step to the side while Grant positioned one hand on the deadbolt and the other on the door knob and whispered, "now."

In the instant that the door flew open, Brad was through the opening, swinging the flashlight at something that moved in the dark. He connected with a hard glancing blow and heard footsteps running towards the stairwell. He regained his balance and followed but heard feet hit the landing and hurry down the last flight. He was too late. Anyway, even in the dark, he certainly could not go any further as he was. He retraced his steps to find his brother examining the door with the aid of a match. A key protruded from the lock.

They heard doors open down the hall and voices wondering what was happening. Leaving the key where it was, they scuttled inside and closed the door. Brad waved the flashlight around and said, "Grant, I think we should take that key out."

"I tried. It's stuck. We'll need pliers or something. Did you see who it was?"

"Not a chance. Think we should call the cops?"

"Remember what happened when we called them before. It took hours for them to turn up. When they did they spent all of ten minutes asking questions and looking at us like we were lab specimens. I say we forget it."

Someone knocked loudly and a voice called out, "Police!" Grant yelled, "Just a second!", and both boys dove for their bedrooms. Moments later they answered the door. Now they stood in the middle of the black hole of their living room in hastily-donned bathrobes facing two plain-clothes policemen. They had not called the police but the police were there anyway. It did not make sense. The only positive thing about the situation was that now there were three flashlights.

The older man introduced himself as Sergeant Griffeth and said, "I wish you hadn't touched that key, son." His glance at Grant clearly condemned him for lousing up a police investigation.

Grant, tall and dark with a runner's well-toned leanness, asked, "How did you know about this? We didn't call."

"You didn't call this in?"

"We'd just closed the door when you started banging on it. We didn't have time."

"Then why did it take you so long to answer?"

Brad, shorter than his brother and more solidly built, brushed a hand through his unruly chestnut hair. "That was because anybody can say they're police. After what happened we weren't sure." That was a lie. The truth was that both boys had been buck naked and it is not easy to find clothing in a pitch-black apartment.

"If you didn't call this in I want to know who did. It was supposed to be a robbery in progress. Constable, when you finish with that door find out who reported this."

The younger officer nodded, then gave a grunt of satisfaction as he finally wiggled the key free of the lock. He placed it into a small paper bag, marked and sealed it, and stuffed it into his raincoat pocket. After closing the door he spoke to the dispatcher on his hand-held and, while waiting for a response, picked up the thread of Griffeth's questioning.

"You're Brad, right? You say you can't identify the person because of the dark, but you think you struck him with your flashlight. Any idea where?"

"I got him a pretty good one . . . upper body somewhere, I think."

The sergeant wrote in his notebook. "And, you say you reported a previous break-in in September when a rock collection was stolen. Tell me about that. What was the value?"

Brad shifted uncomfortably. "Well, you see, it wasn't exactly a rock collection. I mean it was, but. . . . It wasn't what you normally would think of as. . . ." The sergeant pursed his lips.

Grant tried to help his younger brother explain. "What he means is that it was a rock collection—sort of. He's collected rocks since he was real little. He, well, he just likes rocks." It sounded lame. He tried a smile to smooth things over and wished he had just kept his mouth shut.

The sergeant remained silent with his pen still poised

over his notepad and his eyes on the boys. His partner, radio to his ear, did not even try to hide a grin.

"Let me understand this, boys. It wasn't a rock collection. It was more like a collection of rocks. That right?"

"Yes, sir. I suppose that's it?"

"Why did you bother to report it?"

Brad felt himself becoming defensive. "Because the landlord wouldn't fix the door unless we did. I guess he couldn't collect on the insurance or something. Anyway, I thought people were supposed to tell the police when someone breaks into their home. The door jamb was splintered, the lock was broken, the door was damaged, and something was taken. That's robbery isn't it?"

"No, that's B and E. It's just a little difficult for me to believe that someone would break in here in the first place—and take rocks?—let alone try it again."

"Sergeant, believe me, we've tried to figure out who might do it, but it doesn't make any sense to us either."

Momentarily silent, the four of them stood eyeing each other in the small area of light provided by their three flashlights. Finally the sergeant flipped his notebook closed and slipped it into his pocket.

Suddenly, the refrigerator hummed and the lights in the kitchen and living room flickered and then glowed. The four blinked in the sudden brightness and moved about, released from the confines of darkness. With his squawking radio held to his ear, the constable moved through the open doorway into the kitchen. Grant motioned Brad to keep an eye on him while his interest remained with the sergeant. He watched the man make a slow visual circuit of their apartment and tried to see what he was seeing. Books were haphazardly piled on the coffee table, the worn easy chair was at colour odds with the equally worn couch from which a newspaper spilled to the floor. An old kitchen table held a computer. A CD player and tape deck vied for space with a portable TV on top of a crammed shoulder-high bookcase. There were two minuscule bedrooms and a tiny kitchen. Grant suddenly felt protective. Okay, so everything in the place shouted that students lived there. So what? What did he expect? The inventory was almost complete when the man paused to give a second look at the two oil paintings which hung over the couch before plucking his raincoat from the back of the chair and heading for the door.

Griffeth sent the constable ahead into the hall and handed the boys each a card. "Call me if you think of anything else." They both shuffled in embarrassment at the pointed look the sergeant gave their hairy legs and bony feet that protruded from their terrycloth robes. "One other thing, boys, the next time you decide to play cops and robbers, I suggest you put on some clothes first."

Heavy rain muted the light from the street lamps but, even so, every surface looked as shiny as if it were coated in oil. As he stepped outside the apartment door with the collar of his raincoat pulled over his head, Griffeth had the uncomfortable sensation he was walking through a car wash.

When they got to the car, all the windows of the unmarked cruiser were fogged. Constable Stefanyk started the engine, turned the defroster on full blast, and ran the wipers. Helped by the rain that clung and dripped from their coats, the humidity inside the car was high enough to form a rain cloud of its own. Sergeant Griffeth sat in the passenger seat and let Stefanyk deal with it.

Once the windows were clear enough to see and the wipers were slapping furiously, they began to move. Their headlights glared back at them from every rain-slick surface and each falling drop; their tires on the wet pavement sounded like steaks sizzling on a grill. It made Griffeth hungry.

Stefanyk asked, "Do you believe them? I mean, it's

pretty absurd to believe they were robbed for a bunch of rocks, isn't it? And, tonight . . . what was that all about?"

The windshield was fogging again in spite of the defroster's best efforts. Griffeth sighed, wound down his window a few inches, and pulled his coat collar up. It was an inadequate defense against the wet, cold draft. He felt icy water trickle beneath his collar and knew he would have a stiff neck by morning.

"What's your theory?"

"They're university students, aren't they?"

"Meaning?"

"Meaning they're probably covering up damage done during a blast or something. They're all a bunch of spoiled kids."

"Umm?" Griffeth growled. "You can back up that statement, I suppose?"

Stefanyk squirmed a little. Obviously he had said the wrong thing. He had spent the previous three years in Traffic and, for the sake of experience and—he hoped—advancement, he was spending a year rotating through four different units. His current assignment was three months with the Major Crime Unit learning the basic ins and outs of armed robbery and homicide investigation. In his first two weeks he had spent most of his time going through files and writing up reports. He had been more than a little disappointed with the lack of action.

Then, a few days before, because of a plague of flu sweeping the station, he had found himself teamed with Sergeant Griffeth of the prickly disposition and dogged persistence. And what were they doing? Thanks to the flu they were looking at a petty crime that some dodo brain had called in as a robbery in progress and thanks to the rain they were drowning, that was what they were doing. Drowning and probably next up for the flu.

"No, sir, not exactly. What are your thoughts?" The

response was as diplomatic as he could make it. There was nothing to be gained by irritating a superior officer.

Griffeth saw him bite his lip and smiled to himself. "Your experience should take precedence over your prejudices, Carl. The way you talk I'd assume that you had booked every student on campus at least once. Did dispatch give you the name of the person calling this in?"

"No name given. Dispatch listened to the tape but couldn't even tell if it was a man or woman. Said they were calling from a car phone and hung up in a hurry without giving a name. Think it was those kids clowning around?"

The frigid draft was making Griffeth's right ear ache. He rolled his window up again and they drove for several blocks in damp silence.

"Clowning around? No, I don't think so. Their story is so absurd that I think I believe them, and I find that worrying in a way. Why would someone want into that apartment? Why take a bunch of worthless stones? If there isn't something of value worth taking, why go to the trouble? As for tonight? Who knows? That key would never have opened that door. Whoever tried it probably thought the apartment was unoccupied for the holiday weekend."

Stefanyk was having a hard time figuring out why Griffeth seemed to be taking the case so seriously. A box of rocks? Stopped at a red light, he reached into a pocket and pulled out a candy bar. As he peeled the paper and bit off a chunk he felt Griffeth's eyes on him. Talking around a mouthful he said, "Maybe somebody has it in for them. I mean, it's possible, isn't it, that somebody just wants to cause trouble? Or maybe it's a practical joke of some kind, only not very funny."

"Sounds reasonable to me. Look into it tomorrow. Whoever is doing this might get carried away and hurt somebody if he tries it again. Work it in."

"Yes, sir." He did not quite know how to take this. On

the one hand he was being given a case of his own to investigate, on the other he was told to catch a rock thief, something which not only failed to thrill him but seemed downright silly. The most serious sin of all, it seemed to him, was that it could not possibly be considered a Major Crime, however you looked at it. He finished the candy, licked his fingers, and stuffed the shredded wrapper into his pocket.

Griffeth said, "How can you eat that junk?" and shifted in his seat. Just as he had thought, he was stiffening up. His nose tickled and in the nick of time he reached his handkerchief before he sneezed.

"You aren't coming down with this flu, are you, Sergeant?"

"Oh, I doubt it, Carl. I doubt it. If I did my wife would just feed me some foul tasting mixture or other and I'd be back to work in no time. It's probably the threat of her remedies that keeps me healthy."

3. Monday, October 11

At 5:28 A.M. the phone rang on the table beside the queen-size bed. Elie's bare arm snaked from beneath the covers to grab it.

" 'Lo?" It was barely a croak.

The voice of Norm Driscoll, Flannigan's dispatcher, said, "Sorry to wake you, El, but we have an overdue."

Both her eyelids flew open and both feet hit the hardwood floor. She fumbled for the switch on the bedside lamp as she spoke. "Ours? One of ours? Who, Norm, who?"

"No, no, not one of ours. It's some private pilot. The head of the local unit of the Civil Air Search and Rescue Association called. He wants a twin-engine to fly a track crawl at first light. You're a CASARA member, are you willing? It's Thanksgiving Day and you've got that charter this afternoon. It means giving up a free morning. . . ."

She trotted down the hall for a quick wake-up shower. While needles of hot water and apple-scented shampoo washed away the last vestiges of sleep, she reviewed what she had to do. In the case of an overdue aircraft the first vital action was a track crawl. The concept was simple. If weather permitted she would fly at five thousand feet above ground along the path of the missing plane with the spotters searching three miles on either side of the aircraft. They would be looking for the plane or signs of a plane and, with any luck, for a cooperative target, meaning someone alive and capable of assisting the searchers by attracting their attention with something like fire, flares, or a signal mirror. When complete the flight would cover a swath twelve miles wide the length of the track. If nothing was found, the search would widen.

She dressed quickly in Flannigan's neat, green uniform and ran a comb through her damp curls. In minutes she was drinking juice, eating a microwaved scrambled egg and a toasted muffin, and a bare twenty-five minutes after being awakened, she was on her way.

She drove along still-sleeping streets toward the park-verged river, experience guiding her to the fastest early morning route. The metal mesh of Victoria Bridge, a structure that looked like a Meccano project, rumbled beneath her wheels as she crossed it. Downtown buildings, lit at street level by store fronts and street lights, towered over ruler-straight, broad streets she shared with other early risers. Farther along she turned northwest to vie for road space with trucks heading past the airport and out of town.

Even at that hour Norman's cramped dispatch office was already full when she walked in. On the shelf over the U-shaped counter that served as his desk, a scanner with the volume turned low spat out the cryptic messages that only pilots and controllers can properly understand. A fluorescent bulb buzzed and flickered annoyingly overhead. Norm waved a hand by way of welcome and continued talking to Fred Kirk, the local head of the Civil Air Search and Rescue Association. Lars Holmgren, Flannigan's frankly oversized chief flying instructor, leaned against the far wall listening with his arms crossed. Beside him sat the hunched, tense figure of John Gardner, the chief mechanic. John sat, staring into the middle distance, absently kneading a rag smelling vaguely of solvent in his large, calloused hands. Elie nodded a greeting to them both, helped herself to coffee from Norm's pot, perched on the edge of the counter, and yawned.

Norm said, "As far as we're concerned it's a go. If Campbell wants to get sticky about it, that's his problem. He'll be all bent out of shape because he wasn't consulted, but nobody could get hold of him. Anyway, it's better this way because his automatic answer to any question is no. You can set up search operations in the classroom and also use our flight planning facilities. Just make sure you do it in a hurry. If you're already working he'll have to think twice before he starts shouting. Lars is donating his office to the military searchmaster when he gets here later this morning."

Lars pushed his large frame away from the wall. "Understand this, Fred. We're just following Joe's plan of cooperation with an active search and rescue effort. It makes Flannigan's pilots who are CASARA members and any of our unscheduled aircraft available for a search, as well as providing space for your headquarters. We're happy to do it."

"I just don't want you guys on the wrong end of the stick because of this."

"With Campbell we're already there. Let us worry about it." Lars clapped a heavy hand on Fred's shoulder and, before leaving the room, told Elie he wanted to see her.

The phone rang as Touhy James, a CASARA navigator, came in, his arms laden with two large cartons of doughnuts. "Where do you want these?" He was a small man who looked almost as tough as his name sounded and not at all like the competent plastic surgeon he was.

Norm waved his arms. "Listen up, people. That was the CBC looking for info. They've got some absurd story already concocted and they wanted confirmation. I played dumb, but that won't hold them for long. I don't know how the hell they got onto this so fast. Anybody been using a cell phone?"

Touhy said, "I heard a radio news flash when I was in the doughnut shop. It said a small plane crashed and the number of dead isn't known. It's the usual thing: fabricate, complicate, and speculate, speculate, speculate. This is likely to be the only exciting thing to happen on Thanksgiving

Day so it'll get a big play. You're going to have to do a media briefing a.s.a.p., Fred. Kill those rumours before they get any bigger."

"I guess you're right. I'll put something together, but I was kind of hoping that the military would be doing the briefings." The prospect of facing a bunch of reporters filled him with dread.

Norm banged a clipboard on the counter for attention. "Folks, if it's on the news Campbell's sure to hear it as soon as he wakes up. He said he was going to take Thanksgiving off, but this is likely to make him come steaming in any minute. You guys have got to move it."

They streamed down the hangar's central corridor and through the door marked Flight School, leaving Norm to carry out his various dispatch duties by himself. In the large classroom they made short work of arranging tables and chairs and affixing aviation maps with clear plastic overlays to the walls. The coffee pot was plugged in and the doughnuts were put beside the cups. Stacks of maps and various forms were laid out for use by pilots, navigators, and the vital record keepers who would soon arrive. A portable computer and printer found a place in a corner, and three telephone men arrived to string temporary lines.

It was still a good half hour before official sunrise, but the sky was growing light. At 6:50 Elie, Touhy, and four spotters gathered around Fred for a briefing. He stood in front of a map that had a heavy black line drawn from the airport in Saskatoon north to the Downy Lake Lodge airstrip. It was the presumed route that the missing pilot would have followed.

"Okay, everybody, this is what we've got. You're looking for a single-engine Piper, red stripes on white, registration G-Cxxx, one soul on board, a private pilot named Jake Essen. According to the co-owner, the plane should have returned to Saskatoon sometime yesterday morning. The co-owner had a trip planned for Sunday afternoon and was more than a little irritated when he discovered his partner hadn't returned when he'd promised. Anyway, when he still hadn't turned up by the time that storm let loose, he reported the plane overdue.

"Trouble is, the pilot didn't file a flight plan for the return trip and the satellite isn't picking up a signal from an emergency locator transmitter to help pin-point his position. If he crashed somewhere the ELT should have gone off. Every strip and suitable landing area we can think of has been canvassed and there's no sign of him."

"Fred. . . ."

"But, that's only the half of it. His trip on Friday was planned from here direct to the Downy Lake Lodge airstrip." He gestured to the map behind him. "He took off early and closed his flight plan from the air with LaRonge Flight Service at 08:19 local time, but Downy Lake Lodge says that he never landed."

"You're kidding. . . ."

"How do they know. . . ."

"They keep a record of all planes so they can charge a landing fee to anyone who isn't a guest of the lodge. Lord only knows where he got to. He just seems to have disappeared. One scenario has it that something happened before he could land. If that's so then the poor bastard's been down since Friday morning."

Nobody needed reminding of the seriousness of the situation. The only way to find the missing aircraft was to plan the search as carefully as possible. It was tempting to rush to the tarmac, kick the tires, light the fires and go, but all the haste and good will in the world were not, by themselves, going to do anybody a bit of good.

While Touhy drew lines on his maps, Elie went into the hangar to ready the plane. As she started to do the walkaround she heard loud voices coming from the office of the chief mechanic. John's voice roared, "What do you mean it's not done? It's easy enough to check a torque-line shaft. It was on the maintenance schedule for last night. Why wasn't it done?"

"Easy, John." It was Bill's voice, one of the mechanics. "I checked it myself. The shaft spacers had been installed wrong."

"So, put it right."

"Impossible. The damage is done. The shaft could break anytime. It needs a new one, but we haven't any in stock. No supplier is open today, so I'll order one tomorrow when—"

"That's inexcusable. Who did the original work? Who signed it off? Whoever it was is out of a job as of now."

"John, it's not one of our planes and we didn't do the work. The guy flew in yesterday from Vancouver. He reported a bad shimmy in the right main gear on landing and asked us to check it out. I've already told him—"

"Then we'll have to show them how it's done. I don't care how you do it, just get a shaft here today. And, you're on the job till it's fixed, understand?"

Bill exited the office rolling his eyes and whispered as he passed, "Tell him to take a vacation, Elie. He's turned into a regular slave driver."

John, following on Bill's heels, asked, "What did he say?"

She screwed the oil dipstick back on the right engine and said, "He wished us luck on the search, that's all. I meant to ask you earlier, how come you're in today? You should be home with Edna, relaxing and eating turkey."

"Not possible. There were electrical problems on a medevac last night and there's nobody available but me to handle it. My guys deserve some time off and because of Campbell they haven't been getting it. I don't know how long we can keep this up. We're all tired and working way too hard. We're beginning to make mistakes. Just last night Bill. . . ."

She went on with the walkaround while he followed along complaining about the engineer. Whatever he thought, in her opinion and from what she had heard, Bill was not at fault. He had done what he should have done.

"Elie, I'm just plain worried about it."

"Worried about what?"

"The plane you're looking for. Last Thursday morning I got a call from Jake Essen, the missing pilot, asking us to check the elevator control cables because his partner thought they were binding. He wanted the plane for a trip the next morning. I gave him hell for the short notice because that's a hellava job and we're short handed. I got it checked anyway and it's a good thing I did because he was right. The cable was frayed. It could have jammed the controls. We replaced it and most of the assembly, too. Didn't finish till late, but we got it done. I guess what I'm saying is that since we were in such a rush, maybe we overlooked something?"

She paused to study him. Ever since Joe's death he had been working much too hard and, to her eye, had not looked well for some time. At the moment, maybe because he had been yelling, his complexion was red and blotchy, and he was breathing hard. Bill was right, John did need a good rest. But it was not likely that he could be talked into that. Even if he got away he would probably just worry about whether things were being done the way he wanted them done and get no rest at all. The man was so conscientious and meticulous that it was not likely that he would have missed anything. However, the very fact that he was concerned about it was reason enough to keep it in mind.

"And, there's something else you should know. He asked us not to put the rear seats back in. We've got them in the paint room. I got the idea that he was maybe taking something big up to that cabin of his."

"Thanks, that could be important. I'll tell the others. You never know what might help. And, John, try not to worry about that plane. It might be a false alarm. For all we know the pilot could be happily sitting and fishing some place without a clue that anybody is looking for him. It might be the co-owner who got the dates all wrong."

The aircraft was ready for flight and was being towed onto the ramp when Elie stuck her head into the chief flying instructor's small office. "You wanted to talk? I've only got a minute so make it quick."

"Yeah. Come in and close the door." Lars was at his desk, his beefy hands clasped tightly together on the top.

"What's wrong?" She had no doubt that something had happened. He was sitting so rigidly and he usually slouched.

"Heard anything about a sale?"

Elie's eyebrows rose in surprise. "White sale, car sale, what kind of sale are we talking about?"

He visibly relaxed. "You haven't heard anything about Flannigan's being on the market then?"

"You're joking, I hope?"

"Nope. I got a call last night from an old military buddy who's flying for one of the regional airlines. He said the word was out that his company was buying Flannigan's and he wanted to welcome me aboard. I pumped him for information but that's all he'd heard."

"Can Campbell do that? He doesn't have the authority, does he?"

"Damned if I know. One thing is for sure, the regional would only be interested in our scheduled flights and large aircraft. They wouldn't be interested in taking on a flight school or the small charters. The company would have to be broken up. Probably only the pilots who fly the scheds would keep their jobs. There would be lots of us on the unemployment lines including you, me, and the maintenance guys. The fellow who called me is trying to find out more. Keep your ears open, Elie, but don't say anything to anyone, not even to John and Norm. No sense getting everyone even more worked up than they already are. I'll tell you one thing: if this rumour is true, Campbell isn't just going to walk away. I'll see to that."

As the first gentle rays of sun peeked over the horizon to light the undulating underside of the cloud deck with a soft pink glow, Elie led her crew across the tarmac. Before long a small twin-engine aircraft could be seen circling for altitude over the airport. The higher it climbed the more visible it became and the more light the occupants enjoyed. Elie was at the controls and Touhy sat in the co-pilot seat. He carefully arranged his maps while the two spotters on first shift settled themselves as comfortably as possible in their seats and adjusted their headsets. Soon they would be wholly concentrated, their eyes not just moving over the terrain but actually focusing, actually seeing what lay within their search range on the ground below. The overcast diffused the light, eliminating the shadows that, under a clear sky, would have made searching at this early hour more difficult.

As the turn took them over Flannigan's hangar, Elie saw a bright red car hurtle into the staff lot and come to an abrupt halt. A figure got out and ran to the employee's entrance. It was Campbell. They had not taken off a moment too soon.

She leveled off, rolled out on heading, adjusted throttles and RPMs, and trimmed up before punching the intercom switch on the control yoke. "Spotters ready? Visibility range is three miles. Right spotter, that's about the distance to the far bank of the river. Left spotter, see the north-south grid road where it crosses the highway? That's about three miles. Everybody got the range? Questions? Ready?" Both spotters responded through their headsets and the search commenced.

"Driscoll?" Campbell's bellow was punctuated by the staff door slamming behind him and his heels hitting hard down the corridor. At his dispatch counter Norm grimaced and hastily reached for the phone. "Driscoll, what's going on? Why wasn't I informed?"

The dispatcher waved a hand at the slight, almost skinny figure doing its best to fill up his doorway and spoke into the dial tone of the receiver he held to his ear. He was tipped back, looking at the ceiling and the blinking, buzzing fluorescent light.

"Right, right . . . yessir. Just give us a call when you decide. . . . No problem at all, glad to be of service." He replaced the receiver and swiveled around to face the manager. "I wish you wouldn't burst in like that, Mr. Campbell. It's very hard to hear the customer. Incidentally, since your approval is now required for all equipment changes, that bulb needs replacing."

Campbell snapped, "And throw money away? That bulb will be replaced when it burns out, not before. Now, why wasn't I informed about that crash?"

"What crash? Nobody knows if there is a crash. You don't call something a crash unless you know for sure you've got a crash. The guy might not even be missing. It could all be a mistake." He scooted his chair over to his coffee pot and scooted back with a full mug.

"Then why is it on the radio? I'm the one the authorities should have called, not you. Why wasn't I called?"

Norm looked over the top of his glasses. "You don't even know which authorities you're talking about, do you?"

A slender left hand shooed that bit of logic away. "The

news reports say that search headquarters is set up here at Flannigan's. You need my permission for that . . ."

"No we don't. We're following the SAR plan in the operations manual."

". . . and they say Flannigan's is involved in the search. What the hell does that mean?"

"It means one of our twins is up with a CASARA crew looking for it."

"Why, for God's sake? We have nothing to do with this. It wasn't one of ours. It'll give us a bad name. It's an unauthorized use of our equipment and the pilot will not be paid. I want to see him the minute he lands. What's his name?"

"Correction. The use is authorized and the pilot is Eileen Meade, fully qualified and very experienced. And, for your information, the fuel and oil cost is reimbursed and the pilot and all crew fly as volunteers."

"Meade. Of course. I should have guessed."

Norm's patience was at an end. "Mr. Campbell, I don't think you understand. There's a life at stake here. We're trying to find the guy. If he really is in trouble out there he might stand a chance if he's found quick enough."

Campbell's face contorted. He shouted, "You're just trying to undermine my authority, aren't you? You, and a few others around here, didn't want an outsider appointed manager. You wanted the job yourself, didn't you! That's why you continually malign me and why you engineered this fiasco on a holiday when you think I'm not around. You're trying to make me look bad. Well, it won't work!"

A look of disbelief passed across Norm's face. He lowered his voice and spoke just above a whisper. "Nobody is trying to make you look bad. This has always been a good company and a good place to work. We want to keep it that way. You came here without any air carrier experience, but you don't ask for help and you won't take our offers of assistance. We can help you if you let us. We know this business—"

"I don't think so, Mr. Driscoll. You have no management training whatsoever. I know. I have reviewed your file."

Norm stared open-mouthed at Campbell's smug expression, then turned away in disgust and reached for his phone.

Behind his sun glasses Touhy's eyes alternated between landmarks and his map. He kept his pencil point moving along the line on the map to correspond to their path over the ground. As the wind picked up he occasionally requested a small course change to Elie over the intercom, heard over the drone of the engines. Part of his job was to make sure they flew a heading that kept them exactly on the track he had drawn. For accurate spotting it was also important to maintain the exact altitude to keep them a constant distance above ground. Her job as pilot was to make all critical flight decisions and to provide a safe, smooth, stable platform for the spotters. They worked as a team.

The first two spotters were known for their sharp distance vision. Molly and Minerva were sisters in their sixties, CASARA members for years, neither of them pilots. The second team was made up of an electrical contractor named Dennis and a high school senior by the name of Tom. Both Tom and Dennis were private pilots.

They had been in the air approximately two hours and had seen three cars where there should have been none, and reported one fresh highway accident. They also found a splash of orange hung up in a tree that caused their hearts to beat faster as they circled to identify it. It proved to be only a windsock that had escaped from a local airstrip in the storm.

They were close to Downy Lake at the far end of the track and it was time to give the spotters a proper rest. The business of spotting is especially difficult and fatiguing. It is far worse than looking for a contact lens in a deep pile carpet. A spotter in an ordinary aircraft seat must twist about in a cramped space and hold both body and head at an unnatural angle while concentrating on the moving ground for long periods of time. Their eyes must move rapidly and focus continually. The effort produces tense muscles, eye strain, and fatigue. A fatigued, tense, eye-strained spotter is practically worthless. Regular rest periods are a must.

The sky was clearing nicely with spots of milky blue showing through the thinning cloud. They took out coffee and doughnuts and relaxed and chatted while Elie carved large lazy circles in the sky. Dennis, a newlywed, claimed his wife was going to divorce him for missing the first Thanksgiving meal she had ever cooked. Touhy, recently divorced, said Dennis did not know how lucky he was to miss a dry and tasteless bird. Tom said that since they had to miss a turkey dinner, the least Touhy could have done was to get them some fried chicken instead of doughnuts. Touhy said he had tried to bring turkey-flavoured doughnuts, and Minny, fluffing the curls flattened by the headset, asked if he was trying to make them all sick. Molly, with sudden tears in her eyes, said that instead of joking they should all be thinking about the poor man somewhere down there who was not going to have turkey ever again if they did not find him.

Touhy turned, looked over the back of his seat to thrust a stern look and a doughnut at her. "Eat this. It's not like you to fall apart on us. Your blood sugar is probably low. All we can do is the best we can and that, dear heart, is what we are doing. Now, it's musical chairs time again, children. Change spotters. Elie, take it around one more time before we get back on course so these reprobates can get settled." When she rolled out on course they were back to business: searching, always searching.

As soon as James Campbell entered the portion of the building occupied by the flight school, he heard voices. At a trot he headed toward the sound. Lars, at his desk with the phone to his ear, saw him zip by.

The first thing Campbell noticed was that the classroom had been rearranged. Tables were out of place. Groups of people surrounded them, bent over maps. More maps with coloured lines and strange marks all over them were on the walls. Every person in the room, male and female, was dressed in identical flight suits with many zippers and large round crests on their breasts and shoulders. The manager hesitated. He was not sure who these people were. He did not want them around, he wanted to throw them out, but he was afraid they might be military. Ordering them to leave would not be a good idea.

He heard Lars Holmgren's hearty, determined voice behind him, "Good morning, Mr. Campbell, thanks for coming in early to give us your assistance. Someone here I want you to meet." He motioned to Fred.

"Mr. Campbell, this is Fred Kirk, Civil Air Search and Rescue. He's got a media briefing scheduled and he'd like to introduce and thank you for Flannigan's assistance. Wouldn't you, Fred?" Fred looked a little surprised, but he caught on in a hurry.

"Driscoll says the reporters are ready and waiting in the passenger lounge. Time for show and tell, everybody."

Campbell started to protest but Holmgren, towering over him, draped his large arm around his shoulders and steered him down the hall. "You'll do fine. It's a wonderful PR opportunity for you. Here you go. I photocopied the SAR contingency plan from the operations manual for you. It should bring you up to speed. Just read it through and it'll tell you all about what we're doing and the proper terms to use when you tell them how Flannigan's is donating space and making our unscheduled aircraft and pilots available."

"Mr Holmgren! I'm not—"

"Better straighten your tie, Mr Campbell. Incidentally, isn't that a new suit? Very nice."

Fred, his arms full of handouts, trotted ahead of them down the corridor, entered the waiting room, and walked toward the assembled reporters and the whirring, clicking cameras. With a malicious grin Lars shoved Campbell in after him and quickly closed the door.

It was late morning when a waiting TV crew spotted the small white and green twin taxiing onto Flannigan's ramp and moved towards the door to intercept the occupants. They watched while six people, clearly wrung out from their search efforts, clambered stiffly out of the plane. The camera recorded their progress as they entered the hangar, pushed past the human barricade and, outrunning the reporter, dashed for the restrooms. That is the trouble with little airplanes, no toilets.

They then reported to Holmgren's office for debriefing by a member of the military search and rescue team who had set up shop an hour previously. The six searchers were disappointed that they had not found the plane, afraid they might have missed it. There was always the thought that they might have blinked at the wrong time. But each of them was well aware that, however hard they tried, a one hundred percent coverage of an area was an impossibility. It just could not be done. Even seventy-five percent coverage occurred only under optimum conditions. Beyond the window they noticed two single engine high-wings taxi past for the expanded search and hoped one of them would be able to locate the missing plane. Time was so critical.

Even though the CASARA team had not been successful, a thorough debriefing was necessary. Any scrap of information could be important. For that reason, they made individual verbal reports, filled out a special debriefing form, and submitted all the marked up maps and notes for reference. Every bit of it formed part of the search record, which was a legal document. Finding a missing plane is like putting together a jig-saw puzzle without knowing the picture. You never know which piece will be the key.

After going over the flight with the searchmaster, Elie dropped into the Dispatch Office where Norm gleefully recounted the morning run-in with Campbell. ". . . and nobody's seen him since the press conference. It's been downright peaceful."

"How long will that last? I'll bet he's in his office right now concocting previously unknown forms of torture just for little old me."

"Don't be silly, El. He made a pretty little speech and strutted for the cameras. But then, the way Fred set him up, he pretty well had to. Here, before I forget." He handed her a torn scrap of paper. "Campbell won't approve the purchase of any more message pads, the cheap bastard. I took that call for you. Oh, and don't bother checking in with Campbell as requested. You don't have time. Your charter said he'd be here early, in about twenty minutes, so you better go eat lunch."

The message was from Walter Harris. He said he wanted her to call him right away. He always called when he returned from his cabin at Hacker Lake but, in all the years she had known him, he had never called her at work with the request to call him back immediately. While she hastily ate a sandwich she wondered what he could want. There was no time before her flight to find out and she made a mental note to call him that evening, or maybe in the morning.

Maurice Benoit arrived for his flight punctually at 12:30. As he and Elie walked out to the plane he noticed the military search and rescue Twin Otter now parked on the ramp. Bright yellow with a red stripe like a ribbon around it, it was hard to miss. Maurice stood for a minute looking at it, his light blue eyes shining and his snow-white hair ruffled by the breeze. Like just about everyone else in town, he knew about the search for the missing aircraft. During the flight his curiosity spilled over and Elie found herself explaining at length how a search is organized and conducted.

They were flying to the uranium mine Maurice worked for, which was located near the centre of the northern third of the province. As they flew north, the land beneath them changed from rich farm and dairy land laid out almost with the regularity of a checkerboard to irregular fields contoured around copses of bush, or sloughs rimmed by native growth. Then, with an almost shocking suddenness, came dense forest interspersed with hundreds of lakes, rivers, and muskeg that required float planes, boats, or freeze-up to access.

It was while they flew over this largely unspoiled, wild, and terribly beautiful country that Maurice said, "Elie, now it is my turn. Before we took off you asked me about the hunt for diamonds. You have seen in the paper, eh? About the diamonds? Let me tell you. The area we are flying over, down there is one place they are looking for them. They have staked so many millions of hectares it is hard to imagine. But, look at that. It is mostly bog right down there. Can you imagine it? Diamonds down there? So much money to find them. It is a good thing for mining, I think. There will be work for many people. But, I also think, like in the gold rush, many people are going to be very disappointed. But, me, who am I to tell?"

It was getting dark when Elie neared Saskatoon and was cleared for the approach through low scud to land. Taxiing in she realized just how hungry and tired she was. It had been a long day. She wanted to get home, grab something to eat, and fall into bed. But before she could leave she had paperwork to do. When she finally made her way toward the parking lot she peeked into the classroom to find out how the search had gone. She saw Fred and the searchmaster, Captain Bueler, heads together, planning for the following morning, and said a silent, fervent prayer for the missing pilot.

As she walked to her car she saw, outlined by the parking lot lights, what looked to be a large bear rooting through the dumpster that stood against the fence. She grinned. Whatever was Lars doing going through the garbage?

She started the engine, turned on her headlights, and backed out of her stall. When she passed the dumpster there was no sign of anyone nearby. Either she had been seeing things or Lars had stepped back into the shadows. Embarrassed to be seen, perhaps? She shook her head in amusement. But it was just as well that he was out of sight. She was too tired to call to him. She drove on toward home.

4. Tuesday, October 12

"Hey, you two! What were the cops doing at your place again Sunday night? You in some kinda trouble?" The janitor's voice rang up the stairwell as Brad and Grant, hurrying for eight-thirty classes, clattered down the stairs.

"Hey, I'm talk'n to you! Come back here . . . Landlord don't stand for no trouble. You make trouble and you're outa here!" he bellowed after them as they disappeared through the door onto the sidewalk.

"Jeez, he's a loud mouth. In a couple of minutes it'll be all over the building."

"If it isn't already. He's been away since Saturday so somebody had to tell him."

Grant heard rapid footsteps behind them, glanced over his shoulder, and stepped up the pace. At the next corner they joined a small group of students sleepily waiting for the walk light. Across the road the limestone buildings of the University of Saskatchewan looked bleak and cold in the meagre morning light.

"What were the police doing at your place Sunday night?" The husky, slightly out of breath voice belonged to a tall, slender girl behind them. Grant ignored her and the girl tapped him on the shoulder.

"Hey, remember me? Fiona Stewart? Next door? I had to pass your door Sunday night when the power was out so I couldn't help noticing. What happened anyway?"

"Nothing much."

"Come on, cops don't turn up for nothing. What happened?"

"Somebody tried to get in, that's all. Probably just got

the wrong apartment in the dark."

Brad looked quizzically at his brother and nudged him as the light changed.

"Grant. . . ."

"Later. . . ."

Fiona crossed the street and avoided the walks to cut across campus, soaking her runners from the dew-wet leaves and grass. A girl living alone had to be careful, so it was little wonder that she was curious and more than a little concerned about what had happened next door on Sunday night. She did not wonder about it for long, however. She was too anxious to get her supervisor's reaction to the first draft of her master's thesis. She checked her watch and walked faster. The man could get prickly over the least little thing so she did not want to provoke him by being late.

Why he had insisted on seeing this draft was beyond her. It was in very rough form. Probably just to make sure she was on the right track. Maybe to suggest improvements, although she doubted that. She just prayed there would not have to be too many revisions since she wanted to finish in time to get her degree in January. She had a junior geologist position lined up with a mining company beginning in March. It meant experience and a pay cheque every month but the best part was that the company was interested in her thesis topic and field study.

She pulled open the heavy metal door of the geology building, bypassed the elevator, and ran up the stairs to the second floor. Near the end of the hall she knocked on a door. There was no answer, but then she was early. It was only 8:20. To kill time she went back down to the first floor to check for mail. She reached into her mail slot and extracted what was there. It was not much, just two department notices about upcoming lectures. Her eyes kept returning to the hall, checking the faces hurrying by. At 8:35 she returned to the second floor and knocked again on her supervisor's door.

Okay, so he was a little late. She chided herself for her impatience. She had been waiting for almost a week for this meeting. A few more minutes would not matter. She leaned against the wall beside the door expecting to see his compact figure stride jauntily down the hall at any minute.

What would she do if he tried to sidetrack her again? She had told him flat out she was not interested in writing it up as a joint research paper. Why should he get any credit for something she had done? He had been a complete dud as a supervisor, only getting interested—too interested, in fact—in helping her after he saw those rock samples she brought into the lab the previous spring. He demanded to know where they came from and how she obtained them. The intensity of his interrogation was overwhelming and she told him what he wanted to know. Since then his knowing looks and keen interest made her uneasy. If only the department had given her a new supervisor as she had requested, but the committee that decided such things had not yet met. The only good thing was that his interest in her research made her certain she had stumbled onto something really good.

She hoped she had something wonderful. Her boyfriend—ex-boyfriend—had told her that, but then what he knew about geology he had learned from her. Some expert he was. It had taken a while to realize that the guy was also a complete jerk, and a control freak on top of it. Now she just wished he would leave her alone. What was it with some men that they could not seem to understand what "it's over" meant? And all that feigned interest in her studies, that was too much. Almost every day there was a message on her machine. "How are you? I miss you so much. How are your classes going?" or, "Anything new and interesting in your research? Please call me. You know I love you." What nerve. Hardly a case of true love. When they had been together he had tried to run her life. He had even insisted on reading all her papers, always made her tell him all about her work. It had been a big mistake to let him move in. Thank God she had found the courage to throw him out.

At 9:05 she was tired of waiting and entered the office of her supervisor's technician. "Have you seen or heard from Dr. Essen this morning?"

"Nope." Marlene looked up from her keyboard. "His first class is at ten."

"I know. I had an eight-thirty appointment with him about my thesis."

"Then you're late aren't you?"

"I've been waiting for him. I just thought maybe he'd called to say he'd be late or something. Maybe, with all this flu going around. . . ."

"Sorry. Haven't heard a word. You could try calling him."

Fiona looked up the number, dialled, and let it ring. Nobody answered. If he was not at home he was probably on his way.

At 9:30 she scrawled a note and taped it to his door telling him that she was working in the lab. The lab she shared with a couple of other graduate students was down the hall. She walked around the lab table, which occupied most of the centre of the room, and dropped her backpack on the floor beside her desk. She unlocked the bottom drawer, the one in which she kept the rock samples, record of analysis, and the raw data of the magnetic survey she had completed.

Doing the mapping of magnetic irregularities had been a bitch. For days she had tramped around in the bush with a box strapped to her shoulders, her arms aching from holding an unwieldy antenna while she measured local magnetic intensity and fluctuations in polarity. Her entire body had been covered with black fly and mosquito bites. She had ached and itched for weeks. But it had been worth it, really worth it. She had a real live find. The drawer pulled out easily. Because of the rocks, she usually had to tug. A glance told her why. The drawer was empty.

Constable Stefanyk walked into the office at 7:40 holding a large sticky bun. He was twenty minutes early for his shift and proud of the fact, but Griffeth was already at his desk.

" 'Morning, Carl," drawled Griffeth. "Breakfast?"

"Ahh . . . yes, sir."

"Good Thanksgiving, Carl?"

"I worked. How about yours?"

"The wife cooked a turkey, but the day was ruined by a slew of relatives. Exhausting."

Carl wondered what he could say to that and decided to keep his mouth shut.

"Here's the report on the key we brought in Sunday night. Don't bother reading it. No usable prints. The only thing you can hope for is to find someone who saw or heard something."

Carl had already figured that out. He wanted to do a good job so, in spite of his feelings about the attempted B and E, he had spent much of Thanksgiving Day trying to interview apartment residents who were not at home. He got nothing from those who were. He settled at one of the three desks in the room to write up his notes, forcing himself to ignore his superior's assortment of grunts, a voluble phone conversation, and the clatter as Griffeth practically threw the receiver back into the cradle and shoved back his chair.

"Come on. Something has just come up. Shouldn't take long. I'll tell you on the way to the car." Griffeth grabbed his coat and carefully wrapped a knitted red and blue stripped muffler around his neck before he buttoned up.

"Nice scarf." Carl, buttoning his own coat with still sticky fingers, was trying hard.

Griffeth wrinkled his nose. "My wife took one of those learn-to-knit courses at the community centre a few years ago. This was her project. I hate it but it won't wear out. It itches. You have a wife?"

"No, sir. Girl friend."

"Well, keep her away from the community centre. The place is dangerous." They tramped through the building, finally exiting into an alley. "Did you hear about that air search going on?"

"I sure did. It's been all over the TV and radio. Some little plane, everyone killed. I don't know about people who want to fly in those things. Just plain dangerous. More money than sense, I guess."

Griffeth gave a bark of laughter. "I am one of those senseless people who fly those things. Have done for years." He was amused by the look of alarm on Carl's face. "It's fun, Carl. I'll take you up in my plane one of these days. You'll love it." He noticed that Carl's alarm increased. He really was a strange young man.

With Carl behind the wheel, the unmarked car pulled out. As he left the parking lot he asked, "Where are we going?"

"Oh, didn't I say? Sorry. The university."

As they crawled through morning traffic Griffeth picked up his train of thought. "About that search, you have to be careful about believing everything you hear. Rescue Coordination Centre, RCMP and CASARA aren't even sure there's been a crash. All they know is that the pilot didn't turn up when he was expected and nobody seems to know where he is."

Except for the reference to RCMP Carl didn't have the

foggiest idea who or what the sergeant was talking about and he did not much care. He hated planes.

Griffeth continued, "When an aircraft is declared missing the RCMP, local police, and TSB—that stands for Transportation Safety Board, Carl—are contacted. TSB stands by, just in case, and the police units try to locate next of kin. For one thing, nobody wants the nearest and dearest to find out about a missing relative from a news report. For another, we want to get background information about the pilot, aircraft, and the flight. Some little piece of information could help find the plane in time to get everyone home safe and sound. If not, then eventually the info might help the accident investigators piece together what happened and why."

Suddenly Stefanyk jammed on the brakes and skidded to a rocking halt that threw them both against their shoulder belts. A pickup truck had run a stop light and barreled through the intersection directly in their path. Carl's Traffic Unit instincts urged him to follow; his fingers itched to write a ticket. Instead, he radioed the description and licence and again sedately steered the cruiser eastbound toward the river that snaked its way, south to north, through the centre of the city. Griffeth was rattling on about planes again. It took all the accumulated experience of listening to the wrath of ticketed motorists for Stefanyk to mold his features into the picture of a composed and interested cop. The subject bored the bejezzes out of him.

As they crossed University Bridge, Griffeth said, "The aircraft was declared overdue Sunday night and here it is Tuesday morning and RCMP hasn't been able to locate the next of kin. Now the job has been fobbed off on me. Probably think I'm the person to do it because I fly. Maybe they think I know him. I don't, but there's logic for you. It's only a matter of time before some reporter gets hold of the guy's name and it's all over everywhere. I'm surprised it isn't already. No answer at his home when I tried calling so we'll try his work place. Take a left at the next, it'll be faster."

They wound their way through the campus, found the proper building and parked beside a No Parking sign. Inside the building, they examined a chart and headed for the office of the department chairman who was not there. Grumbling, Griffeth returned with Carl to the atrium that served both as a lobby and a natural history museum. There they stood beside a huge fibreglass dinosaur skeleton on its substantial stone pedestal.

"This is obviously going to take longer than I thought. Stick around here and make your presence felt if need be, Carl. Grab the chairman as soon as he comes in and tell him that Dr. Jake Essen is listed as the pilot of an overdue flight. Whatever you do, don't tell anyone else unless you check with me first. And, get the name and address of at least one of Essen's relatives. I'm going to check out his office if I can figure out where it is."

He wandered back to the chart, noticed the crowd waiting for the elevator, and with a sigh headed for the stairs. This was the job he should have given Stefanyk. It would have been far more pleasant to learn about dinosaurs or look at the pretty minerals in the cases lining the halls than to trudge up two flights. The task was made even more unpleasant by the streams of students who found his stolid pace an annoyance and said so. What he thought about being called gramps and worse, he kept to himself.

He found the door with the plastic sign that read, Dr. J. Essen. The door was locked and there was no answer to his knock. Next door he located the technician and learned her name from the plaque affixed to her desk.

"Excuse me. Are you Marlene? I'm looking for Dr. Essen."

She barely glanced at him while she slid a file drawer closed and opened another. "He hasn't arrived yet. Did you have an appointment?"

"Ahh, no. No, I didn't. I'm Sergeant Griffeth, police." He flipped open his badge case. "It's important that we find a relative of Dr. Essen's. I was hoping to talk to him." This ambiguous statement was followed by a boyish smile that was meant to charm the plump and fortyish woman who, he had noticed, wore no rings.

She left the second drawer open and gave him her full attention. "Oh. Well, I can't help you much, I'm afraid. Apparently he was supposed to meet someone at eight-thirty but didn't show up. I haven't heard from him either. Would you like to wait or leave a message?"

"Maybe you can help me. Is there a Mrs. Essen, do you know?"

She gave him a side-ways kind of look. "Now, there maybe I can help. He's divorced, or at least that's what he claims. I don't blame the woman. He's got hands on him, if you know what I mean. At one time or another he's hit on just about all of us. In the mail room, in his office, in the labs. . . . He has a real reputation. Is that what this is about? Somebody file a complaint? About time. . . ."

"Do you know where Dr. Essen went for Thanksgiving?"

She shook her head. "He took Friday off. I just assumed he was taking a long weekend somewhere."

"Is there a colleague who might know?"

"The chairman might, but he's not in. Other than him, I doubt it."

"Do you know where his ex lives?"

"Not around here. Toronto, I think. If you want I'll dig out the address. What is this about?"

"We're trying to locate him. If you've got a key, I'd

appreciate it if I could take a look in his office."

She looked sceptical. "You don't think he's in there, do you?"

"Do you have a key?"

She opened a drawer and removed a key ring. "This is the one."

She hovered in the hallway while Griffeth opened Essen's office and stood looking around at the untidy interior.

"Is this the way it normally looks?"

She poked her head around the jamb. "Yes, pretty much. Anyway, it looks like when I saw it last."

The desk calendar was open to the previous Thursday. Griffeth turned the pages to the current date where a name was written beside a time. "Any idea who Fiona is?"

"A graduate student."

"That the meeting he missed?"

The technician nodded. "He's her supervisor. If you're thinking about his reputation, she can take care of herself. He got her alone a while back and she about broke his arm. I think he got the message."

"Ahh. You wouldn't know if he has an address book would you? We really must get in touch with him and there may be someone listed, a relative perhaps, who knows where he is."

"He always carries it with him."

"Hmm. Too bad. Marlene, if you'll just give me his ex's address—phone number, too, if you've got it—I'll be on my way. I really appreciate your help. If he comes in or you hear from him I'd like you to call me." He produced a card and his charming smile. Marlene produced the information.

Carl liked to drive and when traffic was light he indulged himself. Leaving the campus he saw his chance, floored it, and earned himself a startled, "Was that absolutely necessary?"

"Sorry, sir. My kind of flying, I guess. Any luck getting info?"

Griffeth told him what he'd learned, then asked, "Where did you disappear to?"

"I was wandering around. I went upstairs and found a laboratory room and, this is interesting, the student there was looking for Essen too."

"Did he say why, Carl?"

"She. It's a she. I just told her we needed to contact Dr. Essen and she said so did she. Said to tell her when we found him. She sounded angry about something. Seems kind of strange, don't you think? I mean, you'd think he'd've mentioned where he was going to somebody."

"We know where his flight plan said he was going. He has a cabin at a lake up north. According to his technician, Dr. Essen is very fond of trysts with women. I suppose he could have another little hide-away somewhere. Wouldn't necessarily make that kind of thing known. Where would you take your girlfriend for a weekend, Carl?" He glanced at his constable and saw a red flush start up his neck.

"I don't know. We haven't gotten to that stage yet. Wherever, it wouldn't be anywhere in a plane, that's for sure. I get sick." He threw a quick, apologetic glance at the sergeant. "Sea sick, too. Car sick, if I'm not driving." he added with an embarrassed laugh.

Griffeth nodded with sudden understanding. "No wonder you didn't look thrilled when I offered to take you flying. Not to worry, I won't say anything. Besides, I kind of like the idea of having a chauffeur."

The flight simulator room at Flannigan's was located in a former closet off a corridor near one of the exits to the ramp. A blackboard used for briefing before the exercise filled one wall and was covered with chalk marks. The room was tiny, with what was known as "the box" taking up most of the space. The student sat in a mock-up of a cockpit, his eyes constantly scanning the instruments, his left hand making minuscule changes to the position of the control yoke. Dark circles of sweat under his arms attested to his effort. From where she sat to check his progress, Elie heard him mutter to himself as he wandered slightly off-course and corrected. She waited until his track appeared steady before flipping a switch to freeze the instrument indications for debriefing. "Looking pretty good, Mark."

He stood up and pulled at his shirt to unstick it from his back. "I feel like I've spent a month in a sauna."

"Mr. Holmgren! Stop where you are!" The sharp bark came from the corridor directly outside the room. Mark glanced a question at Elie and they both went to look through the small pane of glass set high in the door. Lars was halfway outside with a student whom he motioned to go on ahead before he turned to face the manager.

"Mr. Campbell, I'm with a student."

"I can see that. This won't take a minute. I've been going over the books. In the last three weeks the flying school has lost five students. Why is that?"

"It's the fees. Our prices are now way higher than our competition."

"Mr. Holmgren, the fee hike was necessary in order to show a proper profit. Management is my job. Yours is to keep the students happy and I'm counting on you to do just that. You must also bring in new students, understand? If you find all that too difficult then I'll just have to find a new chief flying instructor. All that clear enough?" Campbell's wide mouth formed a tight smile. "Go on, Mr. Holmgren. Don't keep the student waiting."

A clearly furious Lars shoved open the door and disappeared. Elie could not blame him for being angry. What she found difficult to understand was that such a supremely self-confident man had not fought back. His job was not just to keep students happy. Among other things he was responsible for the standard of training of all students and for making sure that each flying instructor provided a top-notch level of instruction. For it to be a thoroughly pleasant experience for the student was due in equal measure to a desire to learn and the efforts of a competent and caring staff of a well-run company. Campbell should know that. What he had said was inexcusable. If Flannigan's had lost business it was his fault, not Lars's. She was offended by Campbell's remarks and embarrassed that Mark heard the exchange.

When the hall was clear, she said, "Sorry about that. I don't think they knew we were in here." It was inadequate, but what else could she say?

"Elie, maybe I shouldn't tell you this, but. . . . Well, more than a few students are complaining. The whole atmosphere around here has changed and, like Lars said, the fees are too high. I don't want to, but I'm on a real tight budget so I'll probably have to transfer myself. Why did they go up so much? Rumour has it that you all got raises."

She laughed. "What a lovely idea. I only wish it were true."

He blurted out, "There's something else." He would not meet her eyes and looked uncomfortable. "Last Saturday night a couple of us were in Mufti's. You know the place?"

She nodded. Mufti's was a bar that brought in the best live music it could: rock, jazz, blues, folk. It was a popular place that drew mostly the young but Elie and Don had been there a few times and so had their friends.

Mark continued, "Anyway, Mr. Campbell was there and I overheard—I shouldn't have listened, I know, but I couldn't help it. There were a couple of people that work here. Most of them are charter pilots I think, or maybe some of them fly the scheduled runs, I don't know. Anyway, Campbell was being pretty buddy-buddy with them, but the thing that got to me was. . . . Well, what he said was that he thought women pilots were bad for business, that passengers didn't trust them. I just thought you should know."

In his private and commercial training Mark had experienced a variety of instructors but none of them could get a point across better than Elie and none of them had a finer touch on the controls. Campbell's comments had really bothered him and he had agonized for days about whether to tell her. Now he was not sure he had done the right thing. In fact he wished he had not told her because for a second there she looked stunned. She forced her expression back to neutral and made light of it, her laugh sounding a little forced. Mark gave her nine out of ten for a very good try.

A few minutes later, grateful to be alone, she was in the staff room eating lunch. At least lunch was what she called it. As penance for the doughnuts she had consumed on the search the day before, she had low-fat cottage cheese, a couple of carrots, two sticks of celery, and a slightly desiccated apple she had found rolling around in the back of the fridge. She was not even hungry but, because of her charter to pick up Benoit, lunch could not wait. The stomachs of pilots get used to this sort of thing.

As she crunched and munched she wondered how the search was going. Crews had been in the air now for a day and a half and there was still no sign of either plane or pilot. The longer it took, the worse the probable outcome.

She was mentally shaking her head over this thought when Campbell strolled into the staff room, filled his coffee cup, and actually smiled and said, "Hello," on his way back out. In light of the fact that she had not reported to him as directed after the search the day before, and what she had heard only a few minutes ago, such friendliness was hard to believe. Too hard to believe; in fact, it made her feel distinctly uneasy. She wondered what was going on. The loudspeaker interrupted her thoughts by paging her to answer line three. She picked up the staff room phone.

"Why didn't you return my call? You know I wouldn't call you if it wasn't important?" It was her old friend Walter Harris. His voice was hoarse and he sounded cranky. She remembered her promise of the previous day to call him and kicked herself for forgetting. "They thought I was nuts, didn't they? They didn't believe me . . ." he broke off coughing. He was either getting peculiar in his old age or was even sicker than he sounded.

"Walter, you sound like you have the flu. I hope you've seen a doctor."

"I heard the reports. They have planes up searching, the radio said so, and none are looking where I said," he complained.

"Slow down, I don't understand. What are you talking about?"

With a good deal of vinegar he spelled it out. He had reported to the RCMP that he had been about ready to leave his cabin on Sunday morning when he had heard a plane crash not far from Hacker Lake. It had engine problems, he said, cutting in and out. It was plain that he believed what he was telling her. He was certain, he was positive, he was definite, and he did not like being treated like a senile two-year-old.

She heard him out without comment and thought it through. Hacker Lake was—what?—a good forty-five to fifty nautical miles east of Downy Lake. Was it possible that Essen had crashed that far off course? Stupid question. Of course it was. If, as reported, he had closed his flight plan

Friday from the air he could have been anywhere. All that was necessary was to be in radio range of a flight service station.

"Elie? You there? Did you hear me? I said. . . ."

She found Fred, who went through the record of phone reports received and the few (well-intentioned but proven erroneous) sighting reports that put the missing plane everywhere from Edmonton to Winnipeg. Sure enough, a message was logged from a Hacker Lake RCMP constable. Someone had come into the three-man detachment on Sunday morning claiming to have heard a plane in trouble and then crash. With no aircraft reported overdue the officer thought the man was just an old crank. He filled out a report, filed it, and forgot it. He was off for Thanksgiving and only heard a search was in progress when he had reported for duty that morning.

The military searchmaster talked to Walter. It was partly because the old man had been in the air force, but mostly because of the way he described what he heard that made the difference. Captain Bueler checked the map, measured distances, and then designated the area south of Hacker Lake as a primary search area for the simple reason that it was a real possibility and you just never knew with searches. The military SAR Twin Otter was assigned to the task.

Touhy's medical partners would probably do him damage, but he had decided to volunteer another day to the search. When Captain Bueler asked for spotters for the Otter, he had been the first in line. Tom, the enthusiastic high school student, was playing truant on account of the search and he was right behind Touhy. They were the first two to clamber up the Twin Otter's ladder. They were closely followed by the two military search and rescue technicians (SAR techs) in their distinctive orange jackets.

Various bags and boxes of emergency equipment occupied almost the entire right-hand side of the cabin. Down the left side, one behind the other, stretched a row of single sling seats as uncomfortable as they looked. When the three CASARA spotters and SAR techs were in place, the flight engineer acting as load master stood in the narrow aisle to brief them. He had to hunch over to keep from banging his head. Among other things, he told them how to change spotters at the bubble windows, a tricky manoeuvre that had to be done in such a way that the search was not interrupted even for a fraction of a second. He also pointed out the supply of sick bags. Even the hardiest stomachs were liable to give up during this duty.

Touhy, in the seat closest to the cockpit, was able to peek past the curtain that separated the cockpit from the cabin. He put on his headphones and listened in as the first officer went through the pre-start checklist with the captain. Tom twisted around and watched the flight engineer close the door and secure jumpseats beside the two bubble windows, one in the door, the other in the window across the aisle.

On the trip north the CASARA spotters rotated with the SAR techs to search the track to Hacker Lake. They might as well, they were flying over it anyway. And, who knew? If Essen was not where he was supposed to be, he could be almost anywhere. Two spotters sat sideways in the rear of the plane, their heads stuck in the bubbles, their eyes raking the ground for what did not belong in the complicated picture passing beneath them.

While two spotters worked, the others relaxed and looked out the window, tourists for the moment. The afternoon weather was perfect for flying. The sky was clear, there were few bumps to speak of, and the terrain they flew over was lovely. From the air, towns looked like well-constructed models. Golden stubble fields, pasture, and summer fallow passed by. In each, the tractor tracery was precise and intricate. Each field was neatly outlined by fences or hedges that were yellow or bare of leaves. Grid roads further defined the areas and the whole was punctuated by neat farm yards with wind breaks of poplar or Russian olive. There were orderly villages and small towns with hockey rinks and church steeples, some with the distinctive onion-shaped domes of the Ukrainian Orthodox Church. And, dotted here and there, huge grain elevators sat beside shiny railway tracks. Farther north came the rich, variegated greens of the forest with rivers and lakes that sparkled like dark gemstones in the sunlight.

As they approached Hacker Lake, the spotters changed and Touhy moved into the left-spotting position. The captain let down to a search altitude of five hundred feet above ground and briefed the spotters for a half-mile visibility range. They were now in the intensive "creeping line ahead" search pattern and rolled out on course for the first west to east pass over the trees. Spotting in this terrain was like trying to find a particular thread caught in a moving clothes brush by looking down through the bristles. It was when they were over very dense growth, in the left turn from east to west, that Touhy tensed. He felt his heart rate speed up as he spoke briskly to the pilot through the mike on his headset. He was now in control of where the plane would fly, giving his commands by means of clock reference and distance.

"Captain, left spotter. Roll out of the turn and go straight. Ten o'clock moving to nine, about a quarter mile, there's a bent over top on a fir tree, looks broken. Keep going, and . . . start a left turn . . . now. Tighter . . . more bank. Hold it." He ignored the vertiginous blur at the edge of his vision and concentrated solely on the single tree. "Yes . . . the top is broken, looks fresh, and the one next to it has been clipped. Roll out of the turn NOW. Keep straight. At ten moving to nine, inside a quarter mile, looks like a small one topped. And, coming up at ten-thirty, broken branches on a jack pine. Keep going . . . keep . . . TURN LEFT NOW! STEEP TURN! HOLD IT!" The aircraft almost appeared to pirouette around the tip of its left wing. "Nine o'clock, close in, big spruce snapped clean off about half way down. Keep the turn going. Looks like something light coloured down there. Could be white. Back off the bank a bit, widen the turn. Good, good. Shiny! Something's reflecting light! It's . . . damn, I've lost it! Keep the turn going. I'll try to pick it up again. . . ." Touhy's eyes were glued to the spot that had sparkled for a moment. The pilot continued the turn, completing two full orbits before Touhy spoke again. "Got it! Tighten up the turn . . . looks good, keep the bank. Nine o'clock. Close in. Something's catching the light down there . . . and, there's definitely something light, maybe white. Trees are thick . . . I think that's it but I can't be sure."

In the cockpit the co-pilot inked a heavy **X** on his map and circled it. The pilot rolled wings level and then came around for a right turn. Tom, in the right window, quickly picked up the broken trees and called the plane around for turn after turn to see what he could make out. Slight differences in the light, slight shifts in position, a different set of eyes, and with each completed turn more details were noted. The trees were thick and tall here, the ground beneath them in shadow; they had to guard against allowing their imaginations to see the plane they felt sure was there.

What they could not see, what they wanted to see, were the large registration letters that would positively identify it, not just as an aircraft, but as the missing Piper. They looked carefully at the evident flight path. They saw no signs of scorching or burning. The amount and type of damage to the trees was consistent only with something big and heavy descending through them.

The orange-jacketed SAR techs pulled apart the stacked equipment, put on bush suits, and strapped on parachutes. The Otter began to make the passes preliminary to a paradrop. Long streamers, really lengths of red crepe paper, were released to check wind and drift. They made a message drop to try to communicate with the downed pilot. The jump decision was made and equipment was sent out to parachute to earth. Then Touhy watched the two SAR techs wearing reinforced bush suits, pant legs strapped securely to their boots, visors over their faces, step casually into space and drift down to get caught up in a tree intentionally and lower themselves to the ground by a pulley arrangement called a Sky Genie. As paramedics they would try to sustain life; as survival experts they would preserve it.

The Otter circled overhead waiting for the SAR techs to report by radio. Everyone hoped that they had found the missing plane. They prayed that the pilot was alive. They waited for what seemed an eternity. Suddenly the military co-pilot appeared in the cockpit door. "Good news and bad news, I'm afraid. The good news is that we did locate the aircraft and for that congratulations are in order. It was a difficult task. The bad news is that the pilot didn't make it. The SAR techs will secure the area until RCMP and the accident investigators are on the scene. Thanks for a good job. I just wish it was a happier outcome."

5. Wednesday, October 13

Wednesday morning started with a clear sky, a nasty chill, and a stiff wind that made for bumpy flying. At 10:45 Elie, her hair tousled and her cheeks pink, debriefed and booked her second student of the day for another session, and headed to the staff room for a warming cup of coffee. On the way she plucked a folded paper from her message hole. Curly, a former student, had phoned. He had left two phone numbers, a sure indication that he wanted her to call back right away. She wondered what he wanted, found a phone, and dialled.

"Waste of time," said a voice behind her. She turned to find Curly Griffeth, his ears and nose red, resplendent in full uniform.

"Curly! I was phoning, honest!"

He grinned. "Uniform scares you, eh? Elie, I need coffee. It's really miserable out there."

She sat him at the table in the staff room with its fully-equipped kitchen and a bank of coffee machines that brewed a fragrant gourmet blend. Joe Flannigan had aimed to please. She poured two cups and gestured at the uniform. "I'm impressed. I don't think I've ever seen you in uniform before. What's the occasion?"

"Official luncheon. Awards presentation. I hate ceremonies, but since I'm part of it, it can't be helped. Can you smell moth balls? Martha aired it, but every time I move I smell moth balls."

"Well . . . now that you mention it. But it isn't bad, really. What are you being honoured for?"

"Thirty-five years in harness. I can retire any time but I'm going to hang on as long as I can. Screw those new fascists in admin who want us old farts out. Being a cop is all I've ever been and what I want to do. Besides, if I retire Martha and I will just drive each other nuts." Unexpectedly, he looked a little misty. "You know, I can't quite believe that it was thirty years ago that I was assigned to your father's unit. He was a good man and a very good cop. I learned a lot from him."

His reminiscence caught her by surprise. He was talking about her teenage years, a period of her life during which she had first lost her mother and then, five years later, her father was gone. Becoming an orphan on the eve of your high school graduation does not exactly turn the event into a festive occasion. It still hurt to think about it and she hastily changed the subject.

"Curly, I should warn you, our new manager doesn't allow civilians in the staff room for any reason, so if he catches you in here wave that braid around and go all official."

"I wanted to ask you how it was going without Joe. Sounds like there's been quite a change."

She gave him a rueful smile. "We miss Joe. Lots. Now, you didn't come all the way out here just to show off your uniform and I doubt if you plan to go flying dressed like that, so . . . ?"

"Just a question. I know you have kids. Would two of them happen to be named Grant and Brad?"

She held her cup in a death grip. "Are they all right? What's happened?"

He laughed. "As far as I know, they're fine. Relax. This morning I suddenly made the connection, that's all. Have they mentioned that their apartment was broken into?"

"The first I heard about it was on Sunday. They said it happened in September and that Brad's paperweights, those rocks of his, were taken. The whole thing sounded strange. It worries me. Is that why you're here?"

"Partly. Whoever broke in the first time did a pretty good job on the lock and door."

"The first . . . ?"

"Aha! They didn't tell you about the second attempt Sunday night, did they? Don't want poor old Mom to worry, I think." He leaned back, unbuttoned his jacket, and told her what had happened. When he finished he asked her if she could think of any reason why anyone would want to break in. She could not and asked him if he thought her boys were in danger. He shrugged and asked her about the paintings he had noticed over the couch that looked good even to his untrained eye.

"Those were gifts, one to each of them, from their god-father. He's also the artist. We both have cabins on Hacker Lake and that's where they were painted. Nice aren't they?"

"Valuable?"

"Probably. Walter gets a pretty good price these days."

"Walter? Walter Harris? Good God. That's a possible motive right there."

Elie shook her head. "I doubt it. I don't think anyone even realizes what they are. Anyway, how many students would have an original Harris, not to mention two? Anybody would think they were copies. Besides, if that's what they wanted why didn't they take them? You know, absolutely none of this makes any sense to me."

"I'm having a hard time with it myself. My current partner, courtesy of rotation and this flu bug, is a young man who quite clearly thinks I've gone bonkers even to take it seriously. He's bright but a little strange. I've assigned him to look into it. Maybe he'll come up with something. One other thing, this fellow who was killed in the accident, did you know him at all?"

"Essen? Just to see him. Why?"

"Just curious about why he was found so far off course."

"Lots of guessing going on about that. Everyone has a theory and every theory is different. I want to know why he went down."

"Accident investigators on the job?"

She nodded. "They flew up first thing this morning. We got word they're lifting the engine and assorted bits and pieces out by chopper and bringing it down here for examination."

"Any idea what caused it?"

"You know how it goes, rumours everywhere. There always are after an accident. Reporters keep calling and turning up to talk to anything that looks like it once drew breath. First thing this morning a TV crew did an interview with a flying student with two hours under his belt. Instant expert. We'll probably see it on the six o'clock news." Curly snorted. "One thing though, Flannigan's did the maintenance on that plane and John is tying himself in knots worrying about it."

"I'd be surprised if it was a maintenance problem, knowing him. He's worked on my bird for years. Best mechanic I ever met. Well, let me know if you find out anything." He drained his cup, stood up, buttoned his jacket, which was a bit tight over his tummy, and turned to leave. She watched him move toward the door and wondered how a man with such pronounced shoulder blades ever sat comfortably in a straight-backed chair.

"Incidentally, Martha sends her regards and wonders if you'll bake something for the community centre fundraiser. I'm tempted to torch the place myself. She's taking another knitting class and says I'll be getting a sweater for my Christmas present. Everything she makes itches, but I have to wear it or she feels bad. I wish she'd take up painting or photography, anything at all as long as I don't have to wear the results. Although, come to think of it, having to look at the results might not be such a good idea either."

She walked him to the door and then returned to meet her next student. As they left the building for an hour of take-offs and landings, she noticed Lars, his face tight, coming out of Campbell's office. It did not look good and she wondered what had happened this time. She wanted to talk to him herself, to find out what more he had heard about Flannigan's being sold. Since their conversation on Monday it almost seemed as though he had been avoiding her, but then she reminded herself of how much pressure he was under and immediately dismissed her suspicion as being ridiculous.

During the afternoon the flatbed backed into the hangar. On it was more than an engine and a few parts. From what could be glimpsed during the unloading, all of the plane, disassembled, mangled, and freeform, had been brought in. It was all transferred to the separate but secure room used for painting aircraft and the overhead door was closed against curious eyes. Behind the door two investigators from the Transportation Safety Board were joined by an insurance investigator. If previous investigations were anything to go by, the aircraft would be further dismantled and each system in turn would be examined, tested, and photographed. They had not been working long when another man arrived, identified himself as an RCMP detective, and was shown to the paint room. His presence seemed unusual, but then, accidents were unusual. Before the end of the afternoon mechanics and anybody else who might have immediately useful information were being questioned. Investigators' briefcases filled up with Polaroid photos, rolls of film, tape recordings, and notebooks. And this was just the initial investigation. The final report, which would address both the cause and all the relevant safety issues, would not appear for well over a year.

But that did not stop the speculation that swirled around and sprinkled conversations. Anyone who flies knows that all really juicy aviation rumours appear on the hangar line, fully formed, before eight in the morning. So by three o'clock in the afternoon many succulent versions had already made the rounds and Flannigan's played a role in about half of them.

Joe Flannigan would have known what to do about it; James Campbell did not. While the preliminary examination and questioning was going on, and while Elie flew a multi-engine instrument session with Mark, James Campbell locked himself in his office in his new suit and stewed.

"Cleared for an NDB-15 approach, call beacon inbound. . . ." Beginning instrument pilots are not overly fond of NDB approaches to land. In conjunction with the non-directional beacon, an instrument known as an ADF (automatic direction finder) is used. More than one pilot has had his brain turn to spaghetti while trying to figure out what the little needle, which frequently seems to have a life of its own, is trying to tell him. Mark hated it. He sat beside Elie, talking his way through the non-precision approach from under an instrument hood that looked like nothing so much as a bleach bottle split in half lengthwise and attached to the bill of a baseball cap. The purpose was to prevent him from seeing anything outside the aircraft and to force him to guide the plane solely by instrument indications. On this, his third try, he was doing pretty well. He even remembered to get the gear down. When he was approximately seven hundred feet up and seven hundred feet from the runway threshold, Elie called, "clear of cloud," and Mark lifted the hood.

Spread out in front of him was a brilliant pattern of welcoming lights. A line of bright, yellow approach lights led him to the runway like the stem of a tree leads to the branches. A horizontal row of green lights marked the runway threshold. Running lengthwise along the runway perimeter, spaced at intervals like candles on the edges of a giant Christmas tree, lights outlined the area where he could land. And at the far end of the runway, red lights looked like a large and glorious star crowning the tree. It was a marvelous sight. With a broad smile Mark continued the approach to touch down, adding the white, red, and green lights of the aircraft to the spectacle.

It was a few minutes past six when they taxied in, debriefing the exercise on the way. Mark was hungry, exhausted, and anxious to get home, and Elie was taking her boys to dinner, something she had arranged after talking with Curly. Nothing fancy, just hamburgers. Mostly she wanted to see for herself that they were okay.

Dressed in jeans, blue turtleneck, and a heavy Aran cardigan, Elie left the locker room anticipating a relaxing evening. On the way out of the building she passed by the message boxes. Her full name was typed on the envelope she found. Frowning, she slit it open and unfolded the paper. Neatly typed under the green and gold logo on Flannigan's cream-coloured stationery was a pink slip.

Her face felt hot as she stood there, rooted to the spot, staring at it, she had no idea for how long. The only thing in focus was the paper in her hand. She read it again and again. As of the time of writing, it said, she was unemployed. She was directed to leave the premises and not return; to put her keys in an envelope and slide them under Campbell's door. No reasons were given. She was stunned, as though without warning she had been slammed against a stone wall. She could barely breathe.

Two burning splotches of colour appeared high on her cheeks. Unemployed from the time the letter was written? What was she supposed to have done—receive a psychic message and bail out midway home? Her trembling fingers folded the paper into a neat square and put it in her pocket.

She tried to find Lars, but he was flying. A mechanic said John had gone home. Norm's dispatch office was locked. She found some boxes that had once contained tins of aviation oil, filled them with the contents of her locker and desk, added other odds and ends and carried them to her car. By the time she slammed the hatchback she was angry, really angry.

Campbell wanted her keys, eh? Did he now. . . . Well, the loathsome little maggot would just have to wait. He would get them when she got good and ready to give them. And she was not going to slide them under his door either. Mr. MBA Genius Campbell was going to get them in person along with some splendidly specific advice. Or, maybe she would just push him into a spinning prop.

She started the car and sat behind the wheel taking deep breaths. She had to cool off enough to drive without killing someone—like maybe herself. She had to be calm when she met her boys, too. And, somehow she had to figure out what and how to tell them.

This was not just about her. It directly affected them. She paid the rent on their apartment. An apartment was cheaper than having them live in a dorm. It was also easier for them to get to classes, the library, and track and wrestling practices than if they lived at home. Apart from the break-ins, the arrangement had worked well for everyone. Don's work took him out of town with increased frequency, which made it possible for Elie to accept more flexible flying hours, which in turn gave her a bigger pay cheque and made the apartment possible. Mentally she calculated how long her savings would last. If she were careful, maybe to the end of the first semester.

Night traffic on the street running past the police building was snarled and some fool was tooting his horn. Griffeth shook his head in disgust, but not because of the noise. At his desk he could barely hear it. He was disgusted because someone had turned on the heat. Now the office of the Major Crime Unit was much too warm and had the unmistakable odor of cooked dust. He wrinkled his nose in distaste.

Dreaded uniform jacket draped over the back of his chair, he sat with rolled up shirt sleeves, his shirt collar open, and his tie askew. A styrofoam carton spilling an empty ketchup package lay in the wastebasket beside his desk. Carl entered the office, peeled off his sweater, and looked around for some place to put it.

"Take your clothing off my desk!"

"Yessir. Sorry." He put his sweater back on and was instantly sorry.

"Any luck?"

"Not much. I've spent hours knocking on more apartment doors and talking to people who either weren't around on the weekend or didn't notice a thing. I've heard plenty of complaints about the janitor and the power outage, though. But there was one thing. That girl I mentioned seeing at the university? The one that was pissed off at Dr. Essen? Her name is Fiona Stewart and her apartment is next door to the Meade kids. And, there's something else. She's a graduate student and Essen was her advisor."

"Interesting. Was this girl home Sunday night and did she hear or see anyone trying to enter the apartment next door? That's what we need to know."

"She says not. She got home late, what with the rain and the power failure and all. She said she'd heard that the cops had been called and asked what it was all about. Said that Grant and Brad seemed nice and were quiet enough but she only knows them to say hello."

"Hmm. Not much help there. Okay, shift's almost over so write it up in the morning. Then I'll have something else for you to do."

"I start days-off tomorrow. . . ."

From somewhere under the litter on his desk the phone rang. Griffeth parted the papers and snatched the receiver. Carl watched his superior's usually benign looking features harden almost to granite as he listened intently. When he hung up he swore quietly, then turned to Carl and grimly told him to forget about days-off for about the next hundred years, or until further notice, whichever came first.

Back in the twenties, when it had been little more than a cow pasture for airmail pilots to land, the airport had been located some distance from the northwest edge of the city. Now, the same location boasted a bustling terminal building, four runways and constant traffic, both air and ground. The city had expanded in all directions and now the airport was surrounded on three sides by an industrial district. Elie drove along the service road that ran behind the hangars, joined the street system, and finally arrived at a major intersection. Her intention was to turn on to Circle Drive, the fastest route to the east side and the university district. She found emergency road work in progress and a detour sign pointing her toward the city centre. It was an annoyance, but at this time of night it should make little difference. Rush hour was over and traffic would be light.

In the distance the downtown area created an interesting night skyline with its department stores, office buildings, apartments, and hotels, but Elie neither noticed nor appreciated the view. She was preoccupied by the same question she was asking herself over and over. Why had she been fired? Because she had been part of the search? She had just been doing what the operations manual dictated should be done. Because she had not reported to Campbell as directed? There had been no time before her charter. It could not have been because she was a woman, not in this day and age. Could it? She had never felt discrimination, why now? Besides, she had an excellent record. Joe Flannigan would not have kept her, or hired her in the first place, if she did not know what she was doing. One thing was sure, since one of Campbell's first acts had been to fire some pilots, scheduling was tight. With her gone, even with declining business, scheduling students and charters was going to give Lars and Norm a collective migraine.

Could Campbell be trying to shut down the school before selling the company? Maybe the charter business, too? Was that it? Getting rid of senior staff and creating financial worries for students and passengers was one way of going about it. But if the school was viable—and it was, she was sure about that—it could be sold separately. Come to that, so could the scheduled service and charter business. Flannigan's was known as the best flight training centre in all of Saskatchewan. Shutting it down or weakening it was stupid. Campbell was not managing Flannigan's, he was killing it. But why? He had been appointed to keep the place going. It did not make sense.

She met more downtown traffic than she had expected and crept along as she approached one of the six bridges that spanned the river. To make matters worse, she was caught by every red light. Finally, she crossed the river, made the light at the top of the bridge, and picked up speed along College Drive. To her left was the campus, with lights blazing, a city unto itself. At Wiggins she turned right and a few turns through side streets brought her to a three-storey block of apartments that had seen better days. The only place she found to park was in a tow-away zone with the rear third of her car partially blocking the alley beside the building.

There was grit on the stairs and the banister looked

like she would stick fast if she touched it. She reached the landing and hastily stepped against the wall to avoid being bowled over by someone racing down the stairs toward her. Snatches of music and remnants of food odours came at her at the top of the flight. At the second door on the right, the one with the fresh beige paint and the shiny new lock, she knocked.

"It's unlocked, Mom, come on in." Elie entered as Grant tapped a stack of papers together and stapled them with a flourish.

"How'd you know it was me? Where's Brad?"

"You knock funny, and Brad's in there." He nodded at a door, that promptly opened. A freshly showered Brad grinned at her.

"Hi."

"Brad!" She was horrified.

"Easy, Mom. I got this shiner at wrestling practice. I either had to suck weight or move up a class. I moved up and got creamed, that's all." He did not seem in the least bit troubled by his bloodshot eye, the swollen lid, or the ripening bruise, but she was. He looked like she felt and she wished there were something she could do about them both.

They left the building and piled into the car, which was still where she had left it, all its parts intact. Their destination was a cosy mom and pop enterprise that did not believe in bright colours and lots of light. It was a popular place and crowded when they arrived. They sat in a deep booth of pretend mahogany and red vinyl in the back of the long narrow room and ordered.

"So, . . . Mom . . . We've been wracking our brains trying to figure out how you found out about Sunday. The janitor call you or something? He's hopeless."

"You talked to the police, I suppose?"

"Yeah. They were there and a key was jammed in the

lock. We couldn't get it out. It seemed sensible at the time."

"What I want to know is why you went chasing down the hall without any clothes on. I thought I raised you better than that." Brad froze, looking like a raccoon caught in a headlight. She had to struggle to keep from laughing.

"Who told you that?"

"Curly Griffeth—Sergeant Griffeth to you—is an old friend and he gave me the official version this morning. I'm not so old and feeble that I need protecting from the truth, boys. Not yet anyway."

The burgers arrived in freshly baked buns along with an enormous basket of homefries to share. The familiar odours mingled and, in spite of everything, Elie's mouth watered. When their stomachs were full and their plates empty, the moment she dreaded arrived. She said, "Look boys, I know you can take care of yourselves, but these break-ins have me worried. Don't keep secrets. Talk about it, okay? I'll be honest with you, too. Something has happened that you need to know about and there's no easy way to tell you." She took the paper from her pocket and smoothed the folds before handing it across the table.

"Are you going to call Dad?" Elie's pink slip had been a real downer. They had left the cafe almost immediately and now were parked beside a power pole in the unlit alley alongside the apartment.

"There isn't anything he can do from Los Angeles except worry. I'll tell him when he gets back."

In silence they watched people, students mostly, crossing the mouth of the alley twenty-five or thirty feet ahead, illuminated by street lamps and passing headlights.

"Who's that?"

"Who?"

"The girl just walking by."

"Fiona Stewart. Lives next door. Why?"

"She about ran me over on the stairs when I came in. The way she was running I thought the building was on fire."

"Grant, that reminds me. Why did you lie to her about the break-in on the way to class yesterday morning?"

"It wasn't exactly lying. I don't know, maybe because she was asking the same questions as the janitor. It made me think maybe she was the one who told him. Either way, it isn't any of her business. And if you noticed, she lied, too. She said she saw the cops when she got home, remember? But, she couldn't have seen them through a closed door and, anyway, they weren't wearing uniforms. Maybe she was listening at the wall, I don't know. What I do know is that I haven't liked her since the day she moved in."

"I don't either, but I kind of feel sorry for her. You know that guy who was killed in that plane crash? He was her supervisor. She's got a job if she can finish up in January, but she's afraid now that it won't happen. She told me she's supposed to meet her new thesis supervisor on Saturday. He wants to see her work, but I guess from what she said that's a problem. Some of her stuff is missing or something."

"How do you know that?"

"She stopped by to borrow the newspaper this afternoon and told me. She looked kind of pale and shaky and just stood there staring at the page."

They continued to talk for so long that by the time Elie turned her car onto her street it was nearing midnight. Her headlights picked out the large poplar branch that Sunday's storm had brought down and which, three days later, still occupied the better part of the Stevenson's lawn.

With her arms full, Elie fumbled the key into the back door lock, entered, and dumped the first of her boxes on the family room floor, returning to the car for the second. It was chilly in the house, but she hated the thought of turning on the heat. It meant summer was well and truly over for a long cold time.

She barely glanced at the mail before dropping it all on the hall table. She felt absolutely drained. It had taken a great deal of effort to appear confident and calm during dinner. She certainly had not felt it. The decision to tell the boys had been a hard one to make, but she was glad she had. This was not the time for secrets.

Elie stood irresolutely beside the round oak table in the old-fashioned kitchen with its cream painted cabinets and its red, brick-patterned floor. The light on the answer-phone hanging on the wall over the counter was not blinking. No one had called.

Restless, she wandered from the kitchen through the dining room and into the darkened living room where a splash of light from a street lamp fell across the coffee table and formed a small, dim pool on the carpet. There was no traffic, nothing moved. Across the street a lone upstairs light went out. Everything was still.

A wave of loneliness washed over her, bringing with it a deluge of self-pity that she resolutely tried to push away. She recognised the feelings. This was much how she had felt after the officers came to tell her about her father. Three of them had crowded the front hall, standing almost at attention, clutching their uniform hats. Their faces were masks of despair as the most senior of them haltingly described what had happened. As a cop's kid she had grown up knowing that sudden death in the course of duty could happen, all the same she had never believed that it would. She had stood at the same window then, looking out at the night, feeling so hopeless and lonely, so utterly sad.

Her feet continued to carry her around the house that had always been her comfort and refuge, almost a relative when she was left alone with none. After her father's death

Walter urged her to keep the family home saying it would take care of her. That had made no sense to an inexperienced teenager. A house was something you took care of, not the other way around. But it had been good counsel. With Walter's help, reliable tenants had been found to rent it. Then, when she and Don married, it became her home again. Walter had been right.

She found herself back in the kitchen. What would she do with herself in the morning? Forget about morning, what about now? More than anything she wished Don were home. Just having his arms around her would help. Maybe she would call him after all. No, it was too late. She contemplated a hot bath and bed but knew she would not sleep. She opened the fridge and extracted a beer. Maybe it would help her relax. She twisted off the cap on the way to the family room. Why had she been fired anyway? She flopped onto the couch. Was there some rule about receiving adequate notice? She needed to find out. She untied her runners and took them off. Who could she ask? Call a lawyer, m'dear, that is what they are for. Right. First thing in the morning. Great. Now she was talking to herself.

She snuggled into the cushions and, mostly for company, switched on the TV and flipped through the channels. Murder and mayhem seemed to rule everywhere: Sarajevo, Somalia, Detroit, Top Cops. Depressing. She turned off the sound and reached for the paper.

Front and centre on the first page was the mangled wreckage of the Piper with the caption: "Local Pilot Killed." The accompanying article said that first reports indicated the plane had run out of fuel with no safe place to land. It went on to say the cause was probably pilot error.

A second story gave a somewhat hyped account of the search. James Campbell was pictured with his thin lips curved in an uncharacteristic smile and was quoted saying nice things about the Flannigan's Flying Service pilot—

unnamed—who had participated in the search. Thanks a lot, James. What a hypocrite!

On page three another article was accompanied by a graphic that illustrated both the Hacker Lake accident site and, miles distant, Downy Lake, Essen's planned flight destination. The reporter speculated in a confused fashion about why the plane had been so far off course, making it obvious in the process that she did not have any idea what she was talking about.

At the bottom of the page, Essen's picture appeared with what was really an obituary under the caption: "Geology Professor Dies." Midway through reading it she was startled by the phone. It was almost 1:30 A.M., who could be calling at this time of night?

The dispatcher's worried voice said, "Sorry to bother you so late, Elie, but we've got trouble."

"Norm, I've got trouble. I've been fired."

"Oh, no. Oh, Elie, I didn't know. This is awful. Part of the reason I called was to tell you that John had been fired. Damn it all, this is worse than I thought."

"John, too?"

"Campbell has got to be stopped. He's tearing Flannigan's to pieces."

"You have a particular weapon in mind or do we get to choose?"

"Something slow and exceedingly painful. You can have first whack. Look, this firing business is only half of what I called about. The accident boys want to talk to you at eight tomorrow morning."

"Why me? I can't tell them anything."

"They're talking to everybody they didn't interview before. The RCMP is even questioning people the TSB people have already talked to. City police turned up tonight, too. They're still here. It looks serious but nobody knows why. Go directly to the maintenance office in the hangar, okay?"

She could not see the point but at least it gave her something to do in the morning.

"And, Elie? You know that courier pilot Joe hired right before he died? He was looking for you."

6. Thursday, October 14

With her mind full of trouble, sleep had not come easily and what little she had managed had been fitful. She awoke tense and out of sorts and stood under a hot shower until the water ran cold.

The enormity of her situation was gradually sinking in. One small part of her felt guilty and embarrassed about having been fired while another part said it was not her fault. Which was right? At this point, she did not know. Maybe there had been something she had done, or said, or not done that she should have done. Her thoughts rotated endlessly, she had a headache, and the last thing she wanted to do was talk to an accident investigator. Why did he want to talk to her, anyway?

She made breakfast and forced herself to eat some of it even though her stomach churned. She washed the dishes and checked the time, paced the floor and checked the time, put on her coat and left.

She arrived at Flannigan's much too early for her appointment. Once again she paced, this time at the edge of the hangar floor, keeping out of the way of the ever-present engineers and the tugs that dragged planes from the cavernous interior of the brightly lit hangar into the shadows of the ramp. From time to time she stopped beside the yawning opening to look at the lights of the airport and the glow from the more distant city.

Few people looked at her as they went about their business and few spoke. It was just as well. She could not have responded anyway. A painfully sharp sense of loss had produced a lump in her throat that would not go away. Her parents had introduced her to flying when she was just a child by chartering a plane for a trip. She had fallen in love with the freedom and fun, deciding early on that one day she would pilot a plane herself. When her father was killed, Walter had urged her to learn to fly—she knew now it was to take her mind off her loss—and she never regretted it. She took to it as easily as a fledgling robin. In short order she earned a commercial licence and become an instructor, which paid her way through university. This became her world, where she was at home, but it was hers no longer. She would miss the flying, the people, the purpose, everything. For the first time in over twenty years she felt out of place here, a stranger. She looked it too. Wearing jeans and a heavy black and white sweater amid the uniforms of the pilots and overalls of the mechanics, she looked as out of place as a lamb in a chicken coop.

A courier plane taxied in and the panel truck that had been patiently waiting drove to it. After the transfer of bags, the pilot closed the hatch and walked across the apron, his heavy flight case banging against his thigh with every step. He spotted her, detoured, and motioned her out into the shadows.

"Elie, I can't believe what's happened. The news is all over the airport. Campbell is crazy."

"I can't quite believe it, either. It's a nightmare. I keep hoping I'll wake up. Norm said you were looking for me?"

"Yeah, I was. You helped me a lot when I started to work here so I thought I kind of owed you an explanation. Last Thursday night before my run Campbell came into Flight Ops with a proposition. He said that if I agreed to talk up what he called his restructuring of Flannigan's there was a promotion and raise in it for me. I'm not that kind of person and I told him so. What he's doing stinks. When I turned him down he got real mad. He told me I should thank him for trying to help me and that there were dozens of pilots who would like my job. Even if he doesn't fire me I won't work for someone like that, so I've started sending out my resumé. I just wanted you to know why."

She thanked him for telling her, wished him luck, and watched him cross the hangar floor. He was an excellent and conscientious pilot and she was sorry he would be leaving. He would be missed, but she couldn't blame him. Her stomach was churning again, this time with anger. How many people had Campbell approached and how many had caved in? Is that what he had been doing when Mark saw him at Mufti's? Buying support? If that was not illegal, it was certainly immoral. Campbell obviously cared more about his little power trip than he did for either the company or the employees. Whatever it took, he had to be stopped.

The door to the maintenance office opened. She was summoned and conducted into a windowless room built into an internal corner of the hangar. Only yesterday, when it was John's office, it had been filled with a friendly clutter. Now it was bare, almost Spartan, and somehow appeared to be much smaller. The effect was unsettling.

Two accident investigators conducted the interview. One of them, a tall, pleasant-looking man with kind but fatigue-lined eyes, led her in and introduced himself as Tom Butler. A straight-backed chair had been drawn up to the front of the desk and he gestured for her to sit. Stiffly she thanked him and took her seat, not knowing quite what to expect. Seated behind the desk was a second man. He said his name was Woody. The desk top was clear except for a desk lamp, which was on, a notebook opened to a fresh page, and a tape recorder. It was intimidating.

There was a third man in the room, sitting in a chair against the wall beside the door. Butler introduced him as Constable Dillon, RCMP, who would merely observe the interview. The officer nodded and smiled a smile that did not quite make it to his eyes. Elie took an instant dislike to him and said, "I wasn't aware that the RCMP helped investigate aircraft accidents."

"Sometimes. In this case the plane was found in RCMP jurisdiction and there was a death. We have certain questions to clear up."

This did not quite answer her question but it seemed to be the only answer she was going to get. Butler and Woody took over and did their best to put her at ease. They spoke quietly and calmly. They told her that they each had different roles in the investigation and explained what these were. They tried some small talk and offered her coffee, which she refused. They said that if she wanted a friend or fellow pilot for support during the interview her request would be granted. It seemed to her that they were treating her with kid gloves and she wondered why. She was there at their request to answer their questions and she wished they would just get on with it.

Woody explained that many questions concerning the accident remained unanswered and that they were talking to everyone who might have even a sliver of information. It was important to try to prevent similar incidents from occurring again. He said that, with her permission, they would record the interview. She agreed and, on tape, they had her agree to the interview all over again.

He began, "The company has you listed as both a charter pilot and an instructor. Is that right?" Elie just nodded.

"For the record, Mrs. Meade nodded in the affirmative. Eileen, we need you to give verbal answers, please. Now, I'd like to ask you some questions about Dr. Essen. We know that he did his initial flight training in Ontario, but I wonder if you've ever flown with him. Ever do an insurance check or something like that with him?"

"Never."

"Are you familiar with his plane? Ever fly it? Maybe with the co-owner?"

"The co-owner, yes. I checked him out when he first bought the plane five, maybe six, years ago. He'd never flown a Piper. Since then he's had a lot of work done on it, instruments replaced, new radios, I don't know what all. It got pretty expensive and that's why he sold a half interest in it."

"Then you haven't flown it in some time, that right? Who checked out Essen?"

"The co-owner. I remember him saying that Essen had learned to fly in the same kind of plane and had more flying hours than he did."

"Ever hear him say anything about Essen's skill as a pilot?"

She shook her head, then remembered the recorder and said, "No, sorry."

He asked more questions along the same line but she could tell him nothing. There was a lull during which Elie glanced behind her at the RCMP officer. He sat impassive and expressionless, but his eyes were sharp and intelligent and they never left her. She wondered again why he was present.

Butler, who had been leaning against a bank of filing cabinets with his arms folded, straightened and then draped a long leg over the side of the desk. He said, "Just a few more questions, Eileen. Do you know if Dr. Essen was in the habit of turning his emergency locator transmitter from the armed to the off position after a flight? You ever hear him mention something about that?"

"Is that why we didn't get a signal? It was turned off?"

He nodded and said, "Right."

She shook her head. It made no sense. Rapid deceleration of any type, from a crash to a rough landing, will trigger an ELT to transmit a signal on the emergency frequency, provided it is set in the armed position. There is little point in having an ELT mounted if it is not able to transmit. In Canada, with its vast unoccupied spaces, all aircraft that fly outside a small radius of their home strip are required to carry one.

"Mr Butler. . . ."

"Tom, call me Tom."

"Tom. The newspaper said Essen ran out of fuel. Is that true?"

"Yes. It was fuel starvation, no doubt about it. The tanks were dry." He looked at her oddly. "Why do you ask?"

"Curiosity, mostly. No leaks? Systems all okay? No problem with the flight controls?" It was disconcerting the way they concentrated on her, watching her closely, seeming to listen to the way she said something along with what she said.

"We found no mechanical problems of any kind."

"Does our chief mechanic, John Gardner, know that? He's been concerned."

"He knows."

She was relieved. It was one thing less for him to worry about. Being out of work was enough. "And the plane did go down on Sunday morning?"

"It did. When it was found so far off course, our first thought was that the pilot got lost or disoriented on his Friday morning flight. Now we're sure the accident occurred on the return trip. For one thing, someone heard it crash and the time of that coincides with our other findings. It was Sunday morning."

"It's none of my business and maybe you can't tell me, but I've been an instructor for a long time and I'm interested in what happened. One of the CASARA spotters who was in the Otter told me that since one wing was found separated from the fuselage he thought maybe the plane broke up in the air.

"Woody and Butler exchanged glances, then Butler said, "No. Not a chance. An aerial break-up strews wreckage quite a distance. In this case the wing wasn't far away. He was without power but intact when he went into that forest. I know you were part of the first search crew, Eileen. To put your mind at ease, the result would have been the same if he'd been located minutes after crashing. It was not a survivable accident."

She contemplated her hands lying folded in her lap. After a moment of silence she said, "I've always told my students that if you're in that situation—without power and going into trees like that—that you'll probably walk away if you keep the plane under control, guide it between trees to try to take off both wings at once, and ride the fuselage like a guided missile to the ground. It looks like I've been telling them something that isn't true."

"On the contrary. You're right. We've seen the evidence in other accidents to prove it. In this case it looks like he panicked. From the trees he clipped we think that, at first, he was gliding with pretty close to the airspeed to give him the recommended glide angle. Then, probably as a panic reflex to try to get away from the trees, he pulled the nose up. He gained a few feet but lost airspeed and it was about then that he took out a sizable tree and lost one wing in the process. The end result was that he spun in." She grimaced and shook her head. It was not a pretty scenario.

Woody changed the subject. "Eileen, a while ago you mentioned Mr. Gardner. This morning we learned he had been fired. Any idea why?"

She felt the eyes of the man sitting behind her boring into the back of her neck. It made her so uncomfortable that she almost refused to respond. She turned and glanced at him, then answered honestly and somewhat defiantly, "None. I think it's about the worst mistake Campbell has made. John's been with Flannigan's for more than thirty years and been chief of maintenance for over twenty. You couldn't get a better or more loyal employee."

The tape was turned off, the interview was over. Butler walked her to the door. "Apart from what you think about his firing Mr. Gardner, what's your opinion of Mr. Campbell? You seemed to imply that you think he's made some mistakes since he's taken over."

"I think he has, yes. But, in view of the fact that yesterday he also fired me, I'm not the best person to ask." She nodded to Woody and to the RCMP officer who still sat observing and walked out of the room. As she left, the three men exchanged nods of their own.

The interview left her feeling unsettled. Those men had been after something. As she walked across the hangar floor she tried to figure out what it was. They knew the cause of the accident but still were not satisfied. The cause had been fuel starvation followed by panic and a spin. They were the experts, they should know. It did seem a bit strange, however. She knew next to nothing about Essen, but the man had flown for years. Why forget fuel considerations on this trip? Had he not checked the tanks? Noted his fuel burn? Why was he so far off course? They had not said anything about that. The ELT switch found in the off position? She shook her head. An accumulation of mistakes. It probably would be listed as pilot error like the paper said. Sad.

She checked her watch. It was only 8:20. Too early to call the lawyer she had selected from the phone book. She wandered into Norm's office.

"Interview over?"

"Such as it was. I couldn't tell them much. There was an RCMP observer who just sat there without opening his mouth. I got the impression that he was an investigator of a different sort. Know anything about it?"

"Only that there are a couple of them along with some city police in the hangar as we speak. You going to confront Campbell when he comes in?"

She shook her head. "It wouldn't do any good. Remember, he told me never to darken the hangar doors again. I'm going to call a lawyer to see what, if anything, I should do. I might need to pick up my employment records or something, too. Mind if I wait and call from here?"

"Not in the least. Just try not to frown like that, you'll get wrinkles. You know, I think we could both do with a bite to eat. How 'bout you run down to the staff room and rescue a couple of doughnuts from the charter supplies."

"Splendid thought. Hips be damned! Comfort food is what I need. What kind do you want?"

"Chocolate. With chocolate frosting and chocolate filling. Two or three of them," he yelled after her as she disappeared down the hall.

Every time she tried the law office which, according to their advertisement specialized in labour law, the line was engaged. Were they really that busy or had they taken the phone off the hook? She walked the few steps between the counter and the window watching for Campbell's car. If he caught her it would mean trouble. She dialled again. Busy.

Norm carried on business as usual with much shuffling of papers alternating with coffee drinking, doughnut munching, and talking on the phone. After one call he swiveled around.

"Hold still a minute, Elie. That was Edna Gardner. John's in hospital. She's afraid he's had a stroke."

She could only stare. The bad news just never quit.

"She's pretty upset. She told me John was so keyed up and worried that he couldn't sleep last night, kept pacing around the house, talking to himself. Then, when it started to get light she said he went out to rake the leaves. She found him when she went to call him for breakfast." Norm clenched and unclenched his jaw, causing the little wattle of skin under his chin to quiver.

"This is all because of Campbell. He fires two mechanics and issues that damned pronouncement about everybody being more productive. Christ, he's stupid. He's paying mountains of overtime! John has been coming in early and staying late just to make sure our planes are ready to fly. He's become so compulsive about it that he's been working his men to the point where they've been in here complaining and they aren't complainers. It's bad. You've seen how he's been looking. He can't take all that. A man his age shouldn't work that hard. And then to get fired? Jezzes, El! Campbell's a rotten little bastard who's better off dead!"

Elie reflected that John was not the only one who had become compulsive about work. Norm had too. When he was not in the office his cell phone was in his pocket. Because of Campbell he was on call twenty-four hours a day. If things kept up the way they were going it wouldn't be long before everyone at Flannigan's would be a raging neurotic.

She finally got through to the lawyer. Even this early in the morning the woman she spoke with sounded tired. She also sounded like she knew what she was talking about. When Elie hung up she had two pages of notes and felt much better. Then, as Campbell still had not turned up, she took the chance and went to find Lars.

He was at his desk comparing his credit card receipts to the long list on his bill. "Be with you in a minute, El." He stuck his thick fingers into a pocket of his empty wallet, shook his head in frustration, and shuffled the wallet contents that were strewn about in front of him.

"I can't find the damn thing!" He poked the bill, "This

amount seems too high, but I can't find the receipt. I always keep them." He tossed the wallet on top of the mess he had created, an action that sent a couple of bank statements sailing to the floor. She stooped to pick them up while he leaned his bulk back in his chair, causing it to creak in protest.

"Never mind. I'm so overdue paying it, the interest is worse than the bill. What can I do for you?"

"There's nothing you can do except maybe write a letter of recommendation for me—if you're willing."

"I'm not very good with letters. You write it—really toot your horn—and I'll sign it."

"Thanks. Have you found out any more about Flannigan's being sold?"

"Nothing. But firing you and John seems to me the opening salvo in an active campaign to break up the company. I hope you know I didn't have anything to do with it, El. It came right out of the blue. I wouldn't have been surprised if I'd got the chop, he's threatened enough times. But, you? I was surprised."

She remembered him coming out of Campbell's office and wondered just how surprised he really was. She wanted to ask, but said instead, "Not so surprising. I flew that first track crawl for the search and I didn't report to him afterwards like he ordered. I had a charter. Besides that, I've had the feeling for some time that he was just looking for a reason to let me go."

"The man's a fool. Could he be working on behalf of that regional airline? They wouldn't want to pay any more for Flannigan's than they have to. Think it's possible that's what he's doing?"

"What a nasty thought. It even fits. On the other hand, it's possible that he hasn't any clear idea what he's doing. It's fashionable these days to cut jobs, so maybe that's why he's cutting too. For some reason it's supposed to demonstrate a firm grip at the helm and good management skills. The bottom line looks good for a while because there aren't as many people around to pay, but in companies like ours there aren't any extra people and the business suffers. The average stuffed animal can make the connection."

"Yeah, well, he's not that bright. The man can't be trusted, that's for sure. I know he's up to something and I want to know what it is. I've taken that bimbo he hired and calls his secretary out a few times to try to find out. I've been both blunt and subtle but she won't open up. She's scared to death of him. I've been reduced to going through the trash after dark. I have no idea what I'm looking for but I keep trying. So far, I've found diddley squat. What I really want to do is get into his office to go through his files. I'd like to take a look at his computer, too."

"Be careful. He's such a paranoid he probably uses a security code on that computer of his and he probably locks up the file drawers at night. If he got even an inkling that you might be having such thoughts he wouldn't think twice about calling the police and have you charged with every crime he'd ever heard of. At the very least, he'd fire you on the spot and spread interesting and ugly rumours. You'd never get another flying job."

"Yeah, . . . but, I can't just stand by and watch what's happening. I've got to do something to stop him."

While driving home she wondered whether there really was a way to stop Campbell. Maybe there was something she could do even though she was no longer an employee. But what? By the time she let herself into the back door, the situation seemed hopeless and she was in the grip of an overwhelming compulsion to grab a box of chocolate creams and assume the fetal position in front of the TV. She fought it off by throwing herself into a thorough cleaning of the family room.

The vacuum cleaner made such a racket that she almost missed the ring of the extension just a few feet away. She let it ring, thinking it was probably just another carpet-cleaning pitch. On the other hand, it could be the boys, or it might be Don. She plucked up the receiver as the tape kicked in. It was Norm. He sounded depressed.

"I had the sudden need to talk to a real, live, normal person and, for a minute there, I was afraid you weren't home. I'm going out to eat. I'll transfer calls to my cell phone."

"You usually eat at your desk. Forget to bring your lunch?"

"Nope. This place is getting to me, is all. I've got to get away for a while."

"What's happening?"

"For starters, Campbell still hasn't shown up. But then, after what he did to you and John he's probably afraid he'll be pelted by things soft and smelly. Ha! He should be so lucky. And you were right about those observer people, only they aren't observing any more. They are city police and RCMP detectives and they're all over the place asking questions. One of them named Griffeth says he knows you."

"Norm, what's going on?"

"Damned if I know. They've got everybody upset."

"I'm glad I'm not there. Look, I'm going to make a casserole to take to Edna and I thought I'd have flowers sent to John. Want me to put your name on the card?"

"Good idea. Thanks, El. Talk to you later."

The bay window of the Gardner living room was covered with sheer curtains that managed to keep the sun out without having to draw the heavy floral drapes. The room itself was filled with a little too much dark furniture for the space available, making it look cluttered though it was kept as neat as a pin. Elie sat on a blue brocade couch that sported hand-crocheted arm and head rests and watched Edna, a little bird of a woman, refill their tea cups.

Elie had already reported what she had learned from the lawyer. While Edna wrote it all down, Elie patiently dictated so John could have a full report when he was awake again and able to understand.

"Have another shortcake, dear, and tell me again. I still don't understand this wrongful dismissal business."

"John and I were terminated without a reason and with no notice. We should at least have received what they call payment in lieu of reasonable notice, but we didn't even get a pay cheque. There has to be reasonable cause to be fired like we were, something like theft of company property. The lawyer I talked to said she thought we had a good case and should pursue it."

"That costs money, doesn't it? Lately John has been so worried about money. He worries so much now about everything. And, he seems angry all the time and forgetful! Sometimes he even forgets to change out of his coveralls before coming home, and sometimes I find a gauge or something in his pockets. He never used to do that, Elie.

"The doctor wanted to know when this forgetfulness began and I told him I thought, as near as I could remember, it was about the time Joe died. They were such great friends, you know, but now I think maybe it started before that. I remember the picnic. . . ." She trailed off and her crooked arthritic fingers picked at the embroidery on her linen napkin.

"Did something happen?"

"I'm really not sure. Joe and John spent a great deal of time together that day. They talked and talked. Afterwards, John went off by himself, and after ever so long he came looking for me. He seemed to be upset and said he wanted to go home so, even though it was still the middle of the afternoon, we left. It wasn't like him at all. I remember I asked him if he was feeling poorly and he said he didn't want to stay any longer because he was worried about Joe. He said Joe had told him he was talking to a lawyer about his will. Well, John's one of those people that thinks it's bad luck even to have a will unless you know you're really sick, so I guess maybe he thought Joe was ill. He never mentioned it again, but I guess he was right because Joe died less than two months later. John misses him so much."

"John actually said that Joe talked about his will?"

"Well, yes dear, I think he did."

"Do you have any idea where he would have put it?"

"No, dear. Joe was always very organized so someone should have known where it was. It would have been kept by the lawyer or at the bank or in a file drawer or some place like that, don't you think? But, I guess nobody found it, did they. Maybe he never really had one after all. John could have been mistaken about it. Oh, Elie, whatever shall I do if he doesn't get better?"

Edna was such a sweet woman and so obviously troubled that Elie stayed far longer than she had planned. She was annoyed with herself for getting caught in rush hour traffic, but it could not be helped. Now her car practically rocked from a tape blasting from a car in the outside lane. Her ears throbbed in time to the thumping of the bass. The teenage driver leered at her and turned the volume up another notch. She ignored him and willed the light to turn green.

When she turned down her street she noticed Mrs. Stevenson, hands on ample hips, surveying the offending branch that seemed to have become a permanent lawn fixture. When she saw the car she ran toward it with a loud "Yoo-Hoo!" Elie stopped and rolled down the window.

Mrs. S. stuck her face into the opening and puffed, "When are your boys going to come over and cut up that branch for me?"

"Mrs. Stevenson, they can't. They're both university students, you know. They don't live at home." Besides, she thought, you never even asked them.

"Then how am I going to get rid of it?" Mrs. S. was a complainer who had perfected a whine that filled the interior of the car and threatened to make Elie's ears bleed.

"Perhaps, Mr. Stevenson would have a suggestion?" Her smile was pure saccharine as she stepped on the accelerator.

As she approached her own house her heart sank. A strange burgundy-coloured car was parked at the curb and two men sat on the steps of the front porch. Some religious sect? Vacuum cleaner salesmen? Whoever it was, she did not want to deal with them.

She pulled up close to the doors of the old garage at the rear of the lot, and got out of the car. Coming up the drive to meet her was Curly Griffeth and a rather nondescript young man with medium-brown hair and a mustache.

"What brings you by, Curly? Good news, I hope."

"Elie, I'd like you to meet Constable Carl Stefanyk. We just happened by on the off chance you were home."

She grinned at this outrageous lie. "Of course you did, Curly. And my front steps looked so comfy you just had to have a little sit. Well, here I am. Come on in."

While she put on the coffee Griffeth wandered over to the kitchen window and surveyed the back yard. "Didn't there used to be a brick barbecue in that corner?"

"That went years ago. It fell apart."

"Figures. Nothing lasts forever. Your dad barbecued a mean sausage on it in his day." He picked a yellow rubber glove off the window sill, rubbed it between his fingers, brought it to his nose and put it back where he found it.

"Yeah, he did at that. And when you all came over you had such a good time the racket always kept me awake. I should have called the cops."

"Very funny. I remember a few times when you tried to crash the party. You were a brat."

"I was not."

"Yes you were. You were cute, but a brat."

Funny, she did not remember it that way, but then it was a long time ago. She poured the coffee. "I hope you're here to tell me you arrested whoever burgled my boys' apartment."

He surveyed her over the rim of his cup. "Hmm? No." He dropped his eyes and his voice dripped innocence. "I told you, I just brought Carl by for a little visit."

"Let me guess. Crime is under control so you're out making social calls, right? Next, you'll be telling me I make the best coffee you ever tasted and invite yourself for dinner. Sorry, but there isn't a sausage in the place." She smiled sweetly at the sheepish look he gave her.

"Look, Curly, I'm tired, I'm worried, and I've had enough aggravation in the last few days to last me a lifetime. Please, don't treat me like an idiot. I know you've been at Flannigan's most of the day but I don't know why. What's going on?"

He played with his cup, turning it around and around. He seemed to have become detached and wary. The sudden change bothered her. She glanced at the young man at her right elbow who sat clicking his ball point pen.

"We're investigating a homicide. There's evidence that suggests Essen's plane was tampered with. We believe Jake Essen was killed. Murdered."

"What? Oh, come on. I don't believe it. When I talked to the investigators this morning they said it was fuel starvation."

"That's right. He ran out of fuel."

"They also said that there was nothing mechanically wrong. So how does that translate into murder? You aren't making much sense. Anyway, what have you got to do with it? He was found in RCMP territory."

He ignored her questions and continued to rotate his cup. The young constable continued to click. She saw that he had opened the notebook in front of him.

Finally Curly said, "It's a joint homicide investigation now. RCMP, and us. Sorry, but it's your turn to answer the same questions we're asking every Flannigan's employee."

"Curly, I'm not a Flannigan's employee any more. I've been fired."

"I know. I'm truly sorry about that, but you were employed on Thursday of last week. Can you account for your whereabouts on that day, October seventh?"

She felt her face go hot with indignation. "Of course I can. I worked on Thursday. You can check the flight sheets."

"We already did. There are periods of time unaccounted for."

"What's going on here? Am I being accused of something? If so, I want to know what."

"Now, now, Elie," he began.

"Don't patronize me, Curly!"

"Sorry." He really was sorry, but he was sorry for himself. She was going to make this a tough interview.

The questions continued, going over everything she had done—at least what she could remember doing—on the seventh. After ten minutes she thought the subject was exhausted but Curly was still going strong. Finally he asked if she had gone into the hangar at any time during that day. She replied that she probably had because she usually did. Had she noticed anyone hanging around who did not belong there? No.

He went back to turning his now empty cup. The young man, freed from note-taking for a moment, went back to clicking his pen. His cup was also empty. Well too bad, but she did not feel like refilling them. She propped her chin on her fist and fixed her gaze on Curly's large and shiny bald patch.

Carl felt uneasy. This was the first homicide investigation he had been involved with since beginning his three months with the Major Crime Unit only two weeks before. It was exciting, for sure, but with his limited experience he was just treading water and he knew it. He clutched his pen, slowly and repeatedly pushing the button at the top. He watched Griffeth toy with his cup and wondered what he was up to. Somehow it did not seem professional for him to be slouched in a kitchen chair, playing with crockery. Not when he was investigating a murder. He must have a reason. He had not achieved his reputation for nothing. Maybe he should take notes on his interrogation technique. It might come in handy someday.

And then there was the subject. Her kitchen, her coffee, her cups, and there she sat, silent as Griffeth, staring off into space. Should he be asking her questions now that Griffeth had stopped?

He was curious about her. What would make an otherwise apparently normal woman want to fly airplanes? She was even married. And had children. He examined her as closely as he dared. She had short, thick and curly, reddish-brown hair with a bit of copper and a hint of silver. It was cut kind of like some of the photos displayed in the salon where his girlfriend worked. He thought it suited her. She had a nice friendly smile—except not at the moment—and he liked the way the little lines radiated at the corners of her large, blue-green eyes. He thought the lines might have been caused by laughter or maybe by squinting against the sun. Pilots did that a lot, he supposed. Her other features were—well, they were regular. Taken all together she was kind of nice looking—for someone her age, of course. She was probably not too much younger than his own mother, but his mother was nicely plump. Elie Meade was not. She was slim, graceful, and not very tall so that he wondered how she managed to handle a plane. Somehow, it just did not seem the proper thing for a nice woman to do.

Griffeth pushed his cup around to the left. All he had for motive so far was the suggestion that Professor Essen's love life might have caught up with him. For that reason he was following up on every name in Essen's bloodstained address book. But, even though he hoped something or someone would turn up, it did not seem very likely.

Counting Elie, there were twenty-two people so far who admitted to being in the hangar on the seventh. That meant twenty-two people with opportunity. Griffeth pushed his cup across the mat to the right. Except that the mechanics said that nobody had touched the plane but themselves and they all vouched for each other.

According to them, the job of replacing a control cable was long and tedious and at least one mechanic, sometimes two, had been working on that plane at all times. Curly admitted to himself that he needed to talk this through with someone who not only knew aircraft but was also very familiar with Flannigan's. What he was about to do went against the grain. He placed his cup in the exact centre of the mat.

"Elie?" She was staring at him, her chin on her fist. She did not look happy. "What do you know about beach balls?"

The question so took her by surprise that she burst out laughing. "Curly, I think you've been working too hard." At her elbow the clicking got faster.

"You don't approve, Carl? Well, I don't know what else to do. We can use some help here. And stop that damned clicking! You're driving me nuts."

7. Thursday Evening, October 14

The three of them sat around the round oak table in the kitchen, which now smelled wonderfully of olive oil and garlic, basil and oregano.

"Pass the Parmesan, Carl." A piece of spaghetti disappeared between Carl's lips with a slurp and he mopped his mouth and mustache before passing the fat ceramic mouse full of cheese to Griffeth.

"This is really great, Mrs. Meade. I was starving."

"He's always starving."

"You should talk, Curly, that's your second helping."

"I know. What's this called, so I can tell Martha."

"Spaghetti marinara. It's easy."

"Mmph. It's good."

"Not to mention free. How many murder suspects do you make feed you while you interrogate them?"

"I didn't make you feed us. You volunteered."

"Both your stomachs were growling so loudly I couldn't hear myself think. What else could I do? Besides, I'm as curious about this as you are. Let's get back to the beach balls."

Griffeth pushed his empty plate away and leaned back. "Right. There were four in one fuel tank and five in the other, all wedged away from the filler neck. It's hard to be precise, but we figure that together they displaced roughly half the fuel. That's why he ran short. Tell me what occurs to you."

"Somebody has a rotten sense of humour. The fuel gauges would have lied and the dip stick—assuming he dipped the tanks—would lie, too. Rather horrible isn't it?

Check your fuel and still come up short. How did they find them, anyway?"

"I asked that TSB fellow, Butler, about that. He said that at the crash site they looked at the prop and knew right away that he went in without power so the next thing, I guess, is to figure out why. Before getting to the engine, the most obvious thing to do is check fuel. They removed the fuel caps and used a mirror to check inside the tanks. What they were looking for, he said, was to see if anything obvious was blocking the fuel outlet. What he found was a practically empty tank, mostly just fumes. Draining the tanks confirmed it, so it looked like a case of poor fuel management. The guy had run out of gas.

"The plane was in such a remote place and, since they had to use a chopper anyway, they decided to lift the whole thing out. The insurance adjuster agreed. They had to do some basic disassembly and when they were loading the parts onto the flat bed, Butler said he thought he heard a funny noise that seemed to come from inside a wing. He was curious about that, so when they were examining the plane at Flannigan's he opened it up. There they were, beach balls, five of them. He opened up the other wing and found four. He figures they were wedged well away from the fuel filler, maybe by the force of impact, until moving the wings dislodged them. At any rate he contacted RCMP right away."

"Well, that explains why that officer was at my interview. But, why are you involved?"

"TSB hands over the minute it looks like there's been any kind of criminal activity. The plane was found in RCMP territory so they were called first. Since it looks like the balls were inserted in our territory we're handling this end of things." He held out his cup for more coffee. "Help me, Elie. What comes to mind about those balls?"

"Well, they had to be the inflatable kind, obviously. We

used to have a couple, different sizes—took them to the lake for the kids."

"Where can you get them?"

"Lots of places, and they're cheap enough. This time of year most stores would be selling them off. Heavy plastic or rubber, different colours and patterns, and easy to carry. Just blow them up and let the air out again whenever you want."

"Okay, they had to have been slipped through the fuel filler on the top of the wing and then inflated. How?"

She tried to imagine how to stuff a fuel tank with beach balls. "You'd have to insert them through the filler neck, and you'd have to hang on to the ball somehow while you got the air in." She shook her head. "With so little to grab hold of, and with the depth of the filler neck, it would be next to impossible to blow one up by mouth, but pressurized air just might work. There are tanks of the stuff that are wheeled around where they're needed, like to inflate tires. But, it would have taken time and whoever did it would have been seen."

"That's what I can't figure out. The mechanics say someone was with the plane all the time. Where is the tank kept?"

"Against the wall in the back, usually. It's not hidden, if that's what you're getting at. What I can't understand is how he hung onto the balls while they were being inflated. If they're like the ones we had, when you blow them up you have to be careful not to let go. With the inflatable part inside the wing there wouldn't be much to hang on to, just the little neck, the filler-upper-thingy, whatever it's called."

"Of course! That accounts for the string tied around the piece of plastic attaching the plug. That also explains the aviation gas found inside two of the balls. They probably got away from him and he had to haul them out and start over. Good going, Elie."

"Mrs. Meade, is there any more spaghetti?"

"Help yourself."

Griffeth said, "Carl, you should be ashamed of yourself." Carl looked anything but. He grinned. "Stop thinking about your stomach for a minute and earn your pay. Why were there five balls in one tank and only four in the other?"

Vigorously shaking the mouse over his pasta, Carl said, "Sounds like a riddle. How about this? Something or someone interrupted him before he could finish the job."

"Then we're back to the mechanics. If they're telling the truth, there was no opportunity for anyone to have done it."

"So, someone's not telling the truth." He wound spaghetti around his fork and stuffed it into his mouth.

"If we could only narrow down the time frame."

"Curly, why are we concentrating on that day at all? Why couldn't this have been done some other time when the plane was in its usual tie-down spot?"

"Because the partner, the one who reported him missing, flew the plane on Wednesday, the day before the maintenance was done. He's the one who detected the control problem. We checked the fueller's records. It took 155.2 litres to fill it up Wednesday night. Total usable fuel is around 182 litres. With those balls in place, the best estimate is that the tanks could hold somewhere between 90 and 100."

"Sergeant, maybe it was done when they finished working on it. Overnight, like."

"No. They finished the job sometime around eleven and the plane stayed in the hangar all night. A night crew was working and anyone not authorized to be there would have been very obvious. The plane was pushed out at five and Essen was in the air by six."

"An hour. . . . Isn't that enough time?"

"It would have been harder to do in the dark and in

that time Essen had to load the plane, do a walk-around with a flashlight. . . ." Curly shook his head.

A thought nudged her at the same time that Curly pushed back his chair and stood up. The thought vanished. "Thanks Elie, this has been a help. Back to Flannigan's, Carl. Maybe some of the other interviews have turned up something."

Carl put the car in gear and did a U-turn. "So, is she a suspect?"

"Elie? Of course she is. She knows it too. We've got a list as long as your arm of people who knew Essen's plane was being worked on because they heard John's complaints. They all had ready access and opportunity and all of them are either pilots or mechanics who could have done it without drawing much attention to themselves, and that includes Elie. The mechanics swear nobody could have done it, and so far, there's no motive for wanting it done." The seat belt pressed into his stomach as he leaned forward to reach the car's heater control. He belched.

"Why did you sniff Mrs Meade's rubber glove?"

"For gas. Dismantling and examination of the plane obliterated any usable latent prints on the wing, but Ident found something consistent on all the balls: rubber glove prints. Ordinary, household rubber gloves like the kind she uses."

"Find anything?"

"No, and I didn't really expect to."

"Are they all like this?"

"What?"

"Homicides."

"More or less. Either like this or pretty cut and dried. I've never had one with so many possible suspects, though. It's giving me a headache. Watch your driving, Carl. There's no need to rush."

Carl mumbled something that might have been "sir," but as easily might not. Griffeth gave him a hard glance but decided not to pursue it.

"Drop me off at Flannigan's. I want you to get started on finding out who's selling beach balls at this time of year. See if anybody remembers or has a record of selling nine or ten of them at one time. I want your report by noon tomorrow, if possible."

Carl said the same inarticulate syllable. This time Griffeth smiled.

It was cold in the hangar. The huge doors stood open to admit a plane for overnight servicing. Griffeth pulled his scarf tighter and headed for the maintenance office. Two RCMP constables sat in the warmly-heated room comparing statements, looking for discrepancies.

"Sergeant. We've got something for you. You wanted to know where Essen landed up at Hacker Lake on Friday, right? Our Hacker detachment called to say they had found several sets of tire tracks on an old logging road, three tires, consistent with an aircraft. They took casts where it looks like he parked on the shoulder. They've gone to the lab. And, listen to this, they found some cut pine branches piled up nearby, enough to cover the plane. Interesting, eh?"

"Very. Which brings to mind Essen's flight plan. Deliberately inaccurate, I think. Dr. Essen didn't want anyone to know where he was going and didn't want anyone to discover him while he was there. For the same reason, he probably turned off his ELT to make sure a rough landing or take-off wouldn't set it off. He didn't want anyone coming to look for him. Makes me real curious about what he was up to."

"Hacker Detachment haven't found out where he camped yet. Of course, he might have stayed in or near the plane, but if he did there ought to be signs."

Elie was doing the dishes. She had washed and dried everything but the big spaghetti pot. She carried it from the stove to the sink and submerged it in the soapy water, which came close to overflowing onto the floor. In a flash the little thought that had flitted by earlier came back. She dried her hands and went to the phone.

"Curly, you wanted to narrow the time frame, right? Ask the mechanics if they saw any fuel spilled around Essen's plane and if they did, find out when."

"What are you talking about?"

"Essen's plane was refuelled Wednesday night, right? And it was worked on all day Thursday? And you said those balls displaced about half the fuel? Well, where did the displaced fuel go? Even if it was siphoned off, it had to go somewhere and there was bound to be spillage that would have been cleaned up as soon as it was noticed."

"I'll be damned, you're right. What made you think of it?"

"The spaghetti pot."

He hung up, shaking his head. It had been a very long day and it still was not over. He caught a ride back to the station. It was 10:15 when he dropped heavily into his desk chair and called down to the evidence room for Essen's desk calendar. Before he went home he wanted to take a look at it. If the gods were smiling there might be something obvious. Even if there were not, he might get an idea to chew on. While he waited, he decided to call his wife. Martha liked him to call her if he was going to be late and he was already very late. Damage control was better than no control.

"Martha, sorry I'm late. I'll be home in about an hour. Everything all right?"

"Did you get something to eat? I hope nothing greasy. It's not good for you."

"Spaghetti, Martha. Carl and I had spaghetti marinara

and a salad." He would get points for eating a salad. "And I forgot to tell you— you remember G. P. Ayers' daughter, Eileen Meade? She said she'd bake something for the fund-raiser." He would get points for that, too.

A clerk dropped the evidence pouch on the desk. Griffeth signed for it, adding his name and date to the evidence tag. He withdrew Essen's calendar first. Essen's notes were almost illegible, page after page. He checked the page he had seen in Essen's office. The only appointment for the morning had been with Fiona. For the afternoon, something was written in for one o'clock. It was a scrawled single word and hard to make out. Was it *clam*? Or maybe, *claim*? Claim what? It could be that, instead of a *cl* combination, it was a poorly formed *d*. *Dam*?

Damn! Why was it that nobody wrote clearly any more? He rummaged through a desk drawer, pulled out a bottle of aspirin, went to the water cooler, and swallowed two vinegary-tasting tablets.

He was working away, translating what he could, writing notes in his spiky script, when the phone rang. He waited a few rings, expecting someone on night shift to answer but he finally picked it up.

"Griffeth. Yeah, Russ, I'm still at it. . . . What! Shit! Where? . . . Who called it in? Okay, I'm on my way." With his scarf wrapped up to his ears and still buttoning his coat, he galloped out of the room.

It was cold and, without moon or stars, the night was very dark, but the area where Griffeth stood was brightly lit. It was just off the paved trail that ran along the east side of the river, a favourite place for strolling, jogging, and cycling. Trees, bushes, wildflowers, and grasses of all types grew there profusely. Benches were provided at intervals for resting or for contemplation of the rushing water and nature at its best. But Griffeth was not contemplating nature. He stood beside a group of uniformed officers and looked beneath a large bush in a small area lit brighter than day by a couple of battery-powered flood lamps. He had no intention of crawling under there to examine the body. Looking at it garishly lit through the branches was bad enough. It lay stretched full length and face down. A black cap of dried blood covered the back of the head and what skin he could see had a very peculiar colour to it. The camera flashed again and the photographer made a note before taking another shot. He was trying to get a reasonable photo of the upper torso and head that almost touched the oddly substantial trunk of the bush. Branches kept getting in the way.

The assistant coroner got down on his hands and knees, saw what he could see, and ordered the body dragged out where he could get at it. While he did his poking about, Griffeth retreated up the path to sit in the dark on an orange-painted park bench. It was an excellent vantage point from which to watch. A cold misty rain began to fall. He rearranged his scarf, draping one end over his bald spot. He knew he must look ridiculous but he did not care.

The bench where he sat was set at an angle to the path on a kind of terrace and directly faced the knot of activity forty feet away. He made out a small, round trash collector standing nearby, waist-high on a metal pole. He took out his flashlight and poked briefly through the contents but found nothing that looked remotely like a weapon. It would all be collected anyway in case he was wrong.

He sat down again and looked up the embankment to his right. Behind a parking lot guard rail up there a growing number of gawkers watched the action going on below. They looked like so many vultures sitting on a fence. To them it was nothing more than macabre entertainment provided for free. He wondered if the killer was among them, enjoying the show.

At last the coroner motioned to him and Griffeth

returned to the path and strolled toward the shadowy green ash tree that sheltered the body. At least that was what one of the officers had called it: green ash. His own knowledge of botany was pretty meagre. In this case, the tree looked more like a bush. He had thought it was a bush. The entire east side of the river bank was unstable and at some point had given way and buried most of the trunk of a pretty good size tree. Therefore, he thought, he could be forgiven for calling it a bush. It looked like a bush.

Poles had already been stuck in the ground and strung with yellow crime scene tape, creating a festive-looking large yellow square around the tree and a healthy amount of surrounding ground. He walked past latex-gloved, uniformed officers inside the tape who carefully parted the tall grasses and weeds—or were those wildflowers?—searching the ground with the aid of powerful flashlights. Somewhere down in the darkness to his left, revealed by occasional reflections from lights on the nearby University Bridge, was the river with its tricky current and undertows. The previous summer the water had been so high and fast it had snapped the moorings of the sightseeing schooners and washed them over the weir where they had turned to flotsam. The river was still high, still fast. If the murder weapon, whatever it was, was in the water it was probably as good as gone forever.

The coroner said, "Homicide," and "Twenty-four hours, give or take," and Griffeth said "Full autopsy, a.s.a.p."

A beautiful red setter puppy, dragging his leash, arrived at their feet in a rush and whined softly as he looked up at them with eager brown eyes. Griffeth grabbed the leash and scratched the silky head behind soft floppy ears. "So you're the one who found him, are you? Good boy." The puppy turned his head and whined at a sound that had repeated itself too often. "You're doing much better than your master, little guy. He can't have anything left to vomit, but he's still trying."

He called to a paramedic standing beside a stretcher about twenty feet away. "Harv! Want to see what you can do for him, please?" He motioned toward the forlorn figure sitting in the shadows near a wild rose bush midway up the slope, his head on his knees. Just a man walking his dog along the river who would have nightmares for months and maybe never walk along here again. Griffeth wanted to talk to him, but first he wanted that stomach under control.

Once the body was gone, Griffeth and the man sat side by side on the bench. The dog, worn out now, lay at their feet. The man, pale as a ghost, told how his puppy had raced ahead along the path, sniffed around under the so-called bush, and begun to bark. The man called but the pup refused to come. The man went in to get him, literally tripping over the corpse's outstretched legs. In a panic he grabbed the dog and raced to the nearby hospital where he made the 911 call from a pay phone. That was all. Griffeth sent master and dog home in a squad car.

He remained on the bench deep in thought. Keys and a wallet had been found on the body. He knew the name on the identification and he had never heard a kind word said about him. It was quite an epitaph for someone so young. Now there were two murders to solve, and solve in a hurry. A killer was loose. James Campbell was dead.

8. Friday Morning, October 15

Standing around on the river bank and getting rained on the night before had chilled Griffeth to the bone. A long hot shower before bed and another when he got up had not helped a whole lot either. He still felt cold. He turned up at the kitchen table wearing both a sweater and a tweed jacket, trying to remember where he had put his gloves when he last wore them the previous March.

Behind him, Martha padded softly around in her flowered bathrobe and slippers, giving him searching, oblique looks. From her collection of cookbooks she plucked a slim orange and yellow volume and began to turn the pages.

His grapefruit tasted so sour his mouth puckered, but he ate it anyway. He poured some milk—he knew it was skimmed since Martha was into low-fat—over his oatmeal and sprinkled a little brown sugar over the top. Behind him his wife poured orange juice into the blender and, opening one cupboard after another, added things to it. When the motor roared he cringed at the sound. Before he finished his coffee and the editorial he was reading, a glass full of foul-looking brown liquid was plunked in front of him.

"Drink it."

"What is this stuff?"

"Never mind. It's good for what ails you. You look like you're coming down with something."

"Aw, Martha. I hate these mixtures of yours." But, it never did any good to argue with his wife. He took a deep breath and held it—he just knew it would smell as bad as it looked—and drank it down.

Elie sat at her kitchen table, stared at the toast crumbs on her plate, and gave half an ear to the mindless drivel coming from the radio. She wanted the newspaper and wondered if there was a natural law dictating that the lateness of its arrival would be in direct proportion to how badly you wanted to read it. Actually, all she really wanted was something to do. She pushed her coffee away without drinking any. She did not even know why she had made it. She had drunk too much of the stuff lately. She was getting jumpy.

The kitchen clock read 7:20. As usual she had awakened at six and was already out of bed before she remembered she had no job to go to. Now she was at loose ends. She pulled the little notepad she used for shopping lists toward her and began to doodle. She told herself to get organized, to make a plan, to be productive. Do up a resumé. She continued to doodle and then halfheartedly began a shopping list: paper towels, pasta. After a moment's thought she added: tomatoes, basil, garlic. She remembered her promise to bake something for the fundraiser. Drat. She did not feel like baking; she did not feel like doing much of anything. Propping her head on her hand, she watched a little brown sparrow on the telephone wire try to sun himself in the first weak rays of light. She added bird seed to her list.

A promise to bake meant she had to bake. Bake what? She began to doodle again, becoming aware of the circular patterns on the paper. Circles like little beach balls. Beach balls that had fooled Essen into taking off on fumes. Surely Curly could not think she was responsible, could he? She was certainly seeing a different side of him, one she did not much like. She wondered what kind of cop he had become. There were so many stories of shortcuts and cooked evidence these days. What if the killer was someone at Flannigan's? Someone she knew. The thought made her so uneasy that she got up and walked around. When she heard the paper slam into the front door and plop onto the porch she went to get it.

The headline screamed: "City's Eighth Murder." The lead article was short and concentrated on describing the murder scene on the river bank. There were graphic descriptions from the man who had found the body. There was a picture of the dog. Notification of next of kin was pending so no additional details were given. Sensational but uninformative. Typical.

The business page carried a story on the hunt for diamonds. "Yesterday, Ev-Met Mining announced the results of the bulk-sample of three of its kimberlite pipes." What on earth are kimberlite pipes? She read, "We are very excited by the results,' said the company president. Although the company refuses to divulge exact sizes and numbers, the report states that the best sample, a 42.4 tonne parcel taken from Pipe 2, contained gem-quality diamonds including several that ranged from one to nearly four carats. On the strength of the report Ev-Met stock again jumped in price. The stock trades on the Vancouver Exchange."

She thought a nice, four-carat diamond would come in pretty handy about now. Maybe if she knew what a kimberlite pipe looked like, she could go find one. She turned to the help wanted ads.

Griffeth looked speculatively at Stefanyk, who quietly and carefully threaded his way through heavy morning traffic. His silence and caution spoke more eloquently than words. He was dreading what was coming. They were on their way to witness Campbell's autopsy.

When they pushed through the double doors in the hospital basement an Ident corporal was inking cold, unresisting fingers and taking prints, but the pathologist was nowhere to be seen. The room was chilly and smelled of formaldehyde and other things Griffeth did not want to think about. He noted that Carl remained stiffly by the door taking very deep breaths. At the rate he was going he would hyperventilate and pass out before the autopsy even began. Griffeth clapped him hard on the shoulder and gave him an encouraging smile.

A good ten minutes later, dressed from head to toe in surgical greens, Dr. Clark bustled in, clipboard in one hand, coffee cup in the other. "There you are, Griffeth. Tell me what you can about Junior here before he took to wearing a sheet." It was the line he always used. The proceedings had begun.

The body exterior was examined for signs of violence and photographed. The big Y-cut laid the torso wide open, the organs were dealt with, tissue and blood samples were taken for toxicology, and through it all Dr. Clark droned into his tape recorder and Griffeth took notes. Finally, the plastic bag containing the organs was placed with an audible plop into the yawning cavity, the opening was crudely stitched together and the doctor moved on to the head. As the scalp was excised, Griffeth glanced at Carl who was not only still upright but watching closely and asking questions. Equally amazing, Dr. Clark, difficult and sarcastic at the best of times, was answering them in a civil manner. Would wonders never cease.

When the pathologist picked up the electric saw, Griffeth grit his teeth. The sound always reverberated in his own cranium in a most unpleasant way. Finally, the cap of bone was removed and the brain exposed.

"There it is. What a beauty." Dr. Clark was referring to the huge blood clot that his ministrations had revealed. Once again he mumbled long words into his recorder.

"Excuse me, Doctor, but what is that . . . what you just said, eppa urinal him . . . what?"

"Epidural haematoma? Acute bleeding from trauma,

Constable. It forms a clot. You can see it for yourself. With an injury like this, even if promptly treated, the victim would probably have been rendered severely disabled or even permanently comatose. That's supposing he lived, of course."

Griffeth asked, "Any ideas on weapon?"

"The man was bludgeoned. Mechanism of death was a series of blows that caused a depressed fracture of the skull and tore an artery. From the pressure of expanding haemorrhage and the clot compressing the brain, you get destruction of brain tissue. Add to that the swelling of the brain that accompanies a wound of this sort and what you have is the mess you see before you. Tremendous damage. He didn't stand a chance."

"Yes, but what was the weapon? A tire iron? Something like that?"

"Umm. It's a possibility."

"How long after being hit would he have died?"

"I assume that's both a request for the time of assault and the exact time of death? You know better than that. With this injury it wouldn't have taken long for him to lapse into coma, but death? Maybe a couple of hours, maybe longer. From what the coroner got at the scene and what I see, I'd put the approximate time of death somewhere between 11:00 P.M. and 2:00 A.M., time of assault anywhere between one and six hours earlier."

"What about spattering? Since he was killed outside we need to know what to look for."

"Head injuries, you know, so lots of blood. You saw what he leaked, but much actual spattering? I doubt it. Minimal at most. Most of the damage was internal. That small cut to the scalp could have been closed with a couple of stitches. You'll be looking for something with a fairly smooth, rounded surface, I should think, with traces of blood and perhaps hair . . . maybe dandruff. Your boy had a problem with that."

"Could he have moved under his own steam? I'm trying to figure out how he got under that tree."

"After being hit? It's possible, I suppose, even with the severity of the blows. The nervous system is a funny thing. I've read reports of decapitated men running. . . . Now, what's happening?"

Griffeth looked up in time to see Carl, hand over his mouth, running from the room.

Two men in sweatsuits jogged along the trail past Griffeth, who again stood, along with three other officers, on the river bank surveying the murder scene. It was much easier to see in the midmorning light. Except for the fluttering yellow tape, the whole area looked benign and restful, more like something found on a calendar than the scene of a crime. He drew in a lung-full of cool and sweet fresh air, made all the more fresh and sweet by contrast to the pungent odours of the autopsy room he had just left.

He tried to imagine how the blow to Campbell's head could have been delivered. It certainly would not have been done when the victim was beneath that branch. There was no room to swing anything hard enough to cause that kind of damage. There was barely enough space to crawl beneath it. The nearby area was gently sloping and covered with dry, brown, brittle grasses and wildflowers that would have been crushed had there been a fight. So, there had not been a fight, at least not a physical one, and if physical, not here. He shook his head in disgust. Maybe Campbell had been mugged. Bludgeoning was the frequent result of a mugging gone wrong. Is that what had happened?

He contemplated the tree that looked like a bush. It would have been impossible for someone to drag a body beneath the branches. So how did it get there? After being struck, had Campbell crawled—or perhaps been pushed—under there to die? Maybe. And if so, the blow had to have been struck within a very short distance. He looked up the path to where he had sat the previous night. If the blow were struck somewhere on the path then the slope of the land would have assisted the victim to his final resting place. He drew yet another diagram in his note book.

He moved off the path and one, two . . . four normal steps took him to where the body had lain. Campbell's body had been there, so close to the path, for over a day before being found. How was that possible with so many people using the path? He looked up toward the university. Plenty of windows overlooked this spot. Even at night, whatever happened might have been seen. The parking lot lighting rimming the crest of the river bank was probably bright enough. Even very late the trail was used. . . . No telling who would come by or when. He grunted. He was going to need all the help he could get to investigate this one: extra officers to interview anyone near a window and a public appeal for information from anyone who had used the path.

One of the other officers present bagged and tagged whatever was found by the two constables walking like demented ducks through the sometimes thigh-high weeds. Griffeth, cold hands stuck in pockets, stood motionless nearby, thinking. He was not sure he was starting out right on this one. It looked like a random, senseless crime, but coming on the heels of Essen's death. . . . Flannigan's was associated with both. Were they connected? Work them together? Mostly the same suspects. . . .

After a time he slowly walked north beyond the ash tree. The asphalt trail was level here and the bushes that hid the river from view were dense and almost twice as tall as he was. Orange-red berries still clung to the thorny branches. He remembered that earlier in the fall the leaves had been silvery green, but now they were yellow and lay undisturbed on the ground. Nothing to be found there.

He turned in a full circle, taking in everything around him, then squinted up at the low dull overcast. Snow was predicted and would not be long in coming. They would have to find whatever could be found before snow covered it. He turned and searched the ground on either side of the path as he slowly walked back up the slope, past the yellow taped area where the others worked and past the bench. He followed the path as it made a gentle easterly turn around a lush clump of chokecherry bushes, patting himself on the back for recognizing them. The path wound past another bench that faced west toward the South Saskatchewan River. He stopped there and looked around. From where he stood there was nothing to suggest that anything had happened a short distance away. Across the river the Mendel Art Gallery sat low on the landscaped bank. It all looked so peaceful.

Less than half a mile from where Griffeth stood, Constable Stefanyk, sucking a breath mint, stood in the doorway to Essen's office in the geology building. Students passing by glanced curiously at him as he spoke to Fiona Stewart. "No, Ms. Stewart. I'm sorry." From somewhere behind him came the sound of a file drawer closing, another sliding open, and the clicking of computer keys.

"But, it's my property. It's got nothing to do with anything. I've got to have it back by Saturday to get my work done. My degree depends on it."

"Everything in this office is part of the investigation. I'm sorry, but until it's been released, that's the way it is. If you make a list of what's yours we'll try to locate it and have it cleared as soon as possible. That's the best I can do."

Fiona seemed relieved and disappointed in equal measure. She opened a notebook and wrote, tore out the page, handed it over, and disappeared into the moving stream of students. Carl closed the door and went back to sifting the contents of Essen's desk. In the corner an officer at a computer was reviewing, one after the other, floppy disks lined up in the plastic box beside her.

"Finding anything?"

The woman at the console hooked a loose strand of blond hair behind her ear, slipped in another disk, and punched up the directory. "I haven't any idea about most of this technical stuff. I'm looking for letters, anything really. Here we go, class lists and grades. Might be a clue here, some of these kids aren't doing so well. Think one of them has a collection of beach balls?" The printer began to screech. She entered another file. "Bingo!"

The aroma of cinnamon, cloves, and nutmeg from the spice cake in the oven teased the nose and filled Elie's kitchen with a tantalizing fragrance. To keep herself occupied while it baked she examined the aviation map she had unfolded on the kitchen table, contemplation written on her face.

If, as Curly surmised, Essen's plane had been tampered with before leaving Saskatoon on Friday, then he had taken off with half-tanks, and there had been barely enough fuel to make it to Hacker Lake. He could not have gone further. So, never mind the fact that he had filed a flight plan to Downy. He had made a bee line for Hacker. Why? What was he doing up there? And where had he landed? It was not at the air strip fifteen kilometres south of the lake. RCMP had checked that possibility during the search. If she could figure out what he was doing up there it might give her a clue. Camping? Possible. But, it was pretty late in the season.

She went into the family room, opened a drawer in a built-in cabinet and returned to the kitchen with an ancient, dog-eared survey map covering the area. Every building, gully, stream, and hillock was on it. She spread the survey map on top of the aviation map. Now where could he have landed? The entire area was trees or water. She pencilled a mark in the approximate location of the crash site. Walter had heard the plane. If it had flown over the lake he also would have seen it. She examined the area between the pencil mark and the lake. There. Logging road. Long abandoned but maybe still serviceable enough. It wound around some but there was a straight stretch that looked long enough to take-off or land. The road stopped about half a kilometre from the beach at the end of a small inlet. She knew the spot. It was the family's favourite picnic area, but they had always reached it by canoe. There was a small rocky beach and behind it a rock bluff topped with a dense growth of spruce and pine and a plentiful supply of deadfall for a fire. All in all, the place was a beautiful and perfect place for a campsite. If that was where he had gone she could not blame him. But why not file an accurate flight plan?

Stefanyk replaced the phone on Essen's desk and put on his coat. Campbell's keys had been found in his pocket, but his car could not be located. Griffeth believed that since Carl had so recently been a member of the Traffic Unit he was the perfect candidate to find it. That car could contain something, however small, that could point to the identity of his killer.

It was between classes when Stefanyk eased away from the curb near the geology building to begin his search. He felt pulled in a dozen different directions. He was supposed to find out who sold those beach balls, he had been forced to watch that damned autopsy, he had been told to help turn over Essen's office, and now he was supposed to find Campbell's car. On top of all that he was, presumably, still responsible for finding the thief with the penchant for swiping rocks.

He had to stop every few feet for jay-walking students who did not give his car the barest glance before walking into the road. The arrogance of it annoyed Carl. It confirmed his opinion of university students. He moved slowly on. Ahead, another pack of students was about to cross the road. He stopped again and impatiently waited as they strolled in front of his car. It would feel good to give the lot of them a ticket.

He watched their faces to see if he spotted any of the students he had interviewed the day before. There was a profile that looked a little familiar. The profile became a momentary front view as the student glanced in his direction. Carl smiled. It was one of the Meade kids, and look at that shiner! And Griffeth thought he was so innocent. Wait till he hears about this!

Edna called, her voice pouring through the phone lines and into Elie's ear in a torrent of relief. The doctor said that John was suffering from exhaustion and dangerously high blood pressure but not a stroke. He was being kept in hospital for treatment but he was allowed to see a few friends. Would Elie please visit?

Of course she would. At noon she entered the multi-storey lobby of University Hospital. The place reminded her more of a strangely quiet shopping mall than a health centre. There was everything from a snack bar to a pharmacy. Next to the information desk, in a pretend sidewalk cafe, yellow and white patio umbrellas protected twenty-four white plastic tables and chairs from an imaginary sun. Like shop fronts, the reception desks of departments such as pediatrics, family medicine, and opthamology faced the lobby. Patients in robes and slippers sat in wheelchairs or pushed their intravenous units as they milled about or clustered in hushed groups with visitors. Elie barely avoided upsetting an I.V. contraption as she made her way into an elevator. She stepped off on the correct floor and, several false starts and wrong moves later, she found the right room just as an aide carried out a food tray.

John's appearance was a shock. He looked haggard and far older than his years. He lay flat in the bed by the window morosely watching big fat snowflakes that slowly drifted past.

She spoke to him softly. "Hi, there. How are you feeling? Edna said you could have visitors."

"I guess so. . . ." His voice was thin and weary. He lifted the arm attached to the I.V. drip and gestured to the curtains drawn around the other bed. Tears came to his eyes. He whispered, "They put me in a room with a sick person, Elie. I shouldn't be here. And I don't need this I.V. thing either. There's nothing wrong with me."

"John, you gave everybody a scare. Exhaustion is not funny, and neither is high blood pressure. You're here to rest and recover. You'll be out hale and hearty in no time at all." She perched on a chair beside his bed.

"Out to do what? I can't rest in here. All I can think about is losing my job."

"I know. Me too. It's hard. Maybe it'll help if we talk about it and compare notes."

He told her about finding his termination notice lying on his desk on Wednesday around six when he was leaving for the day. His reaction had been the same as hers: stunned disbelief followed by anger. Both had gone to tell their families, neither had quite known what to say. Even now, it seemed unreal. A lifetime of work, effort, and loyalty down the tubes. For a while they remained silent, both occupied with their own thoughts.

Then in a weak voice he asked if the police had figured out who had fooled with Essen's plane. She shook her head.

"They're still working on it and, as far as I know, we're all still suspects."

"It's not bad enough we lost our jobs?"

"John, that plane was worked on all day, right? At any time were the engineers away from it? Waiting for a part, on a coffee break, anything like that?"

"No. Well, let me think. . . . Around five-thirty, no it was closer to six, I took the whole crew out for pizza. The way they were working, they deserved it. I called ahead and it was ready when we got there. We weren't away long, less than an hour. I had my cell phone so I could be reached . . . " The fabric of the oversized standard-issue blue hospital gown moved with a shrug of his bony shoulder.

"Was any fuel spilled in the hangar that day?"

"How did you know about that? We found a little fuel under the wings and mopped it up. It was just breather discharge from the change in temperature."

"Are you sure? When did you find it?" The grey-painted hangar floor was kept immaculately clean so any spill, particularly of a hazardous substance, was noticed immediately and promptly cleaned up.

"After dinner. Oh, I get you. If it was going to drip, it would have dripped in the morning just after we pulled it inside."

"Sorry you're feeling bad, John." The voice belonged to Griffeth who had silently appeared at the foot of the bed. A nurse cruised past him to the bedside with a tiny paper cup and a glass of water. She dropped a pill from the cup into John's hand. He took one look at her expression and swallowed it like a lamb.

"Doctor said you could have visitors but not a party. Sorry, it's nap time." She shooed them both out of the room before John could even say hello to his new visitor. In the corridor Griffeth grabbed Elie by the arm and headed for the elevator. "Let's get out of here. I hate hospitals." He put his finger on the down button and pushed it repeatedly. As the doors opened, he said, "Besides confirming that fuel spill, did he say anything else?"

"He said he took his men for pizza somewhere around five-thirty or six. They were away about an hour."

"What time did you say you were back from that charter?"

She gave him a dirty look. "That's amusing, Curly. I told you it was probably around seven, but since I can't check the flight sheets myself. . . ." She shrugged.

"You haven't remembered seeing anyone?"

"No, but then, I wasn't looking either." The doors opened and the two crossed the lobby with Griffeth leading the way with unseemly haste. As soon as they were outside he came to a sudden halt and breathed deeply a few times, almost as if he had been holding his breath. A light dusting of snow covered all the cars in the lot and a trail of footprints followed them as they began to walk. As they approached her hatchback he began to cough, covering his mouth with the tail of his scarf.

"You coming down with flu?"

"I'm fine," he sounded grumpy. "I have to be. Martha fed me one of her mixtures this morning. I'm now protected against all germs and evil spirits at least to the end of the week. Awful stuff."His expression was comical. She hid her grin and mentally congratulated the formidable Martha. She unlocked her car but he stopped her from getting in.

"Elie, I'm sorry to tell you this but you might as well know it now. It'll be public knowledge soon." His expression was not funny any longer. "I need all the help I can get to figure out who killed Professor Essen. We've got another body on our hands and the two deaths could be connected. It was James Campbell we found last night on the river bank."

She could not find her voice for a long moment.

"Campbell?! Absolutely nobody liked him, but I can't believe anyone would have killed him!"

"Believe it. And I want you to be careful. Until we get a handle on this, everyone is a suspect and anyone could be next. Call me if you think of anything, even if you think it's not important. I mean it, Elie. Be careful." He turned on his heel and walked away, leaving her rooted to the spot.

9. Friday Afternoon and Evening, October 15

In the hospital lot Elie sat in the car while the wipers frantically swatted the snowflakes almost before they had a chance to land. Campbell had been truly obnoxious, a manipulator, a rotten manager, and a bully, but murdered? It shook her. She remembered the last time she saw him. It was in the staff room when he had smiled at her and said hello. Maybe she was judging him too harshly. But, to be honest, she had to admit that she did not feel any particular sorrow that he was gone. What she felt was more like relief and she was ashamed of herself.

What troubled her most was the obvious question of who could have done it. Curly seemed to think Flannigan's was involved somehow. She had trouble getting her mind around the thought. There were plenty of people with good reason to hate the man, but who among them would actually kill?

She also wondered if Campbell had put into motion something which could not be stopped. Lars had said the company was on the market, maybe even already sold. Had he learned anything more about it from that friend of his? One thing was certain, she would have to tell him about Campbell's death. He would probably cheer at the news. It meant his job as chief flying instructor was safe and, even though his salary was not high, he really needed to keep it. He had alimony payments to make and the bank statements she had seen indicated that he was carrying a crushing debt load.

She should also tell Norm. As company dispatcher he needed to know. On a purely personal level he would also be delighted, although, knowing him, he would probably miss his daily skirmish with the man.

The thought that she should tell them finally got her moving. It was not until she got to the pay booth and had to ransom her car that she realized how long she had been sitting. When she got home she went straight to the phone and dialled Lars. He was not in his office so she called Norm. He answered on the first ring sounding almost obscenely happy.

"Yo, Doll. How ya doin'? What's up?"

"My, you're chipper."

"And why not? Our esteemed leader still hasn't favoured us with his presence. That's a whole day and a half of peace and quiet. Everybody's smiling. . . ."

"Not for long. That body they found by the river? It was Campbell."

There was silence on the line, then he cleared his throat and said, "Come again?"

"You heard right. I was just up visiting John—he's going to be okay by the way—and Sergeant Griffeth turned up and that's what he said. Campbell's dead."

"Hooo boy. . . .So we expect the police to clutter the place up again asking more questions, eh? Thanks, I'll pass the word. I just hope the cops understand when they see general mirth and merriment instead of tears."

Mirth and merriment because of a violent death? The world was spinning off centre. She shook her head and grimly punched the rewind button to listen to her messages. There were three. The first was from California. Elie listened to it while looking at the snow dusting the grass. Don cheerfully reported that he had spent the previous lunchtime at the hotel pool and now was suffering the pain of terminal sunburn. Ah well, at least he sounded more relaxed than he had for a long while.

The next message said her boys had chili in the slow-cooker and invited her to come to dinner at six-thirty. It was exactly what she needed to chase away the chill she had felt since learning about Campbell. She called their machine and accepted.

The last was from Walter. He sounded hoarse and unhappy and wondered plaintively if she had forgotten his phone number and address. It made her feel guilty. There were two peach pies in the freezer reserved for Christmas. She took them both out, grabbed one, and headed for his house to make amends.

He greeted her at the door of his studio, a remodeled three-car garage complete with skylights and a large northern window, all of it kept almost unbearably neat. He led her in, relieved her of her coat and the pie, and gestured to a cedar-paneled wall where his latest works were hung.

"What do you think?" Covering the walls at eye level were his twelve latest paintings, each one a northern scene from somewhere around Hacker Lake. He was famous for them. She took her time and inspected each in turn. He expected this. Behind her he leaned on his cane, wiped his rosy nose on a snowy hanky, and awaited her verdict. Every year, for as long anyway as they had been neighbours at the lake, they had gone through the same ritual. He always said she was the first to see them framed and hung. Part of the game was for her to identify where each had been painted. Most of the time she did. This year it looked as if he had painted scenes from his row boat looking in-shore.

The first one brought a warm jolt of surprise. There was a wooden dock in the foreground with a canoe overturned on it. In the background, barely showing through the trees, was the Meade log cabin. She could practically smell the pines and hear the water lap the shore.

"Walter, it's perfect!" She wished she had the money to buy it, but now there was no chance of that.

She had to guess the location of two of the paintings,

but most were familiar. One of the series was of their favourite little picnic area. It was just as it appeared when they rounded the rocky point at the mouth of the small inlet. It looked inviting with its protected beach of dark stones, magnificent tall trees on the ridge behind it, the sun glinting on the quiet water.

"Better than ever! They're wonderful."

He smiled proudly. "Then we better toast the muse, don't you think?" He limped across the room to a counter displaying orderly rows of jars of brushes, freshly washed and folded rags, cotton and latex gloves, boxes of paint tubes, turpentine, linseed oil, all the accoutrements of the artist. From a small under-counter refrigerator he took a bottle of sparkling wine and expertly extracted the cork. A pot-bellied stove in the corner sent billows of heat throughout the room. They settled for a chat beside it in matching, worn leather chairs. The room was comfortable and cosy, and the wine and company were good.

For a while they talked about the paintings. Then he told her all about the lake since she had last been up. He reported that the pesky old bear they all called Old Titan had, as usual, made a nuisance of himself. One day he had kept Walter from leaving his cabin for the entire morning by lying down for a nap in a sunny spot at the foot of his stairs. That episode had prompted Walter to complain to a local trapper which, in turn, had provoked a laugh and the advice, "Better the bear you know. The next one might be much worse." Elie was amused. Old Titan could be a bit of a terror but he was as much a part of Hacker Lake as the water and trees. She could not think of the place without him.

Walter turned the conversation to the investigation into the plane crash. After all, he considered himself involved, almost a participant, since it was he who had heard the plane and his report that had sent the searchers to the right area. "Have they caught up with the culprit yet?"

"Not yet, and I don't know that they ever will at the rate they're going. Everyone at Flannigan's, including me, is on the list of suspects. What makes it even worse is that the body they found near the river last night is, or rather was, the manager who was appointed after Joe died."

He chuckled. "So you're suspected of doing him in too, eh? No doubt on one of your more bloodthirsty days. It must be hard, but you just hang in there. Just do your job. The police will sort it out eventually."

"That's part of the problem. Wednesday was my last day. Campbell fired me."

"Uh oh. Why did he do that? Is business that slow?" She shook her head and gave an elaborate shrug.

"You mean he didn't say? He should have given you a reason, Elie. That's no way to treat people or to run a company. What kind of person was this what's-his-name anyway?" Walter had become so indignant that a little wine sloshed over the edge of his glass onto the floor and he did not even notice.

"It's best not to speak ill of the dead."

"That bad? I'm sorry to say it but, murder or no murder, you are all better off without him."

"I keep thinking that this wouldn't have happened if Joe's will had been found. He must have made one, Walter."

"Of course he did, smart man like that. His company meant everything to him, didn't it? Of course it did. He wouldn't have neglected an important detail like that. Like everyone else, I liked the man a great deal and respected him. Did I ever tell you that he personally used to fly me around? I always kept an eye on the buildings I designed as they were going up. Edmonton, Calgary, Winnipeg, Regina. . . . I flew around a great deal in those days. But, that was a long time ago now. . . . I remember sitting in his office. He had a big old logo on the wall, nice touch that."

"The new manager took it down."

Walter snorted his displeasure and, with the aid of his cane, got up to refill their glasses from the bottle in the fridge. When he returned he looked thoughtful. "You know, that logo meant a great deal to Joe. He designed it himself and it hung outside on the south wall of the hangar from the first day he opened up until he had a bigger one painted. Take a look at it. Look inside the frame he had made for it. If there's a backing, check behind that. I'll lay odds you find something important, even if it's not the will."

At first she dismissed the suggestion as absurd. But by the time he had eased himself back into his chair she had decided to find a way to check the logo, even though it seemed a pretty strange place to put anything. He said, "What does Don think about you losing your job?"

"He doesn't know about it. He's at a conference in Los Angeles, bless his sunburned little heart. Brad and Grant know though, but they have problems of their own. Their apartment has been broken into. But, not to worry, the thief wanted some of Brad's rocks, not your paintings. Says something about the thief, doesn't it."

"Ah well, that illegal line of work has never been noted for attracting geniuses. Then again, it might be an art critic. They aren't noted for genius either. Are the boys all right? They weren't hurt, I hope."

"No. They're fine, but I'm not. I'd like to get my hands on the person who's doing it. The police don't seem to be very interested. It makes me mad."

Walter chuckled. "And you a policeman's daughter. Shame on you. But I don't blame you for being worried about the boys, and I don't like the sound of what you're telling me, either. Break-ins on top of murders? Could it be possible that someone at Flannigan's . . . ? It does seem more than a little strange to me that two people connected with the place are dead."

"I hope not. . . ."

"Think about it, Elie. It worries me. And you be careful. If I were you I wouldn't trust anybody about now." Great. Now Walter was sounding like Curly. If this kept up it would not be long before she started sleeping with the lights on.

"Walter, visiting with you has been a pleasure but I've still got things to do. I promised the boys I'd come eat some of their lethal chili tonight, so I better get going. Thanks for showing me the best paintings yet. And you take care of that cold."

"I'll feed it your pie and the rest of this wine."

She drove to the hospital as quickly as traffic permitted. She felt better for having visited with her old friend, and seeing his paintings had been a treat. They had also jogged her memory and now she had a question, a question that could only be answered by John. He lay flat on his back with an arm over his eyes and she tip-toed only part way into the room believing him to be asleep.

"I'm awake, Elie."

"I'll only stay a minute. You feel up to talking?"

He lowered his arm and she saw that his eyes were rimmed with red. "Anything's better than just lying here. God, I hate this place. Do you know they put rails on my bed at night? I feel like a god-damned baby in a fucking crib!" He angrily wiped at the tears that suddenly overflowed onto his cheeks. She took his work-worn hand in hers and stroked it as she would a child's.

She said, "Nobody likes being in hospital, but you'll be back home soon," and handed him some tissue. "John, I've been thinking about something you said. Why were the rear seats out of Essen's plane? When they brought in the wreck did you see what was in it?"

"Yeah. The usual. Regulation survival gear, sleeping bag, flight case. . . . The investigators went through it and packed it all up. Come to think of it. . . . Hand me my cell phone." He dialled a number at Flannigan's and spoke to one of the mechanics.

When he finished he dropped his hand together with the phone as though the effort of holding it to his ear had been too great. He wearily closed his eyes. Elie took the phone from his fingers and replaced it on the bedside table. "Well?"

"Nothing important. Bill helped pack it up. Essen was a geology prof. . . . Well, rocks, is what he had. Seven canvas sacks full of 'em. Bill, who hefted them, said each sack had to weigh over twenty kilos—that's more than three hundred pounds total. That gave him weight and balance problems. The rear seat was out so he could pile the bags in a box made special to keep the weight close to centre."

Griffeth stood at the window of the Major Crime Office. He had the sniffles. He wiped his nose absently on a piece of tissue as his eyes roamed over the afternoon traffic and passing pedestrians without really seeing anything. He was deep in thought. He had tossed out the mugging theory and was working on a more plausible motive for Campbell's death. Either hate or revenge were much more likely, and that fit just about everybody at Flannigan's Flying Service. Particularly suspect were the employees who had been fired. Now, if he could just come up with a logical motive for Essen's death he might be getting somewhere.

He crossed the room. Where were those in-depth checks he had requested? They were taking too long. What were computers for, for heaven's sake? Stefanyk was taking his own sweet time checking on those beach balls, too.

At his desk he pushed around the files and papers that once again littered the top, located his legal pad and uncapped his pen. He paused to study the scale drawing of the river bank that hung on the cluttered bulletin board on the wall beside him. If he was hoping for inspiration it did not work. He recapped his pen and bad-temperedly plucked papers from the chaos in front of him, stuffing them into their proper folders. If he did not always find it necessary to pull files apart when he studied them there would not always be such a mess to clean up. But he always pulled files apart. It was the only way he could work.

He picked up a sheet of three-hole notebook paper with a note stapled to it. If he was reading Stefanyk's scrawl correctly, the note said that Fiona Stewart wanted her belongings from Essen's office but some of the items could not be located. Should the items they found be returned? Should they let her in to try to identify which rock samples were hers?

He printed a large NO on the note. He had no intention of turning anything in that office over to anyone until he was finished with it. Miss Stewart could wait. He read through the list of items—thesis draft, computer print-outs (17 sheets), rock samples (32), charts (3)— and stuck it in a folder.

Much more interesting were the copies of some of Essen's letters. He shuffled through them. In mid-September, Essen had contacted Ev-Met Mining with a proposal and a promise of a report by mid-October; however, no draft of a report had been found. Again he wondered what Julian Essen had been doing at Hacker Lake.

Once again Elie climbed the filthy apartment stairs, keeping a wary ear and eye out for anyone flying down. She had changed for the occasion. After all, how often do your kids invite you for dinner? Her heels sounded loud on the treads, and her knees beneath her pleated skirt felt the draft in the stairwell.

In the apartment Sarah and Sammy sat together on the couch. Sarah said, "The guys are in the kitchen and won't let us help. It's making us a little nervous."

"I'll take the pie in and see what they're up to."

"You can't come in!"

"I don't come in, you don't get pie!"

Grant appeared in the doorway. "We don't get pie, you don't get chili! Thanks Mom, this'll be great for dessert. Okay, we're almost ready. Mom, you sit at the end, Sarah on that side and Sammy over here. Sorry, we're a little crowded. . . ."

Elie whispered, "Anybody know what's going on?"

Sarah laughed. "I've been giving Grant a hard time about his cooking."

The room was suddenly plunged into darkness and there was a great banging of pan lids. Brad's voice intoned, "Laa-deez und gennel-mens, Cheef Grant und hees cree-ah-shun! A mo-ment of see-lance, plize." Sammy giggled.

Suddenly a blue flame appeared from the direction of the kitchen and (if you ignored the footsteps) seemed to float across the room, finally coming to rest on the table in front of them. *Chili flambé a la Grant.* They burst out laughing.

The chili was actually quite good, which surprised everyone, including the cooks. They were just finishing when there was a knock on the door.

"Constable Stefanyk, police." It really put a damper on the occasion.

Grant swung the door wide. "Come on in. We're just finishing dinner. You're in time for some of Mom's pie."

Carl's growling stomach said "yes," but his mouth said "no." He was also beginning to doubt the wisdom of his bright idea. He wanted to solve the case he had been given and had decided to try to get an admission from the kid with the shiner. He still believed the boys knew who had done the B and E. But obviously a party of sorts was going on. Two attractive coeds and Mrs. Meade were looking at him. He had not anticipated this.

"Did you find out who broke in?"

Stefanyk looked at Brad. "That's quite a shiner you've got there. Another burglar or just a fight?"

Brad spoke deliberately, "Look, Constable, I realize you think this whole break-in thing is total malarkey but it happened, just like we said it did. And for your information, I don't make a practice of getting into fights. My black eye came from wrestling practice. Ask the coach if you don't believe me."

"I will. What's his name?"

Brad told him and added directions to find the office in the maze of the phys ed building. Stefanyk was not pleased by the ready answers and the steady eyes. He also did not like Mrs. Meade's expression. It was a painful moment.

"Actually, I was in the vicinity and just stopped by to see how you were doing and learn if anything else had happened."

Grant said, "Well, thanks, Officer, but there's nothing new," and closed the door firmly behind him. "Anybody buy that? Jeez, what a jerk . . . !"

Over pie and coffee the conversation rehashed the break-ins. That was how Elie learned that sometime the previous spring, on a weekend when apartments were being vacated and new residents were moving in, Brad and Grant had kept their door open, their coffee pot on, and had helped to carry stuff up and down the stairs. One of the people they had helped move in was Fiona Stewart who, while the boys had been wrestling with her boxes of books, had helped herself to coffee and, they suspected, to some of Brad's rocks. At least several of his favourites had gone missing during that time.

Grant volunteered, "She's the one you were asking about the other day, Mom."

"These walls are pretty thin, boys. She might hear you."

"Who cares. We're just talking. You should have heard what went on in her place. After she moved in she threw some pretty loud parties, and then some guy moved in with her. They fought. Often. Everybody on the floor heard them. Then there was one final blow-up. It woke just about everybody in the building. They were yelling and throwing stuff . . . pretty grim to have to listen to. Fiona left town the next day and was gone for weeks. So far this term her love life's been pretty tame. At least, it's been quiet."

Around nine they left the apartment and headed downtown where Elie dropped the four young people off at Mufti's. She checked the rearview mirror before pulling out into traffic and heading for home.

Ever since the subject had come up she had been thinking about those rocks. What suddenly made them so special? She glanced at both side mirrors and frowned. She was concerned about her sons and worried about their safety. It annoyed her that the police were not doing much to sort out the problem, if anything at all. Certainly, if Stefanyk thought he had anyone fooled by that insulting performance earlier in the evening, he could think again. She made sure all the car doors were locked.

Curly had told her he was bright but she had her doubts. She was beginning to have her doubts about Curly, too. She adjusted the position of the rearview mirror. She hoped he was one of the good guys, but he did not seem to be getting anywhere with either murder investigation. She did not think much of being considered a suspect either, although that could not be helped. But his pleas for her assistance were a bit much. She suspected that they were just a ploy to get her to talk and she did not like being played for a fool.

Her eyes flicked over the mirrors again and her heart beat faster. She was positive now. The same vehicle had stayed three cars behind ever since she left the apartment. At first she thought she must be mistaken and to convince herself she detoured twice, backtracking through streets. Now she was passing Mufti's again and the car was still there. She felt the hot rush of fear. There was no mistake. She was being followed. She did not recognize the car, could not read the plate, and could not get a good look at the driver. She thought about Curly's and Walter's warnings and changed lanes without signaling. The car behind changed, too. The game was not funny. Was this what had happened to Campbell? She wanted to lose whoever was back there, wanted to be safe at home, but she did not want to lead him there.

A block ahead a convenience store occupied the corner lot. She pulled in and as casually as possible strolled to the doors. Through the glass she watched as the vehicle went around the corner. The street it turned down was narrow, with cars parked on both sides. Perfect. She raced back to her car and rocketed out of the lot before he could get turned around. At the next light she sneaked a left on the yellow and zigged and zagged her way through side streets all the way home. She did not see anyone behind her but, to be on the safe side, she doused her headlights before turning into her street. When she pulled into her own drive she was shaking with relief.

She got out of the car with her house key ready but came to an abrupt halt twenty feet from the back door. Someone was on the steps, practically invisible in the dark. She turned on her heel and ran for her car.

"Stop! Elie, we have to talk."

She stopped and turned, anger flaring from adrenaline overload. She had recognized his voice and now Curly held a flashlight so she could see his face. A squawk from a police portable came from his overcoat pocket.

"It's kind of late for a visit, isn't it, Curly?"

Griffeth found the edge to her voice perplexing. She was not being her usually friendly, helpful self. "I thought you, of all people, would understand. I have to talk with you. Can I go in and sit down?" His tone was hopeful.

It was clear that he did not intend to leave and she could not stand there all night. "Curly, this better be important. . . ." She opened the door and motioned him into the family room. He walked to the fireplace and eased himself into Don's favourite wing chair with a sigh of pleasure. She remained standing. She still wore her coat and she did not invite him to remove his.

"Something troubling you, Elie?"

"Lots of things. Carl is one of them and you're another. I know you've got a job to do and that I'm one of your suspects, but coming here at this time of night amounts to harassment. What is it that can't wait until tomorrow?"

"What about Carl?"

"He's harassing my boys like you are me. That the way you solve cases these days? Wear people down so they'll say anything you want?"

"I don't know what you're talking about."

"He stopped by their apartment at 7:35 tonight and practically told them he didn't believe their story about the B and E. Carl needs a bit of work, Curly."

He grunted. "I'll talk to him. Elie, I'm here because I checked the Air Traffic Control records. You landed at 6:20 on the night the plane was tampered with and the mechanics returned from dinner at 7:15."

Was he accusing her of murder? Seriously? It had been a real mistake to let him in the door. Did she look like a marshmallow he could roast at will?

"Think what you want. I didn't do nasty things with beach balls but I can't prove it. Since you're a pilot you might remember that it takes time to taxi to the hangar, time to unload passengers and baggage, and then there's the paperwork. You probably also think I killed Campbell, don't you? Well, I'm going to foul up that nice theory, too, Mr. Ace Policeman. Wednesday evening I flew with a student and after we landed, I did paperwork, changed my clothes, discovered I'd been fired—a truly memorable moment—packed up my stuff, and went to dinner with my boys. We ate at Calder's Cafe. You can check. I paid by credit card. Anything else rattling around in your head, Sherlock?"

Lord, he hated it when women got testy. "You're right about still being considered a suspect. I can't help that. But you can see what I'm up against here. I need help with this. That's why I came. About the only thing we know for sure—keep this to yourself please—is that Hacker was Essen's destination all along."

"Any idiot could have told you that."

His eyebrows shot up. "What? How?"

"You're a pilot, you should know. Fuel consumption. He didn't land at the airstrip either and the only other place halfway suitable is the old logging road south of the lake."

He whistled. "You knew that all along?"

"I could say I did and make you feel real bad, couldn't I? Actually, I found the road by looking at a map this morning. It's the only logical place."

"We have the tire casts. That's where he landed, all right. We also think he cut brush to cover the plane so it wouldn't be seen from the air. What do you make of that?"

"I don't know, you're supposed to be the detective. Your RCMP buddies didn't happen to find out where he camped or what he was doing up there, did they?"

He shook his head. "Not yet. Those are questions I want answered, too. Suggestions?"

Silently, every movement deliberate, she went to the cabinet, opened the drawer, got out the map, opened it up, and pointed to the beach on the inlet. Griffeth took one look and asked to use the phone to call the RCMP detachment at Hacker Lake. Elie made him call collect.

As soon as Griffeth drove off, Elie kicked off her heels and ran upstairs, still buzzing from adrenaline. He had confirmed it. Essen had used the road as a landing strip. From the silent ELT, no rear seat, and the incorrect flight plan, it was obvious that his destination of Hacker Lake had been no accident. She stripped off her clothes, let them lie where they landed, and pulled on jeans and a sweater. And, his cargo had been rocks. From where? The beach? The beach was where Brad's rocks came from. Fiona had taken Brad's rocks and she was Essen's student. Essen had gone to Hacker Lake. If his rocks were the same as Brad's then those rocks were connected with murder and Brad and Grant could be in even more danger than she had thought. Speculation was useless. She needed to know and there was only one way to find out. She tied up her runners and ran back downstairs.

The parking lot at Flannigan's was shaped like an **L**, with the short end running along the south side of the huge, two-storey building. It was close to midnight when she pulled in. There was a door on the south side that was always kept secured because it entered the hangar proper. She unlocked it and entered, wishing she had prepared a story about why she was there. If she were caught creeping around she would need something that sounded at least halfway believable.

Private planes, crammed in at all angles to make the most of the space, occupied almost all of the south side of the hangar floor and a single work light at partial power lit the area. All the night shift mechanics, thank heaven, were fully occupied on the north side.

In the dimness she almost fell over a portable power

washer and just managed to side-step it, the dripping gloves, and snaking hose. John had told her which store-room contained Essen's things. Quietly, her dark clothes blending with the shadows, she moved toward it behind the cover of aircraft. With luck one of her keys would open the door. She tried first one and then another. The fourth key went in easily and started to turn, but stopped. As quietly as possible she jiggled the key around in the worn old lock. Something pinged softly and the key turned. She twisted the handle with hope in her heart. It opened. Softly she closed the door behind her and stood still in the dusty dark-ness, one hand on the knob for orientation, the other hold-ing a small flashlight.

The flashlight cast a puny beam but it was relatively easy to tell which of the many boxes and cartons held what she was looking for. The sides bulged from the weight. She opened one and wrestled the topmost sack around until she could get at the knotted drawstring. She shone the light into the bag, withdrew one of the stones to examine, and then pulled out others. To her eye they all looked like Brad's rocks, exactly the same.Something cold and heavy settled in the pit of her stomach.

She replaced the samples, closed up the box, and turned to another. As she opened the flaps she heard a noise that seemed to come from just outside the door. She killed the light and stood motionless, her heart racing. It felt like she stood for hours in the silent blackness before she heard the sound again. It was not outside the door. It was in the room with her. At first she remained where she was in the hope she would not be discovered, but reason said that whoever it was knew where she was, otherwise why would he be there? She decided on confrontation, snapped on the light, and swung around. The beam swept in an arc to set-tle on two unblinking red dots staring at her. Her heart lurched and tried to run away without her. Then, in a sudden flurry of motion, the dots were gone. The squeak and scrabbling of tiny feet told her it was a mouse, even more frightened than she was. She almost cried in relief.

When her heart rate had slowed to somewhere near normal, she began to examine the contents of the second box. In it she found Essen's flight case, under a sleeping bag. She opened it and found pretty much what she expected: circular computer, flight supplement, and maps. Lots of maps, but some were not for aviation. She pulled one of these out to find a survey map with the Hacker Lake beach area circled. She refolded it, put it back, and took out another. This one looked completely different. It had numbers all over it and strange markings that meant nothing to her. While returning it to the case she noticed Fiona Stewart's name neatly printed on the back side under the title, *Preliminary Ground Magnetic Survey of the Hacker Lake (West) Area.*

10. Saturday Morning, October 16

From the kitchen counter the radio played softly and the coffee maker emitted little burbling sounds. Elie tried to do a neat job of wrapping and labelling the spice cake she had baked for the fund-raiser but she seemed to have acquired an extra thumb. Twice she made a hash of it and had to start over. The problem was that her thoughts were not on the task. They kept revolving around what she had discovered at the hangar the previous night and she did not like what she was thinking.

She had lain awake most of the night trying to figure out what made those rocks so special to so many people. At one point she had even climbed out of bed and gone downstairs to look at her Mother's Day rock. She had wished then that she had taken one of Essen's samples to compare with it. Maybe they were not quite the same. Maybe she was mistaken. But, if she was right? Both Essen and Fiona had gone out of their way to collect those stones. Now, Essen was dead and Fiona alive. Did that mean that Fiona was in danger, too? Or did it suggest that she had killed her advisor?

Another question: what were Stefanyk and Curly doing about the break-ins? Nothing. That investigation was definitely on the back burner and maybe off the stove entirely. Okay, so they had a couple of murders to solve. And, okay, finding a killer was way more important than solving a B and E, but Fiona could be involved in both and Elie doubted if Curly was even aware of her existence.

In a way Elie felt sorry for the girl. Fiona was having a tough time trying to finish her degree and, according to the boys, her taste in men was seemingly dreadful. But all that aside, she had also known Professor Essen and her boys suspected her of swiping some of Brad's rocks the previous spring. Somehow or other, Fiona had to be involved.

Elie's father had always considered a crime a crime, each deserving of a solution. She believed that, too. She also believed that her boys could be in danger. Therefore, since Curly was busy trying to pin murder on somebody at Flannigan's, she decided that she would just have to do a little something to figure out who was breaking in to her boys' apartment. If that meant getting the goods on Fiona in the process, so be it.

Griffeth was not a happy man. His wife had fed him a different mixture that morning, one that had taken a great deal of effort to swallow. It was far worse than the other stuff. From the slime still clinging to the roof of his mouth he suspected she had put cod liver oil in it. He could barely get it down without gagging. He brushed his teeth to eliminate fish breath and escaped from the house, afraid if he did not that Martha would try to smear his chest with something smelly or hang a clove of garlic around his neck.

So when Griffeth arrived at work he was in a foul mood made worse by his stuffy nose and the stifling heat of the office. He cursed the architect who had designed the place with one thermostat for six offices and hermetically-sealed windows. He felt like smashing one to let in some air. He plunked himself into his chair and violently blew his nose.

There were messages and a stack of reports on the desk in front of him. He pushed them around irritably rather than pick them up. Stefanyk had found out that five gas stations, three hardware stores, Canadian Tire, Zellers, and several other places had sold summer toys right through the Thanksgiving weekend, but nobody remembered a large sale of beach balls. And that was just on the city's east side. He was still checking the rest of the city. He had not found Campbell's car either. Besides driving around wasting gas, what the hell was he doing? There was nothing yet from the Hacker Lake RCMP Detachment, and Griffeth's uncharitable assessment was that they were all just sitting around on their asses up there among the pine trees.

He cleared his throat, which felt like used sandpaper, and thumbed through his notebook. He still had no idea where Campbell had gone when he left Flannigan's on the day he died. That bugged Griffeth. Campbell's secretary said that the manager had walked out of his office with a couple of letters in his hand shortly after four and had never returned. So where had he gone? What had he done? Griffeth thought there was something, besides Flannigan's, that linked Campbell with Essen. Why could he not figure out what it was?

In the unmarked cruiser, Constable Stefanyk prowled streets, alleys, and parking lots with a gritty determination born of the dressing-down he had received from Sergeant Griffeth because Campbell's Mazda still had not been located. Since the body had been found on the river bank and the keys had been found in a pocket, Carl reasoned that Campbell had driven to the river. Of course if someone had stolen the car, or it was in a garage, it might take forever to find. No, no. Bad thought. He would find it.

By nine o'clock he had worked up an appetite. He searched his pockets for a candy bar but came up empty. He decided to head to a convenience store to get one—okay several—and a coffee, and so turned down a leaf-strewn street. Before he went half a block his progress was halted by a tow-truck parked askew in the street, the driver on his hands and knees putting a rig under the wheels of a disabled car. Stefanyk waited patiently, but by the time the street was clear he had put his coffee break on hold.

At 8:40 Elie raced into the red-brick community centre, dropped off her cake, raced back out to her double-parked car and, duty done, drove downtown. She went twice around the block to find a place to park, inserted coins in the meter, and checked her watch. It was going to be tight. She raced off and at precisely 9:00 A.M., breathing hard, she opened a heavy door and found Maurice Benoit waiting for her in the lobby of his company's corporate headquarters. She had called to ask for this meeting early that morning and had been surprised that he had so readily agreed. He ushered her into the elevator, inserted a key and pushed a button, and they descended to a basement floor. She followed him along a corridor and into a small and very cluttered office filled with filing cabinets, the tops of which were laden with books and stacks of paper.

"Elie, let me introduce you to Robert Gilbride, our chief geologist. Robert, meet my favourite pilot and my friend, Eileen Meade."

Gilbride launched himself from behind his computer-filled desk top with his hand extended. Fine sandy hair fell over his forehead while the bottom of his face was covered with a coarse and curly chestnut beard. The two unlike parts were joined together by a tanned and pleasant face. The face smiled. "It's a pleasure. Maurice doesn't allow just anybody down here. He keeps me locked up in this dungeon, you see, rarely seeing the sun. . . ."

"What nonsense!" thundered Maurice. "This clown you see before you got back only yesterday from a mining conference in Rio de Janeiro."

"Maurice says you've got some questions for me." Gilbride's merry blue eyes searched her face. Under their gaze she flushed. She felt completely foolish. When she had called Maurice, this had seemed like a good idea. Now she was not so sure. To cover her embarrassment she dove into her purse and pulled out a list of questions.

Maurice said, "Before you begin, Elie, I confess that I am very curious about why you wanted this meeting."

She told them about Brad's rocks. She explained that Essen had been carrying over three hundred pounds of samples from Hacker Lake when he crashed. She mentioned the geology graduate student who conveniently lived next door to her boys, whose advisor had been Essen, and who had been hired by the same company that was looking for diamonds. To her way of thinking, she told them, there were just too many coincidences. She did not really know what to ask. She just believed that some of the answers lay with those rocks.

Gilbride whistled softly. "You may be right. Let me see those questions of yours." He read down the paper and looked up with a grin.

"You don't want much, do you? This is what geologists are paid to know, and what makes or breaks a mining company. Anyway . . . here we go . . . how to begin?"

He looked at the ceiling and bounced lightly on his toes. "We'll begin with kimberlite. You want to know what it looks like and what a kimberlite pipe is, right? All righty. I wish I had pictures to show you. . . ." He stopped bouncing and focused on her.

"Kimberlite. It was named after the Kimberley mine in South Africa and is a type of material that was pushed up from deep under the earth's crust by volcanic action millions of years ago. It's the host rock that sometimes, but not always, contains diamonds. The deposit is frequently found where the crust is thickest, and it has the shape of a giant carrot—you know, fat and round at the top and then tapering as it goes down. It can go down for hundreds and hundreds of feet. That's what we call a kimberlite pipe." In his enthusiasm, Gilbride had bounded over to a blackboard on the wall beside the door and drawn what appeared to be a carrot.

"So, next. . . . What does kimberlite look like? Ha. That's part of the fun. Kimberlite doesn't have a look, or rather, it has lots of looks. Deep in the Kimberley mine they called it 'blue ground' because it looked blue. But, up near the surface it changed and was called 'yellow ground' because of its yellowish, mustardy cast. I've seen samples from other areas that were a dark grey, while others were as green as an olive."

"I always thought it was green. . . ." said a perplexed Maurice.

"Oh, it can be, it can be, but it doesn't have to be, you see. That's my point. It can be any number of colours."

"Mr Gilbride . . . ,"

"Rob, just Rob."

"Rob, if it can be any colour, how do you know it's kimberlite?"

He laughed. "That's how we earn our keep. The colours I've been talking about, the colour of any rock at all, are due to the mix of different minerals that make it up. It's only when you find a vein, like a gold or silver vein, that the mineral is nearly pure. Also, the surface of the rock weathers and frequently hides the colour you find in crushed or freshly cut rock. So, from the outside, if you were walking over the occasional outcropping, our kimberlite would look like almost any other rock. Since it is made up of differing amounts of associated minerals you probably wouldn't know what you were walking on."

"So how . . . ?"

"The fun part. We do aerial electromagnetic surveys and the results tell us where to collect samples—earth and soil samples. We screen, process, and examine them. It's kind of like asking around to find a spot that looks good for fishing and then throwing in a line. If we catch something good, something big, we're going to stick around and keep fishing. Well, if we're fishing for diamonds and we find what we call indicator minerals then we stick around. We probably drill some holes. We want to see how big the kimberlite deposit is, the breadth of the outcrop, and what it contains. Maybe we don't find much and maybe we find diamonds. If we do, then, just maybe, we've found ourselves a great fishing hole." He was back to bouncing again.

"So. If we have kimberlite and some indicator minerals do we have diamonds? That's the hundred-million-dollar question. Not all kimberlite has diamonds and even if it does there may not be enough or they may be of such poor quality or so small that they aren't worth going after. It's all pretty much a game of chance with educated guesses thrown in by experts like me. The better the surface samples, the more interest there is in looking further."

"Robert, the samples collected by the professor. . . ."

"I'd have to see them, Maurice. It would be helpful to know if he was collecting stuff at random or was going for a specific area."

"He had maps. One of them looked pretty much like that one." She pointed to one of the several charts pinned to the wall. "A notation on the back read: 'preliminary ground magnetic survey of western Hacker Lake,' or something like it."

"Then he knew exactly where he was going. Interesting. I'd love to see those rocks."

She reached into her purse. "They looked like this. Careful of the paint. Brad gave it to me when he was little."

Gilbride stood stock-still and directed all of his considerable energy at the rock that filled his large open palm. Then, with a wave for them to follow, he raced out of the office and down the hall to a lab. They found him bending over a low-power binocular microscope to examine the rock that lay in a pool of bright light. When he straightened up his face was serious.

"Where did you say this came from?"

"Hacker Lake. We have a cabin there and this is from a little beach area where we—What's the matter?"

"You wanted to know what kimberlite looks like? You've been looking at it. This is kimberlite, Elie, and not just any old piece either. In this one little piece, and just looking at the surface for a moment, I've found an indicator mineral. Come over here and look."

Under the glass she looked as directed to the tip of the shiny metal probe he used as a pointer. "Under this fluorescent light your kimberlite is almost an ultra violet purple, so dark you'd almost swear it was black, not what you'd expect at all but look here. . . . This bit that looks like a small piece of a green pea is chrome diopside without a doubt."

He turned the rock and slowly moved the lens over the surface again. "There. . . . Oh boy, I don't believe it." Again he directed her to look where he pointed. "That—right there—that washed-out-looking little crystal, it's just a single crystal, Elie. . . . That's what we call a kimberlite garnet. Can you see this rim around it? Kind of like a rind on an orange? That's called a reaction rim. They're so unobtrusive that I almost missed it. Garnets like this are found near the source, very near the source, and it's the source you want to find. You see? Two indicators on such a small piece. . . . " He practically smacked his lips.

She looked at the rock sitting in the pool of light. The tiny coloured crystals were what had made the rock pretty to Brad and the perfect Mother's Day gift from a five-year-old.

"Do you have any others with you?"

"In the garden. . . . "

"I'd like to take a look at them." He turned suddenly

toward Maurice. "Do you know if there are any claims registered around Hacker Lake? Elie, when you were last up there at your cabin, did you happen to see any stakes or poles? There would have been a tag. . . . "

"I don't think so. I'm pretty sure."

"It's all public record, Robert. I'll try to find out on Monday. I'll look into whether Essen had a prospector's license, too. You go and look at those rocks. What you find will help Elie, I think. You know, I am so excited and curious about all of this that I want you to call me and tell me what you find."

She gave Gilbride her address and pushed back through the doors onto the sidewalk. In the time she had been inside, the street had come alive. Traffic had picked up and pedestrians strolled along window shopping or strode by with purpose. When she got to her car she found a parking ticket decorating the wind screen. Drat one-hour metres anyway. With the inevitable ticket, parking on a downtown street was an expensive proposition. She peeled it off, threw it into the glove box, and eased into traffic. A moment or two after she got home Gilbride's four-by-four hustled into the drive and squeaked to a halt.

She took him around the house and pointed out the garden. Together they stood and surveyed it, Elie with alarm, Gilbride with confusion.

"Where are they?"

"Gone—Missing! And look at my flowers. . . ." Someone had made a meal of her garden and stolen Brad's stones. Large plants leaned over at crazy angles, small ones were crushed, bare earth showed where rocks once lay. Elie was stunned.

To one side, a drift of seemingly undisturbed leaves covered a portion of the plot closest to the house. She knelt and carefully brushed the leaves aside. A large clump of long-since-spent creeping phlox was nestled happily amongst the largest stones of Brad's collection. Gilbride let out a happy whoop, selected the rocks he wanted and carted them off to his lab with the promise to call as soon as possible with whatever results he found.

Elie stood, hands on hips, surveying the damage to her garden. There was no doubt in her mind that the rocks were what they were after—or was it she? Why? She examined each of her poor plants. They would need to be trimmed back and protected over the winter for even a chance of survival. Mounds of leaves would be good. She went to the garage for the secateurs and rake and got to work.

She would have to tell Griffeth about her garden. Maybe it would finally convince him that someone was really stealing rocks. It might make him do something about the break-ins.

She would have to tell him about Essen's cargo, too. But, how to do it without asking to be hung by her thumbs? He would definitely take a dim view of her sneaking into Flannigan's and poking through Essen's stuff. Maybe, somehow, she could get him to look in those boxes. But she could not just tell him to do it; he would want to know why. Worse yet, he would want to know how she knew what was in them. She had to tell him as soon as possible, and there had to be a way to do it without admitting anything. She pondered the problem as she worked.

Curly knew about the boxes. He had to. At some point, he had probably even looked at the contents himself. But he had obviously missed the significance of those rocks and the maps. To be fair she could not blame him for that. A bunch of stones was what you'd expect a geologist to have. How would he know they might mean diamonds? And everybody knew that pilots required maps. The assumption would have been that they were all aviation maps. For all her suspicions, until she had talked to Rob Gilbride and found her garden looted, she had not been sure of the extent of their importance herself. Still, with the obvious connection of the samples and map to Hacker Lake it seemed to her that Griffeth should have made the connection to Brad's rocks and the break-ins, as well as to Fiona's involvement. And if he had make the connection then he was missing the point. Somehow she had to make him see and understand the point. Unless he had deliberately dismissed the point. Elie thought about that as she wielded the rake. To dismiss the importance of the cargo, Curly had to have a prime suspect in mind. She wondered who the unlucky person could be. She remembered all Curly's visits and all his questions in the last few days and her stomach twisted. The prime suspect was probably herself.

A proud Carl marched up to Griffeth's cluttered desk. When it came to ideas you never knew which ones were the good ones until you followed through. As it happened, this one had been splendid. "Sergeant, I found Campbell's car. Ident is going through it now. "

"Good. About time. Where?"

"Police compound, sir. It was hauled away from the university parking lot at the top of the river bank at 9:00 A.M. on Thursday, the fourteenth, on orders of University Security. They're pretty slow with the paper work up there. Traffic unit still hasn't received a report. I just got an idea and went and looked."

"Well done." He sourly noted Carl's pleased smile and barked, "Don't just stand there. Get back on the street and find out where those damn beach balls came from."

One look at the jammed shopping mall parking lot and Elie wondered what had possessed her to wait until Saturday afternoon to do her grocery shopping. With a long list and nothing in the fridge there was no choice. She had to get on with it. She cruised up and down looking for a parking place and finally found a spot in a far, inconvenient corner. She rescued a cart from between two cars and pushed it through the doors.

By the time she got to paper products she had most of the items on her list and there were fewer carts in the aisle. Not many people, it seemed, browsed for toilet paper. She tossed paper towels in the basket and reached for garbage bags.

"Elie, yoo hoo. . . ." The shrill voice came from behind an overly- full cart coming toward her down the aisle with all the majesty of an ocean liner.

She pasted a smile on her face and said, "Hi, Mrs. Stevenson. How are you?" and hoped she looked happier at this encounter than she felt.

"Well, I've been better." Mrs. Stevenson looked reproachfully at her. "I always thought we helped each other in our neighbourhood. I could have used some help to clear up my yard. Now, I know you said your boys are in university, but they come around. They could have helped. And, Eileen, being a student does not excuse being rude, you know."

"Excuse me? Who was rude? When was this?"

"Just last night. Grant's the older, taller and thinner one isn't he? Well, he was riding away from your place on his bike with his backpack and a toque pulled over his ears. He looked right at me. I know he saw me but he didn't even wave. When he was visiting he could have. . . ."

"That doesn't sound like Grant, Mrs. Stevenson. It must have been someone else."

"Coming out of your driveway? I think not, Eileen."

"When was this?"

"Last night, I told—"

"What time?"

"Time? Oh, it was exactly 7:30. We always watch "Grand Ole Opry Live"and it was just coming on."

Elie's mind was no longer on shopping, but somehow the cart finished filling and the groceries got to the car. She was ready to lay odds that it was Fiona that Mrs. S. had seen. Somebody riding a bike, and wearing a toque and backpack. Somebody slender like Grant. The silhouette would be similar enough to fool Mrs. Stevenson. But, it had not been Grant. Grant had been eating chili.

11. Saturday Afternoon and Evening, October 16

Stefanyk, half-eaten candy bar held between his teeth, applied the brakes and came to a slow and careful stop in front of the Meade house. He was trying not to disturb Sergeant Griffeth who, from the open mouth, closed eyes, and head lolling on the headrest, he supposed to be asleep. He was mistaken.

The minute the engine was cut Griffeth grunted, unfastened his seat belt, and rubbed his aching temples. Only moments before it had occurred to him that Essen's death could have been a red herring, the death meaningless, designed solely to throw him off the track. With Campbell the real target. He doubted it, but it was worth thinking about when he had a spare moment to himself, like in the bathtub. He did some of his best thinking in the tub. He wished he were there now and not sitting in a cold car that smelled of chocolate.

Elie was out shopping, he knew that. But he needed to talk to her again and she could turn up any time. Anyway, the wait would not be wasted. It was a good time to think. His eyes travelled up and down both sides of the street. Curtains twitched in the house next door to the Meade's and he made a mental note of the address. It was always nice to know who the neighbourhood busybodies were. They came in handy from time to time.

He again put his head against the rest and tried to concentrate on the Essen case. What had the man been doing at Hacker Lake? Had he met someone? A woman, perhaps? If so, why the great secrecy and who could it have been? His forehead felt as if it were being squeezed in a vice. He shifted his position, saw Stefanyk take another slow bite through chocolate and caramel and his stomach turned. He found a bedraggled roll of stomach mints in his coat pocket, picked a bit of fluff off one, slipped it on his tongue, and made himself as comfortable as he could to review his list of suspects for both cases.

Front and centre was Lars Holmgren, chief flying instructor. He was big and powerful, ex-military and no-nonsense, a thirty-five-year-old man of direct action and, Griffeth believed, easily capable of murder. Two of his instructors had been let go without warning, the fee hike had lost students, and Campbell had threatened his job if he did not cooperate. Judging from financial statements and credit reports, losing his job was something Holmgren could not afford. His professionalism was being challenged, his position was being undermined, and Elie, his most senior instructor, had been fired. The man certainly had motive enough to kill Campbell, and his claim to have been home alone the night of Campbell's murder made him a most promising suspect. However, he was clear of any suspicion of tampering with Essen's plane because at the time the tampering had probably occurred he had been on a cross-country flight with a student.

Then there was the chief of maintenance, John Gardner. He had worked for Flannigan's longer than any other employee but Campbell had not done him any favours either. His staff had been cut, and longer working hours and greater productivity had been demanded. John had managed all that at great personal cost and been fired anyway. More than enough motive to kill, but when his state of health was considered Griffeth had to put him at the bottom of his Campbell list. It was a different matter, however, when it came to Essen's death. It had required no particular state of health to put those beach balls into the fuel tanks and Gardner had repaired Essen's plane, which had given him ample opportunity. Griffeth hoped he was wrong; he had always liked John, but all the same John was at the very top of his Essen list. He could not fathom a motive, but that could come later.

The dispatcher, Norman Driscoll, was another good candidate. Even as a private pilot, Griffeth had never understood the roll of dispatcher until he began the investigation. He found the job interesting. The dispatcher has to know the location and condition of every aircraft at every given minute, including when it is scheduled for routine maintenance and when it is in for snags. Likewise, he has to know his pilots and to make sure they get enough flying hours, while ensuring they get proper rest periods and do not fly more than regulations permit. He also has to be mindful of safety and to take into account the weather at destination and all along the route. All of this is often necessary at short notice. It is like being a juggler. It takes a person who can stand the stress.

Griffeth found the man interesting, too. Driscoll was in good health, an inveterate bachelor of fifty-eight, who seemed to have no life outside of work, and made no secret of his hatred for Campbell. He had openly opposed and publicly challenged the manager on several occasions. The night dispatcher had been fired, so to pick up the slack, Driscoll worked or was on-call more or less twenty-four hours a day, both at home and at Flannigan's. His presence in the hangar at odd hours could have given him ample opportunity to tamper with Essen's plane. At the approximate time of Campbell's death he claimed to have been having a quick dinner at a local cafe, but nobody could remember him being there and he had not kept the receipt. He was, therefore, a real possibility as the killer of both men.

Then there was Elie. He did not want to believe her capable of murder but stranger things had happened in his experience. She disliked Campbell with good reason, but she had an unbreakable alibi for the night of his death. However, much as he hated the thought, she was a definite possibility as Essen's killer. For one thing, she knew too much. In Griffeth's experience, that was always a red flag. Some of the knowledge came from being a commercial pilot, some from working for Flannigan's, but she also had that connection with Hacker Lake, the B and E and the stolen rocks. And, she had—too easily?—come up with locations, explanations, and helpful suggestions, like the ones about those damned beach balls. Lately, she also seemed preoccupied and defensive. And, in all the years he had known her, she had never spoken to him the way she had the previous night. That really bothered him. He asked himself where he would ordinarily put such a person on his narrowing list of suspects, and shook his head sadly at the answer.

The rustle of paper as Stefanyk crumpled his candy wrapper interrupted Griffeth's thoughts. "Sergeant, you going to bring her in?"

"No." Griffeth rearranged himself. "I prefer to talk to people on their own turf and preferably one-on-one. I get more information that way. In cases like Essen's, where we've got damn-all in the way of hard evidence, it pays to tip-toe around."

The radio resting on the dashboard squawked a message and Griffeth straightened, checked the rearview mirror, and told Carl to wipe the chocolate off his mouth.

From way down the street Elie could see the burgundy car sitting in front of her house again. Damn the man! What did he want this time?

She pulled into the drive and noticed the curtain move on the kitchen window next door. Don was out of town and strange men visited the house at all hours of the day and night. Lordy, what must the neighbours think?

She opened the hatchback and called out sweetly, "Curly, can you and Carl give me a hand with the groceries, please?" If they were going to turn up all the time, drink her coffee and eat her food, they could jolly well help carry it in.

She filled the coffee maker with freshly ground beans and, while it dripped through to fill the kitchen with a welcoming aroma, she unloaded the carrier bags that had been placed in the middle of the floor. From what had become his place at the table, Curly noticed the flashing indicator on her answering machine. "Aren't you going to listen to your messages?"

"They can wait. I have to get this stuff put away." She opened the freezer door and filled the frozen juice dispenser with cans.

"Elie, where were you last night?" She reached into another bag and put the meat into the freezer, taking the time to arrange it all neatly. She did not like Curly's question or the way that he asked it. If she stalled long enough maybe he would ask something she did not mind answering. She closed the freezer door and began to put vegetables away.

"Elie?"

"Why so interested in what I do with my time, Curly? More to the point, what business is it of yours?"

He waited until she started to unload the canned goods. He tipped his chair back, balanced on two legs, and smiled like a naughty child. "Why were you at Flannigan's last night, Elie?"

"Quit that! That chair is old. It'll break." She gave him the look he deserved.

He shifted his weight and allowed the front legs to fall with a thud. He was pleased with his little stunt. He had her full attention.

She examined him through narrowed eyes before opening the cabinet where she kept the mugs. If he knew where she had been, it must mean he was having her followed. The tail the previous night had been pretty obvious, but then maybe he wanted her to know she was being watched. She poured the coffee and took the mugs to the table. On the other hand, maybe the tail had been obvious because it had not been a policeman. Maybe he knew where she had been because, in spite of her caution, somebody at Flannigan's had seen her creep in and reported it. She put milk, sugar, and spoons on the table while Curly just sat and waited with a smug expression.

Finally, she sat herself down. "Curly, you can believe this or not—and you probably won't—I was planning to call you. I think I know who took Brad's—"

"I know you're concerned about your boys, but that's another issue. Tell me about Flannigan's."

"I'm getting to that. You're absolutely infuriating, you know that? Just sit there, drink your coffee, and hear me out."

He listened, directing Carl to fill up his notebook as she talked. He interrupted, "Wait a minute. You mean those bags . . . those rocks are the same kind as Brad's? And, that engineer, geologist, whatever, says they're valuable?"

"Not by themselves, at least I don't think so. But, valuable to someone interested in finding diamonds. Don't you see, Curly? I think Fiona took Brad's rocks because she realized what they were when she saw them last spring. She could have shown them to Professor Essen. Brad made no secret of where he found them so they would have known where to go. Fiona spent time last summer in the field. The maps in Essen's flight case are for Hacker Lake and have her name on them. Doesn't that tell you she was up there? Essen had the same maps with him and we know that's where he went. Fiona and Essen had to be working together."

"You've got it all figured out, don't you, Elie?

Unfortunately, there're things you don't know. For instance, Fiona made a list of her belongings that she believes were taken by Essen without her knowledge. In addition to rock samples she listed maps. She says she found them missing on Tuesday when she was supposed to meet him. So you see, she may be a victim in all this, too."

Elie decided she was not ready to exonerate Fiona just yet. "Curly, I'm not so sure she's the victim you paint her. I think she's the one my neighbour saw riding away from my house last night."

"Come on, Elie, what proof do you have?"

She did not have any proof, but the set of her jaw said she was not about to give up. Curly waved his cup for a refill and relented a little. "Okay, let's assume for a minute that you're right. How does this sound? Fiona sees Brad's rocks last spring and helps herself. She finds out where they came from and goes there for her summer study. Essen sees what she brings back, appropriates her research including maps and samples, and goes off on his own, starting where she left off. But, she needs samples to do whatever, so in September she breaks into the apartment. Now it's October and for some reason she needs more rocks so she tries going into the apartment on Sunday, probably thinking it was unoccupied for the holiday. That didn't work so she raids your garden."

"Not bad, Curly, but just for argument's sake, consider this. Fiona takes Brad's rocks last spring, she finds out where he got them and selects Hacker Lake for her field study. She comes back with her own samples at the end of August, so why would she have broken in to take Brad's rocks a week or so later? It doesn't make sense. And, what about the attempt on Sunday? Why would she have tried it then? From what you've said she didn't even know her stuff was missing until two days later."

"Umm, good point. You realize your arguments are

helping her, don't you? But, if she is the one who raided your garden, it could have been because those rocks of hers did go missing over Thanksgiving and she claims to need samples from Hacker Lake. That does make sense." He motioned to Carl that they were about to leave.

"Now," he added, "if you promise to leave the detective work to us professionals, I'm willing to forget all about your trip to Flannigan's last night. I kind of hate to admit it but I think you may have turned up something important there. We'll take another look."

She watched them drive off before she closed the front door and returned to punch the rewind button on the answering machine. The message from Norm to call sounded urgent, but then all his messages sounded that way. She dialled.

"Elie, glad you called back. Couple things . . . first, I got a message for you. One of your students wants you to call him. Something about transferring? He says you'll know. I've got his number. . . ."

"Give it to Lars."

"Whatever you say. Now for the real reason why I wanted to talk to you. What are you doing for dinner? That husband of yours has gone and left you all alone, so how about a date?"

"Norman!"

"Seriously, Elie, you need a friend and we need to talk. It might as well be over dinner. We both have to eat. Six o'clock?" He mentioned a downtown restaurant.

"Make it seven."

"Six-thirty and there'll still be time to visit John."

Their table for two was beside the railing on the mezzanine, overlooking the bar and general hubbub on the floor below. Soft music played, smoked glass sconces provided subdued lighting, waiters resembling long-legged penguins in black ties, white shirts and cummerbunds scurried about with napkins draped over their arms. The only jarring note was Norm's cellular phone that lay at the ready beside the single deep pink candle in its cut-glass holder in the centre of the rose-coloured cloth. Teetering on the edge of the table a Plexiglass wine bucket threatened to fall along with the half empty bottle of white wine it contained. He reached for it and refilled both their glasses. "We're going to need another bottle of this."

"Right, and get picked up for drunk driving on the way to visit John. Good plan."

Norm took a last bite of his calamari and sighed happily. "I love that stuff. Come on, cheer up and eat your salmon. You've hardly touched it."

She picked at it. "Norm, what do you know about this new fellow who's taking Campbell's place?"

"Nothing, except that he starts on Monday. When the word went around the fear and trembling started, I don't need to tell you. Lars said he—"

"I should call Lars about that student so he knows—"

"Elie, you're not listening. When we heard we were about to get another new manager, Lars and I decided we needed to find out about him—you know, his qualifications and that. So Lars said he'd grab him as soon as he walked through the door to tell him everything that's been going on and what needs doing.

"Then I got to thinking that we don't even know how they appoint a manager for companies in our situation. I wanted to find out because I didn't want another total jerk on the scene, you know? Anyway, I talked to a nice lady who said they only appointed people with relevant experience, and preferably one acceptable to the employees. So, I told her that when they'd picked Campbell they'd really messed up. Well, that worried her big time what with what's happened, so she pulls the file. When she gets back on the line she tells me that Campbell did have a positive reference from right inside the company. I asked her who wrote it and she said. . . . Guess who, Elie. Lars. Lars—who makes noises like he hates Campbell—recommended him."

It was preposterous. Lars? It had to be a mistake. He had not even been willing to write a letter for her, why on earth would he write one for Campbell? It was completely out of character.

Norm drained his glass. "You don't believe it, right? But it's what the lady said. She even spelled out his name to make sure it was the same person."

"Maybe it's a different Lars Holmgren."

"Yeah, real common name. I thought you didn't like coincidences, Elie."

"I don't, but . . . I don't know. Look, Lars would have to know Campbell to give him a reference, right? Did it look to you like they knew each other? Would Campbell have fired people out from under the nose of the person who had got him the job? Would he have threatened to fire Lars like I heard him do the other day?" She wished she could tell Norm that Lars suspected Campbell of trying to sell the company and was trying to find out what he could. That should convince him. If it were true. But then, come to think of it, she only had Lars' word for it. The salmon flipped in her stomach. It was an awful feeling when you began to suspect your friends.

They skipped coffee, left the restaurant together, and then separated to retrieve their cars. She stood under a street lamp beside her hatchback and rooted around in the bottom of her purse for her keys.

"Hi, Elie, over here. It's Mark. You coming or going?" He stood under a street lamp on the pavement nearby.

"Hi there, yourself. Good to see you. I'm going . . . if I can ever find my keys."

"Too bad, I was kind of hoping you were heading

down to Mufti's. They've got a great band tonight. Anyway, I'm glad I ran into you. I wanted to talk to you about where you think I should transfer to finish my instrument rating and then this morning I was talking to the dispatcher and he said you're coming back. Is that true?"

Loyal Norm and his big mouth. "That's a bit premature, Mark, I don't know what will happen."

"Will you call me and let me know? I'm willing to bite the financial bullet and stick with Flannigan's. I'd rather not change instructors in midstream."

"Sure will, glad to." Her fingers finally closed around the heavy brass disc of the key ring which always sank to the bottom of her purse like the *Titanic*. "Mark? Before you go. . . . That night you heard Campbell in Mufti's talking about women pilots? Do you happen to remember who he was talking to?"

He looked around like he did not want to be overheard. "I don't know most of the names, but Holmgren was there and he didn't say a thing. I thought he should have, but all he did was sit there with his mouth shut. Sorry, Elie. Call me when you know, okay? See ya."

She drove along broad dark streets, moving from one light-washed bit of pavement to another, catching more than her share of red lights in the process. What Mark had said meshed with what she already knew, but it did not explain why Lars had kept quiet that night or why he had not told her what Campbell had said. Maybe she had been reading him wrong. Perhaps he had known all along that she was going to be fired. And it even could have been Campbell who told him Flannigan's would be sold. It was a disquieting thought. One she did not want to believe.

There was not much visiting time left but she parked and went up anyway. She would want visitors if she were stuck in a hospital bed. Besides, John needed all the support he could get. As she entered his room she heard Norm talking about how good his fried squid had been, how fruity the wine. John countered sarcastically with how light and fragrant his cup of tea had been with just a hint of orange in the Pekoe. In the next breath he demanded to know the latest gossip. She smiled. He still looked sick, but he was on the mend. When Norm told him that Lars had written the letter of reference for Campbell, John's eyebrows pulled together in a frown. He said he did not believe it. She added what Mark had told her moments before and his eyebrows rose. "I never thought they knew each other. It ever seem that way to you, Elie?"

She shook her head. "Anyway, just because he was in Mufti's when Campbell was shooting off his mouth doesn't mean he was Campbell's friend or that he agreed with him. I can't believe he wrote any letter either. . . . " At least she hoped not.

John said, "What the hell was Lars doing in a bar with Campbell in the first place? It doesn't sound right. And, when he heard him talking rubbish he should have said something. He should have defended you. . . . "

"I don't need defending, John. . . . "

"The hell you don't! Everybody does sometimes. You turning into one of those damned feminists? Besides, what are friends for except to stand up for each other. Flannigan's has always been like family, everybody pulling together and helping out. You know that." He turned back to Norm. "I don't think Lars understands that—you know, the closeness. He hasn't worked for Flannigan's long enough. I've been in here since Thursday morning and he hasn't visited or even called. At least he could have sent a card."

"Maybe Lars' divorce affected him. I heard his wife really screwed him. She got a big settlement. That could've soured him on women, maybe on people in general. He's in debt and behind in his alimony, I know that."

Elie laughed at the two grey heads nodding in unison

at this bit of wisdom and said, "Oh, for heaven's sake, you two are really reaching." She tapped Norm on the arm. "You don't get rich working for a small aviation company, you know, or haven't you looked at your pay stub lately? Or, maybe all the profits go to the dispatcher, in which case, why did I pay for my own dinner?"

John snapped, "Don't get snarky, Missy. We're trying to figure out how to keep Flannigan's afloat. Joe would expect it. Campbell has really fouled things up. If Lars hadn't written that letter we wouldn't have had to put up with that piece of shit—Sorry, Elie. I should watch my mouth."

"Listen you two, we don't know for sure that Lars really did write it. We don't even know if it really exists. None of us has seen it. We should check the signature at the very least. It just doesn't sound to me like something he would do. . . .

Neither of them looked like they wanted to hear her opinion so she gave up. A gloomy silence settled over them and both men sent withering looks in her direction. To break the silence, she asked, "John, when are they going to turn you loose?"

"What? Oh. My blood pressure. . . ." His hand flapped impotently above the covers and then lay still. "I don't know. Maybe Monday. Doctor didn't say for sure."

Visiting hours were over. Norm picked up his coat and said, "Time for the pretty ladies to tuck you in, John-boy. Sleep tight, don't let the bed bugs bite," and ducked the paperback that sailed past his ear.

12. Sunday, October 17

The world beyond the window was a white and lacy confection. Hoarfrost covered every twig of every branch and every blade of grass. It was lovely. It was also cold. In a comfortable old grey sweatsuit and sneakers Elie puttered around the kitchen putting on coffee, mixing a pitcher of orange juice, and thinking about Don. He had been gone now for a week. It seemed like an age. She missed him terribly and could only hope things were going better for him in California than they were for her at home. They probably were. They had always operated on a no-news-is-good-news basis and, except for the gloating sunburn report, she had not heard a peep from him all week. But then, maybe he was delaying the bad news until his return. Like she was.

She took her coffee into the family room and decided a fire would be just the thing. As she loaded up with wood from the stack beside the garage her breath came in little smoky puffs. She built the fire and sat crosslegged on the hooked rug in front of the hearth, cheeks flushed from the heat, watching the blaze.

With nothing better to do she got out the photos she had been meaning to sort and put in the album. On the rug she spread the prints from Flannigan's annual June picnic. The first shot was of Flannigan's baseball team that never managed to win a game with Norm, their manager. The next two were of Joe. Joe with an enormous smile presenting the golf trophy to Lars; Joe walking and talking with John, both of them holding dripping ice cream cones and both looking very serious. She studied the photos closely. Joe seemed to be the picture of health, yet less than ten days later he was noticeably ill and five weeks after that he was dead. He had been one of a kind and larger than life. She missed him.

Another envelope of pictures had been taken up at the lake in July. She smiled at the photos of Don and the kids mugging for the camera, displaying a string of fish, swamping the canoe. She could almost hear the shouts of laughter. It had been a happy two weeks. She came to a photo of herself and groaned. Don had strict orders never to take a picture of her in a swimsuit, but he always did it anyway. Suddenly there was a clamour of bike bells and voices in the drive and she hastily stuffed the offending photo under the rug.

"Hey, Mom, let us in. It's cold out here."

Grant and Sarah, Brad and Sammy, their faces red, their noses dripping, rushed inside and huddled in front of the fire.

"Is there anything to eat, Mom? We came for breakfast."

"Even if you'd had breakfast you'd still want breakfast."

She served them mushroom omelets with fresh chives and parsley, crisp bacon and mounds of toast. They ate in front of the fire, passing photos around while they chewed.

Grant said, "Hey, Mom, one of your pictures got under the rug. You hid it didn't you? Come on, 'fess up. You didn't want anybody to see that ancient swimsuit did you? Some year you really ought'a break down and get a new one."

Sammy volunteered the information that swimsuits were on sale all over town at great prices, and Sarah asked if there were any baby pictures of Grant. Elie winked and told her to come over some afternoon, and Grant howled, "Mom!"

"Are these people your relatives, Brad?"

Brad looked over Sammy's shoulder. "Nah. Those are people Mom worked with. They have a picnic every June, invite families. It's fun. That's Mom's old boss, he died a while back, and that's Grant in a three-legged race with Dad." He held up three prints she had set aside as discards. "Mom? Where did you take these?"

"At work, in September, to finish off a roll. That blur is Norm, he moved, and the other two were supposed to be shots of some really spectacular clouds."

"Circular file 'em. All you can see is the parking lot."

"Wait, who's this guy beside the little Mazda convertible?" asked Sammy.

Brad looked more closely. "Grant, come look at this."

"I'm not all that interested in Mazdas, Brad."

"No, just look."

He looked and said, "I'll be damned."

"You know him?"

"Sarah, remember when we were talking about Fiona and her noisy love life the other night? This is the guy. I'm sure."

"What?"

"Yeah, Mom. This is the guy. Who is he?"

She had to look over their shoulders and between their heads to see who they were talking about. Almost out of the frame was the rear half of a red Mazda and lifting the trunk was James Campbell. Curly had to know about this. She went straight to the phone. When he answered she almost did not recognize his voice. "Curly? Is that you? You sound dreadful."

"Just a frog in my throat. It'll clear. What do you want? I'm busy so be quick about it." A grumpy frog in his throat. She decided to make him work for the information.

"I just thought you'd like to know something, that's all. It'll keep. Probably. Sorry I bothered you. Keep warm."

"Know about what?"

"Oh, you undoubtedly know about it already. I don't know why I ever troubled you. . . . Have you seen a doctor?"

"What are you talking about?"

"It's probably not important—"

"Elie! Stop playing games. Why did you call?"

"Just to tell you something about someone."

"Who?"

"Fiona Stewart."

"What, for God's sake?"

"She had an affair last spring."

"So?"

"So, Curly, it was with James Campbell. G'by, Curly. Take care of yourself."

"Elie? Eileen!"

She hung up with a satisfied smile. Sometimes it was lovely to get your own back.

The kids rode away at noon with the last of the frost falling from the trees like light snow. Overhead the bright clear sky made it seem warmer than it really was. It seemed to Elie like a good day for a walk, a decision only partially prompted by the thought of checking out the swimsuit sales.

Friday's snow had long since disappeared and once again it looked like fall. The air was crisp and smelled of damp leaves. She walked west, past the Lamner's neat lawn that dared a leaf to fall on it, past the Smith's where the kids raked leaves to jump in and throw at each other, and past the Stevenson's (thank heaven, Mrs. S. was nowhere in sight). A block further on she crossed the street and cut obliquely across the little park with its single bench beside a single tree, the most direct route to the river.

So Campbell and Fiona had been lovers, eh? If Brad had not seen that picture she would never have known.

Fiona's advisor was dead; her exlover was dead. Never mind the rock thievery, things looked bad for Fiona. Elie did not want the boys anywhere near her. The very thought gave her shivers.

Sarah and Sammy did not liked the idea either, backing Elie when she practically ordered her sons to spend the night at the house. However, the effort to persuade them took a bit of astute horse trading. She promised the boys that if they came home they could use her car to get to campus for as long as they stayed. It was a concession she could live with. One of the argumentative sticking points was their individual opinions of Fiona. Everyone thought she was a tad peculiar, but neither of the boys believed her to be the dangerous character their mother and the girls thought she was.

With her eyes flashing warning signs, Sarah had disagreed with Grant. She held the opinion that it was better to be safe than sorry and that it was easier to give someone the benefit of the doubt at a distance.

Sammy, raising Elie's eyebrows in the process, had argued that there was probably sufficient evidence to charge Fiona with at least one count of theft under one thousand dollars; that the act of stealing indicated a lack of social responsibility regardless of the value of the items taken; and that her social irresponsibility might indicate a readiness to solve her problems by eliminating the person seen as causing them. Sammy was in prelaw.

While her thoughts meandered, Elie's feet carried her down leaf-littered sidewalks, past comfortable, slightly sleepy older homes, past a young man wrestling a heavy old storm window up a ladder. Could Fiona have killed her advisor? She would somehow have had to sneak into Flannigan's, know which plane was his, know about the air tank, insert and inflate each ball, and then disappear again. It seemed very unlikely for someone unfamiliar with the hangar. But that did not let her off the hook. Not to Elie's way of thinking. Murder is said to be a crime of passion, which led her to think it much more likely that Fiona had killed her exlover. She experienced an unexpected moment of sympathy for the girl since she certainly understood how angry you could get with James Campbell.

Discordant honking interrupted her thoughts. A flock of geese in close but lopsided V-formation, long necks stretched straight and great wings flapping, flew low over the river heading south. She stood still and watched them out of sight. As they disappeared she felt a kind of longing, as if she had been left behind. She smiled at the thought and wished them a flight without buckshot. She walked on, her thoughts rambling and by the time she joined the river bank trail, she had come to the conclusion that if solving these murders depended on her mental powers then the bad guys had little to worry about. All the same she could not let it go.

She strode along past a clump of chokecherry bushes, then on past an orange bench where an elderly couple rested. Where had Campbell been found? Under which of the many bushes? A few inches of yellow tape fluttered as she walked past what looked to be a short ash tree. She strolled on past a copse of tall leafless bushes with rust-red berries, then around a bend she stopped at a high point where she looked out over the river as it rushed along and hurled itself in a froth over the weir. She had gone far enough. It was time to turn back. Somewhere along this trail Campbell had lost his life. She wondered if his mother was living, and if she was, what agonies she was enduring. It must be awful to lose a child.

Could Fiona really have done it? Elie looked up the bank to the university and noticed the number of small paths that led from the trail, each providing easy access to the university grounds. The killer could simply have walked across campus. A student would not have been noticed at all.

Not many blocks from where Elie walked, Griffeth and Stefanyk climbed gritty stairs, walked down a dirty hall, and knocked on a door that needed fresh paint. Fiona opened it as far as the chain permitted and looked from one to the other without saying a thing.

Stefanyk said, "Ms. Stewart, this is Sergeant Griffeth. He would like to ask you a few questions. May we come in?"

"I suppose. . . ." She released the chain and stood aside. Stefanyk took a seat at the dinette table and opened his notebook. Griffeth took off his coat and settled into a beige easy chair, all the while taking in details. The place was neat and tidy and even Griffeth's stuffy nose could smell the floral room-freshener. Clearly she was a better housekeeper than the Meade boys, but their apartment, a mirror image to this one, seemed to him to have more character.

Fiona perched gingerly on the edge of the matching beige sofa as far away from Griffeth as she could get. He smiled and thanked her for the opportunity to clear up some details. He apologized for his hoarse voice, popped a cough drop in his mouth, tried to clear his throat, and finally began the interview.

He began by telling her how concerned he was that her work had apparently gone missing at the same time as Professor Essen had been killed. It was necessary, he told her, to be clear on the details because it might help catch the person responsible. When she nodded cautiously he rewarded her with his most affable smile.

"Fiona, when did you last see Professor Essen?"

"Wednesday afternoon, the sixth. I gave him my thesis draft and he said to meet him at 8:30 on Tuesday, the twelfth, to talk."

"And you think that he somehow got hold of your maps and samples without your knowledge?"

"Yeah. The last time I saw them was late afternoon of Thursday, the seventh, so it's the only thing that makes sense."

"I agree with you. He left for his trip up north the next morning. In his flight case we found an intricately marked map of Hacker Lake with your name on the back. I assume it's one of the missing items, but I'm afraid it's evidence for the time being."

"I need it. . . ."

"I know. We could probably make it available to be copied, if that would help."

"Yeah, thanks, it would. But I need the original back eventually."

"Noted. Now, I'm going to ask you what I'm asking everyone. In the week following Thanksgiving, where were you between the hours of six P.M., Wednesday the thirteenth, and one A.M., Thursday?"

"Wednesday? I'm a lab assistant and by the time I get the place cleaned up . . . I must have gotten home . . . well, I usually get home about quarter to six . . . fixed something to eat and then studied. Why?"

"Didn't go out? Anybody see you come in?"

"No to both questions."

Did she know that her advisor had been doing a project for Ev-Met Mining? No, she did not and she seemed bothered by the question.

Griffeth croaked, "That news seems to trouble you. Why?"

"Well, I didn't know, that's all. That's the company I'm supposed to work for if I ever finish my degree. It probably doesn't have anything to do with me, but Essen knew about the job offer so. . . ." She let the sentence trail off with a worried frown.

What was left of Griffeth's voice was failing fast. "Do you know if Professor Essen was acquainted with someone named James Campbell?"

She looked startled and shook her head. "How would I know who he knew? He was my advisor, not my friend."

"But, you knew Campbell. Tell me about him."

She leaned over and straightened an already tidy pile of magazines on the coffee table.

"There's nothing to be nervous about. You knew Campbell well, we know that. Tell me about him."

"I knew who he was, that's all. . . ."

He croaked gently, "You knew him better than that, Fiona. He lived with you for a while, remember? What kind of person was he?"

She looked frightened. "Just a person."

"How and where did you meet him?"

"At a party."

"Whose party? When? It could be important."

"Okay! It was a bar. Happy?" Angrily she crossed her arms and glared at him. Noticeable red blotches had appeared on her cheeks.

"Go on."

"Well, it was last spring. He'd been doing some special project or other for airport management in Edmonton, only Transport Canada cut the funding so he came here looking for work. He seemed nice enough so I included him a time or two when I was having friends over."

"And?"

"Well, then. . . . Then we. . . . Well, he seemed very interested. Like that, you know?"

"Came on pretty strong then, eh?"

Her recollections seemed painful. "Oh, yeah. He took

me out to dinner, got tickets. . . . Look, is this really important?"

"Then he moved in?"

She looked away. "Yeah. He was subletting a place and
had to move out. That's what he said, anyway. I thought it
was just until he could find another place. As soon as he
moved in everything changed."

"How?"

"He kind of tried to take over. He was always telling
me what to do, always quizzing me about my work, and he
always wanted to know where I was and who I saw. I was
just trying to do him a favour. I didn't know . . . I tried to
make him understand I wasn't interested in a serious rela-
tionship, you know? He didn't see it that way. We argued.
He had a rotten temper. It was more than I could take. I
finally worked up the courage and told him to leave."

"That when he threw stuff around?" She looked surprised. He smiled. "The walls in this building are pretty
thin. So, you kicked Campbell out and disappeared for a
while. Where'd you go?"

"That was when I did the field work for my thesis. I
was away for about two months collecting samples, taking
geomagnetic . . . sorry, you wouldn't understand."

"So you just wandered around up there doing this?"

"No, no, I set up camp at the lake where I did my stuff,
fished a little."

"If the fishing was good would you mind sharing the
name of the lake? My luck is usually rotten."

"No problem. It's a small one called Hacker Lake. Go
to the west end; there's a good place to camp and the fishing is great."

"Thanks. Campbell still around when you got back?"

"Oh yeah! He called and called. That's why I got the
answering machine, to screen the calls. I didn't want anything more to do with him."

"You said you need your samples. We found all sorts of rocks in Essen's office. Could you pick out yours if we showed them to you?"

"I don't know. . . ."

"Maybe, since you have other samples now, you don't need the originals."

"What do you mean?"

"The ones you collected Friday night. You were seen by a neighbour. Around seven-thirty wasn't it? Riding away from the Meade's on your bike, knapsack full of rocks—must have been pretty heavy."

She sat as if flattened against the back of the couch. Griffeth opened his mouth to speak but his voice had completely gone. With a look of apology he peeled another lozenge off the roll in his pocket and sucked it while he waited for her to speak. She did not, but it did not matter. Her reaction said it all.

He whispered, "Around the time of that B and E next door, did you notice anybody strange hanging about or hear anything that struck you as odd?"

She turned away from Griffeth and looked accusingly at Stefanyk. "I told you days ago that I didn't notice anything."

Griffeth looked disappointed. "Too bad. We need all the help we can get." He pulled a paper out of his pocket and made a show of skimming through it, then looked up with a smile. "I think that does it, although a question or two may still come up that I'll need to ask you later. Thanks, Fiona, I really appreciate your help."

He smiled and stood up, put on his coat and moved to the door with Carl in tow. All the while he chatted amiably in a hoarse whisper about absolutely nothing at all.

Elie's walk was invigorating and she arrived at her back door with pink cheeks and a red nose. Now that she had tons of time on her hands she decided to go walking more often. She hung up her coat, put her palms against the refrigerator door, and stretched out the backs of her legs. And, what the heck, Grant was right. She really ought to break down and get a new swimsuit. Tomorrow she would hit the sales. Trying on swimsuits wasn't *that* much of an ordeal. She laughed at the thought. All that fresh air and exercise was softening her brain.

The phone rang and for a moment or two she thought she had an obscene caller. She finally identified the whispers and gasps and said, "Hi, Curly. Why aren't you home in bed?"

"Can't. Need to talk to your boys."

"Why? They're studying in the library, or should be, but they'll be here for dinner around seven."

"Seven is fine. What are we having?" Griffeth's social graces were pathetic. She decided to give him a taste of his own medicine.

"I'll only feed you if you bring the wine. We're having chicken."

To his credit, Curly Griffeth knew a good wine. He also knew that his welcome was wearing pretty thin in the Meade household so he brought two bottles. It might have been the copious amount he had eaten, or perhaps the fact that he had consumed several glasses of the chardonnay, but for whatever reason Griffeth seemed relaxed for the first time in days. The finishing touch was a snifter of Don's brandy with coffee. He appeared to throw caution completely to the winds and tell them, in a whisper, about his interview with Fiona.

When he stopped for comments, Grant asked, "Mom, sorry for raising a sore point, but wasn't it Wednesday that you got fired and we went for burgers?"

"A day of infamy. Curly, Fiona said she stayed in

Wednesday night, right? Wrong. She almost knocked me over racing down the stairs. Grant, about what time did I get there?"

"It was after seven, maybe even seven-fifteen. When did we get back, Brad?"

"Pretty close to ten, I think. That's when we saw her again."

A pleased smile hovered on Curly's lips as he took notes. Finally, he put away his notebook and asked about Elie's pink slip. He said that copies of all eight had been found in Campbell's office and the general impression was that they were intentionally insulting and humiliating. What did Elie think?

"You've seen them so you don't need me to tell you. That's the way Campbell was. He had to demonstrate his power and everybody else's insignificance."

Griffeth snorted. "As mellow as I feel at the moment, if you told me you'd bumped off Campbell, I probably wouldn't do a thing about it."

"You expect us to believe that, I suppose?"

"Of course. Now if Fiona had received a demeaning little love note like that I could probably build a good case against her."

"Maybe, in a way, she did. From what you said, and what the boys heard, that's the way Campbell treated her."

"Something to think about. Thanks for dinner and the information, everybody." He got to his feet and reached into his pocket. "Grant, here are my keys. Please drive me home before I fall asleep."

13. Monday, October 18

A deep and overly enthusiastic male voice promised a beautiful day with moderate temperatures and a coupon for a free car wash to the first five callers with the magic word. It was another Monday morning. Car doors slammed, the engine revved, gravel crunched, and Brad and Grant were away for classes. Elie cleared the table, poured another cup of coffee, and sat down with the paper.

A few minutes later an excited Rob Gilbride called and reported he had found indicator minerals in the rock samples he had crushed. He had also found a single tiny microdiamond, cloudy, flawed, and minuscule, significant only because it was a diamond. And, he reported, a policeman named Griffeth wanted him to take a look at Essen's samples. He could hardly wait.

She had barely hung up when the phone rang again. It was Maurice and he was brimming over with good humour. "Robert and I, we have been talking, Elie. We believe that we know why Professor Essen went up there, for sure. It is common practice for the independent prospector, when he finds something that looks good, to try to sell the information to a mining company. We know that the professor had a prospecting licence and he had contacted Ev-Met Mining with a proposition to give them information about Hacker Lake. I found this out last night at my club when I happened to talk to someone very important at this company. I just happened to be at my club, you know?" Elie smiled at the vision of Maurice, master conspirator. He was having a ball.

"So, Robert has told you, yes? If he says it is good, it is

good. So . . . we don't pass by an opportunity, eh? I myself have a prospecting license. I have decided that when we finish talking I will go to the Recorder and stake a claim of at least fifteen-thousand hectares with Hacker Lake in the middle. We don't waste time. After we make the claim, we keep quiet for a while. We see what happens."

"What are you up to, Maurice? Your company going into diamond mining?"

"No, Elie. We do this for investment purposes, or maybe just to protect a very beautiful place. I will stake the claim in the name of G. Berm. Nobody will know who that is. In these matters we are always very secret. We don't want anyone to know anything until we know what we have in the ground. G. Berm, Elie. The name is from the first initials of you, your boys, Robert and me. So, what do you think?"

"How much do I have to pay?"

"For now we pay only a recording fee, which is peanuts. I take care of that. After that, we just sit. There is no requirement to do anything for a while. Even in the second year of the claim we need only spend twelve dollars a hectare on exploration. We can afford that, eh? Do not worry. There will be much time to decide what to do."

She felt a little giddy. To be involved in the hunt for diamonds, even in such an insignificant way, was a heady experience. If this was the diamond equivalent of gold fever it felt great! Her enthusiastic little tap dance across the kitchen floor was interrupted by the phone. Curly's testy rasp told her to come down to the police station right away.

"No can do, Curly. The boys have my car."

"Take a cab," he barked, and hung up.

She thought his bad temper was probably due to a hangover, and if it was, it served him right. It would not hurt him to cool his heels for a while. On the other hand, he was a policeman with ongoing murder investigations. If she had learned nothing else as a youngster, you did not mess with things like that. She called a cab.

Forty minutes later she arrived at the police station and had to endure the suspicious stare of the constable behind the service desk while he phoned up to confirm her visit. He continued to keep an eye on her while she paced the beige and brown clay tiles, waiting for her guide. Finally, a harried officer ushered her into the elevator and then down a corridor, and more or less shoved her into a small room containing three desks, a table and entirely too many people.

She stood by the door looking around. Nobody seemed to notice her at all. Across the room, Curly was holding a meeting in front of a bulletin board crowded with photos and charts. As it was he who had summoned her she waded in and joined the crowd. Maybe she could pick up an interesting tidbit of some sort. Unfortunately, as she peeked around a shoulder he spotted her, pointed to his desk, and ordered her to go sit down.

His desk top was a mess with papers and files everywhere. One file toppled as she sat and it took only the slightest nudge for Elie to get it to spill its contents. Letters, notes, bills, even one of Lars' VISA receipts from Mufti's slithered towards her. A photocopied bill told her what Campbell's new suit had cost and that the purchase date had been October seventh. A pencilled note in spiky script read, "8:45 P.M." Campbell shopped late. There was a dry cleaning receipt also dated October seventh, with "gas" written on it. Now that was interesting. One gas-soaked suit at the cleaners and a new one purchased. Well, well, well. Now, that was a surprise! A little tweak was required to free a few more sheets. There was a multipage memo written on Flannigan's stationary. As she skimmed it her face grew hot. She could not believe what she read.

"Finding all that informative? You took your sweet

time getting here, didn't you?" The raspy voice behind her sounded cross.

"It wasn't my fault. I had to take a cab. It cost me ten-fifty, double that to get back home. Are you going to reimburse me?"

He merely grunted and hauled her out of his chair and over to the table, which was partially covered by a plastic cleaning bag.

"Is this Campbell's suit?"

"It looks like it. Until he bought the new one he wore the same thing every day."

"Thank you. You may go now."

"That's it?"

"That's it." He went back to his desk with her on his heels.

"You dragged me all the way down here for that? What was the big rush?" He ignored her. She pointed to the papers spilling from the file. "Curly, do those bills mean that Campbell killed Essen?"

He sat down without answering and began to put the files haphazardly back.

"If you won't tell me that, then what about Fiona? Have you—"

"Go home, Elie."

She took a deep breath and tried again. "Okay, I'll go, but first I need to copy that memo. Can I borrow—"

"No. Go home."

"Curly, that memo is important. Haven't you read it? I need a copy."

"Go home. Campbell's dead. It doesn't matter any more."

"Like hell it doesn't," she exploded. "Seven of us were fired by that piece of human refuse with his cockamamie ideas on management. That memo—"

"Okay, okay, but later. Reporters are bugging Media

Relations, and Media and the chief are breathing down my neck. Remind me in a couple of days. Now please go away. I'm busy."

And to think she had fed him dinner and Don's brandy the night before. Curly Griffeth was a very exasperating man.

She had to part with more money to get back home and was still fuming when she arrived. She vowed that one way or another she was going to get a copy of that memo and no official run-around was going to put her off. The little red light on the answering machine blinked its greeting. Once again Norm seemed in the midst of a crisis. What could be happening now? She dialled.

"Elie, we've got a big problem. Lars didn't come in this morning and I can't get hold of him. The new manager is ready to quit! Incidentally, he seems like a nice guy. Lots of experience and he's got a pilot's licence—private—but at least he knows which end of a plane goes first. We may have a winner, but for this to happen on his first day isn't good. We've been holding the fort and rearranging instructing schedules as best we can, but we need you."

"Lars is probably just sick. There's a lot of flu going around."

"I don't think so. He would have called, and anyway why wouldn't he answer his phone? Please come in, Elie. We need you."

"I'm glad to hear it, but that's the manager's call."

"Then, will you at least go over to Lars' place? See if he's there and find out what's going on, okay? He's never done this before and with all this crazy business lately I'm worried."

"You're right, it doesn't sound like him. All right, I'll go. I'll call you later."

Norm was right. It was crazy business and it was

equally crazy for Lars not to call in at least . But then, he was keeping very much to himself lately. She had been expecting a call from him for days. There had been ample time for him to get more information, so the suspicion that he was avoiding her returned. Maybe he did not call to report because, with Campbell dead, they had nothing to worry about. On the other hand, maybe once set in motion, something like that could not be stopped. She wished she knew.

She dialled Lars' number and let it ring. His tape answered and offered to take a message. She shouted over it to get him to pick up. When he did not, she called again with the same negative result. How was she going to get to his apartment? She could not afford to take another cab, and the bus with a transfer would take over an hour. The boys had her car but she had their bikes. She wheeled one out of the garage and started off.

Lars lived in one of the several three-storey apartment buildings that made up a complex on the southeast edge of the city overlooking a golf course. It was a long ride and by the time she pedalled into the parking lot and dismounted her legs were wobbly and crying for rest.

Right away she spotted the ancient Cutlass. Lars never walked anywhere if he could help it, so that pretty well meant he was home. She locked the bike to a Tenants Parking Only sign, and in the lobby she leaned on the button beside Holmgren. There was no response.

From the few times he had entertained she knew his apartment was on the first floor overlooking the seventh hole. She went around the building on rising terrain until she identified the right balcony, found a long stick, and banged on the metal railing. When that brought no result she threw pebbles at the sliding glass door. Any normal person, even one suffering with the flu, would investigate the noise she was creating. Why did he not at least look out the window?

It might have been an optical illusion, but she thought she saw a small circle of light on his living room ceiling, the kind a table lamp might throw. She got a grip on a railing support and awkwardly, sneakers gaining purchase on the rough brick wall, she pulled herself up. By the time she landed in an untidy heap on the cement floor of the balcony she was winded and had a whole new respect for cat burglars.

She caught her breath, expecting his large frame to appear at any minute. She pressed her face to the glass door and saw that the light came from the lamp beside the couch. An untidy pile of newspapers occupied the coffee table and a pair of sneakers lay on the floor beyond it. Nothing seemed amiss.

Except. . . . She looked again. One of the sneakers seemed to have an ankle attached to it. The sliding door was locked and knocking on the glass and calling out did no good. She climbed over the railing, jumped to the grass, and ran.

A block away she wrenched the phone from a startled veterinarian's receptionist, dialled 911, then climbed back on the bike and tore back to the apartment to hunt up the caretaker. She had the worried man beside her when the ambulance and a police car careened into the lot and came to a dusty halt.

They seemed to take forever in that apartment and the long delay convinced her that Lars needed more help than anyone could give him. She was close to tears as she sat on the grass beside her bike. It was a welcome surprise when his bulk, tightly secured to the stretcher, was wheeled out. They would not have a tube in his arm and oxygen going if he was dead. She scrambled to her feet as the medical parade approached. As they passed by, a barely conscious Lars held up a single finger in mute salute.

A uniformed policeman took her by the arm and told

her Sergeant Griffeth wanted to see her right away. He loaded her, bike and all, into his cruiser. She asked him questions as they drove, but she might as well have been speaking Gaelic. All she got in the way of answers was a polite silence.

Griffeth met her at the door of his office and steered her toward his desk. "Who knows you went to that apartment?"

"Norm. He asked me to go. Lars didn't turn up for work and didn't answer the phone. Norm got worried and when he told me about it I got worried too."

"Since finding him, have you talked to anyone?"

"No."

"Good."

"Why?"

"Keep quiet about it. Don't tell anyone, Elie. I want whoever did this to think Holmgren is dead."

"Talk to me, Curly. I thought he'd taken sick."

"Sick doesn't involve stab wounds and a savage beating. Fortunately, the man is in excellent shape in spite of the blubber he carries, which, incidentally, cushioned some of the blows and also served to staunch some of the bleeding. The paramedic said it probably saved his life."

"I can't just keep quiet. I promised to call Norm. He's probably driving himself crazy wondering why I haven't."

After a moment of thought he agreed. "Okay, call. But, be careful about what you tell him. Just report that Holmgren won't be in and let him draw his own conclusions. Call from here. I want to hear what you say. And Elie, one more thing. I don't want you alone at any time, particularly at night."

She told him he was being silly, that there was absolutely no reason why she should be in any danger. But even as she spoke she noted the dead serious expression on his fatigue-lined face.

"I wouldn't have thought Holmgren was in danger and look what happened to him."

Curly's scratchy voice underscored the warning. It made her feel distinctly nervous and, with her own voice shaking a little, she made her call. It was a brief conversation that ended with Norm cursing loudly as he hung up.

It was one o'clock when Carl drove her home and unloaded her bike from the back seat. In a stiff little speech he told her to stay inside, keep her doors locked, not to admit anyone into the house but police and family, and to call right away if anything seemed amiss. She stood solemnly on the driveway and listened politely. In her own familiar surroundings the warning seemed distinctly misplaced, but she promised to follow his directions anyway.

After a sizable lunch (all that exercise had left her famished) she phoned John to tell him what she had discovered in the memo that morning at the police station. He came on the line in the middle of the first ring.

"John? How are you doing?"

"I'm not sure. I'm looking at what I was served for lunch. It's a bowl of soup that has kind of grey and black and green lumps in it. Any idea what kind it is? I'm afraid it's a specimen of some kind."

"Very funny, John. You've obviously been in there too long."

"Tell me about it. I'm just waiting to be pronounced fit as a fiddle so I can go home. Anything new and different in the outside world?"

It was a pleasure to hear him sounding more upbeat and full of energy than he had for weeks. "John, I was down at the police station and—"

"They finally caught up with you, eh?"

"—I got a fast look at a copy of one of Campbell's files. He had a whole hit list with reasons to let people go and dates and checkmarks after the names of everyone he had fired. There was also a page which outlined his plans for the pension fund. He'd already changed the terms without consulting anyone. It indicated that you were fired so you would get only a termination payment. By the time anyone else was ready to retire there wouldn't even have been a pension fund!"

"The little shit! Who all was on that list? What about Norm and Lars?"

"Yeah, both I think. But, the list was a long one and, like I said, I only got a fast look. I'm going to get a copy, John, and—"

"Just a minute. . . ." She heard a woman's voice in the background and he whispered, "I have to go. Doctor's here. Thanks for the news."

Some things were looking up. John was going home and, with what she had learned, they both stood a good chance of getting their jobs back. She just wished she had been able to spend more time looking at that file. There was nothing that had flat-out said she had been fired because she was a woman, but she found it interesting that she was the only one whose sex had been noted in the memo. Mainly, it looked as if Campbell had been determined to get rid of all the old timers, undoubtedly because they most vociferously opposed his plans. She was going to sit on Curly until he coughed up that copy. Maybe, if she played her cards right, she could persuade him to let her read the other stuff, too. She stretched out her legs, which were beginning to stiffen up. What a morning!

Curly had told her he thought the attack on Lars had occurred sometime Sunday evening. The only good thing about it was that he had been sitting at her dining room table at the time. For once he could not consider her a suspect. That was a relief. He had also said that the blows to the heads of both Lars and Campbell could have been delivered by the same weapon. Therefore, he was looking for a person known to both Campbell and Holmgren. That was a terrifying thought because the only people she could think of who fit the bill were Flannigan's employees. She did not want to believe that. There had to be someone else. Maybe Fiona?

The more she thought about it the better the possibility seemed. She reasoned that Fiona and Campbell had met at Mufti's and Lars had been seen there. Therefore, it was possible—maybe even probable—that Lars was acquainted with Fiona. In fact, she was the type of girl Elie thought Lars would find attractive. Then too, Fiona was the only person she could think of who also had close contact with Professor Jake Essen, and that put her right back at the top of the suspect list. Did it not?

But, what if Lars had never met her? What then? It was inconceivable that anybody at Flannigan's could be a cold-blooded killer. It was a small company. Elie knew everyone, some better than others, but she could think of no one who would do such an awful thing. But then, that is what friends and neighbours always tell reporters as the culprit is led away.

She wandered around the house wishing she had not promised to stay indoors. She felt confined. Aimless glances out one window after another only confirmed that the windows wanted washing. She stood in the living room and watched as leaves detached themselves from the weeping birch to swirl about in the wind like a flock of confused canaries before settling gently on the grass. It meant more raking. Why was it that trees never dropped all their leaves at once?

A tense and subdued Fiona sat across the small dinette table from Sergeant Griffeth who, this time, had come alone. The remains of her macaroni and cheese congealed on the plate she had pushed aside. "Sure you don't want a hamburger or fries? I brought two of everything. It's on the department. . . ."

She shook her head. He opened the bag so that the reek of onions that followed him into the room intensified. He arranged his dinner, picnic fashion, in front of him.

"Why are you here again, Sergeant?"

He produced a pocket tape recorder and placed it beside the french fries. "It's dinner time, I'm hungry, and I thought this was a fast and easy way to clear up some final details. Incidentally, it won't be public until tomorrow, but we believe we know who killed your advisor."

"Who?"

"Sorry, the name will have to wait for the announcement. I just thought you'd be relieved to know." Griffeth took the top off his burger and squeezed mustard from a plastic pouch. He studied the result. "Does this look like double onion to you? I ordered double onion."

Fiona wrinkled her nose. "Trust me, Sergeant, that's double onion."

"Go ahead, help yourself to those fries. My wife says they're better for you than these burgers. She says this is fat pretending to be protein." He took a big bite, chewed and swallowed. "This is not double onion."

"What details do you need to clear up this time?"

He talked around another bite. "Mmph. 'bout those rocks. Mrs. Meade is a very nice lady and she says she doesn't want to press charges for stealing them from her garden." Actually, Elie had said, "People would think I was crazy person if I pressed charges for something like that!", but it was close enough.

"You did take them. I know you did."

She looked at the table and confirmed it with a little nod.

"I don't know anything about geology. What made Essen want your research so badly?"

"I think he was trying to sell it to Ev-Met. He must have gone to Hacker Lake to get photos, some samples of his own, and to see what the place looked like. He'd have to be at least a little familiar with the area to convince the company the material was his. But if he sold them my work there wouldn't have been any reason for them to hire me. I could have been in trouble with my degree too, if he claimed it was at least partially his work. I don't know what I would have done if that had happened.

"Anyway, the department assigned me a new advisor and he wanted to meet last Saturday morning. He told me to bring all my work. Everything! I printed out another copy of my thesis draft, that was no problem, and I had my field notes, but I didn't have maps or my samples. . . ."

"So you helped yourself to Mrs. Meade's garden and hoped those rocks looked enough like yours to fool the professor." Griffeth shook his head and made little tsk-tsk noises. "Fiona, why didn't you tell me this before?"

"I didn't think my problems had anything to do with anything."

"Not really an excuse, is it? Now, let's talk about the night Campbell died. Your previous statement was that you were home all evening from about five-thirty, but that was a lie, wasn't it? We know you left your apartment at approximately seven-fifteen and returned shortly before ten."

She groaned and looked at the ceiling. Griffeth went right on eating, apparently oblivious but watching closely.

Sounding resigned, she said, "Okay, I know I should have told you. It's just that it's so complicated! Remember I told you about Campbell bothering the hell out of me so I had to screen my calls?" Griffeth nodded. "Well, he got someone I know to phone me a little after seven, Wednesday night. As soon as I started talking, James got on the line. He insisted he had something real important to tell me, but he'd been leaving that message for days. This time he said it was something about Dr. Essen, that he couldn't talk about it on the phone, and to meet him in the bar of a restaurant on Eighth Street at seven-thirty . . ."

Griffeth popped the top on a can of soda and glanced at the tape recorder to make sure it was still running.

". . . so anyway, when I got there, he just sat there smiling that superior smile of his. I asked him what he wanted to tell me, but he didn't say anything till he'd ordered us a couple of beers. Even then he didn't say much and I was sitting there thinking I'd been had, you know? I was starting to leave but he grabbed my hand and said he loved me and what he'd done proved it and that I should take him back. I asked him what he was talking about and he said that he'd fixed it so that Essen wouldn't give me any more trouble. . . ."

She stopped talking and stared into the middle distance for so long that Griffeth finally asked, "What trouble was he talking about?"

"See, this is my second year in graduate school. It's a two-year program. The whole of last year Essen ignored me completely. He was absolutely useless as an advisor. I did everything on my own." She went on to explain how, when Essen had seen her field work, he had become too friendly, too helpful. How he had tried to get her to write a paper with him, a paper he would receive credit for, even though he had done none of the work.

"So when he backed off and agreed to read your thesis, you thought he'd changed his mind?"

"Yeah, I did. Now, I know different. It was just another way for him to get his hands on everything I'd done." Her face crumpled. Griffeth almost felt sorry for her.

"Fiona, how did Campbell find out about Essen?"

"He knew I wanted another supervisor when he lived here. A couple of weeks ago I met up with a bunch of other grad students at Mufti's and I told them what Essen was doing. I wanted their advice, you know? Anyway, James was there, hanging around, buying beer for everybody, and being a total dweeb. He heard everything."

"Okay. Tell me exactly what he said Wednesday night."

"He didn't spell it out. He just acted like I should be grateful! I didn't like what I was hearing so I just got up and ran out of there. He followed me into the parking lot, and he was yelling. To get away I had to run across Eighth Street in the middle of traffic. I almost got myself killed. I ran into an alley and hid behind a supermarket garbage bin. I haven't any idea how long I was there, but I stayed until I thought it was safe to go home."

"Was he driving that night?"

"Probably. I sure didn't stop to find out. Yeah, I'm pretty sure . . . he must have been. That car was his pride and joy."

"Fiona, did you kill James Campbell?"

"No! No, I didn't. That's the honest-to-god truth. I think I hated him and he really had me scared, but I didn't kill him."

Griffeth thought that probably, finally, she had told the truth. He wadded up his napkin and began to tidy up the table, stuffing the wrappers back in the bag.

"Thanks for your cooperation, Fiona. Sure you don't want this extra burger and fries? You could freeze it or something." He looked dubiously at his cold and soggy offering and did not blame her for emphatically turning it down.

"Sergeant? Since I'm telling you stuff . . . I'm pretty sure that the real reason James kept calling me was because he knew what I'd found. I think he was more interested in the diamonds than he ever was in me."

Her voice was unsteady and it looked to Griffeth like tears could flow at any moment. But once her confession had started she seemed determined to hold nothing back. He had seen it happen many times before and did not say a word.

"And . . . and on Thanksgiving weekend? When the power went out? That person who tried to break in to Brad's and Grant's place next door? I think that was James trying to get in here. He still had a key. When I kicked him out he wouldn't give it back so I changed the lock, but I don't think he knew that. With the power out it was pitch black and you couldn't see a thing. I heard someone rattle my door knob and fiddle with the lock. It scared me. I kept quiet and pretended I wasn't here. Then, a few minutes later, I heard the same thing happen next door. That really did it. I knew he was determined. I had to report it—I wanted him caught—but I didn't want to get involved, you know? That's why I said I was calling from a car phone and hung up real quick without saying who I was. See, if it was James and his key didn't work, he would keep trying thinking he just got the wrong door in the dark."

Elie was fixing dinner. She stood at the counter, chopping onions and blinking back tears. The phone rang but she ignored it until she heard Norm's voice talking over the taped message. She picked up the receiver with smelly hands and a mighty sniffle.

"Elie? You okay?"

"Onions."

"Oh. Look, I know it's late notice but, if you can make it, Phil—that's the new manager, Phil Mylanski—wants you out here for an interview at seven tonight. That okay by you? It doesn't give you much time…"

"Great! I'll be there, no problem. Tell me more about him. What's he like?"

"Oh, I think you'll like him well enough. Sorry, gotta go . . . medevac on the frequency. See you soon. . . ."

14. Monday Night, October 18

In Griffeth's opinion the temperature in the office was no longer too hot. In fact, he felt chilled. He sat at his desk in his overcoat and scarf, pawing through files. He hoped Fiona was right about Campbell and the key. That attempted break-in was an irritant, mostly due to the fact that Elie would not leave it alone.

He found the manila envelope containing the pathology report. Campbell's every mark and bruise had been meticulously listed in the neat little boxes. With a wet thumb he found the page in his notebook where he had taken down Brad's statement about hitting the would-be thief with his flashlight. He referred again to the report and the photos, smiling over the dimensions and appearance of the contusion on Campbell's outer left shoulder. It was not, of course, absolute proof but under the circumstances it was good enough. He tossed the file back on his overflowing desk top, straightened his back and wondered if any of the others in the room could hear the pops and cracks coming from his spine.

He opened the top desk drawer, stirred the contents, pulled out a roll of stomach mints, popped one in his mouth, burped, and decided Martha was right about his diet. From now on, no more burgers. He slouched in his chair, sucking the mint, thinking. Essen's case was all wrapped up and, thanks to a routine report of pilferage, he even knew where the beach balls came from. Ten had gone missing from an outside display at the Co-op Home Centre near the airport. Nine were found inflated in the fuel tanks of the plane, and one uninflated ball was found behind the spare tire in the Mazda's trunk. It was a nice tidy little detail.

But there was no time to bask in his own glory. There was still Campbell and the attack on Holmgren to figure out. Could Campbell have been killed because he murdered Essen? No. Not if the same person had attacked Holmgren. It did not fit. As with Campbell, there had been blows to the head, but with Holmgren there had been even greater violence. Why? Was he dealing with someone who was growing to like violence and so inflicted greater damage with each attack? Lord, he hoped not.

Holmgren had to know his assailant. He had buzzed him in and opened the door. Judging from the condition of the apartment it was probably an unexpected caller. Griffeth wanted Holmgren to tell him who it was—hoping to God he would remember and be able to tell him. The results of concussion were so damned unpredictable.

Carl's sudden appearance in front of his desk startled him. "What is it, Carl?"

"You feeling all right, Sergeant?"

"Just tired, and I should have had tea and toast for dinner instead of the garbage I ate. Anything to report?"

"A uniformed—same guy that was tailing Mrs Meade—is posted outside Holmgren's door like you wanted. Sergeant, I saw him when they brought him down from surgery. He's hooked up with tubes and monitors all over the place. The doctor said that under the circumstances he's doing real good, but I don't know."

"Any idea when he can talk to us?"

"The nurse wouldn't even guess. She said they had to keep him sedated and even if he was conscious he might not make much sense. They'll call when he comes to."

"We'll just have to be patient. Go get yourself some dinner but don't take long. We've got work to do yet tonight." He slid lower in his chair and yawned.

Stefanyk felt like telling him to go home to bed, but it was not his place to comment. The man was grey all over, not quite the colour of the guy he had just seen in hospital, but not far from it, either. Why could he not just admit he was sick? He threw his coat over his arm and left the sergeant to himself.

In a matter of seconds Griffeth looked like he was asleep, but he was not. Not quite. His head rested against the back of the chair with his wadded-up scarf serving as a cushion. His feet rested on top of the muddle in the bottom drawer, his overcoat was lapped across his stomach, his eyelids drooped.

If he could not get a simple identification from Holmgren then he would have to work it out the hard way. When had the attack occurred? From the clean dishes in the washer and the skillet found soaking in cold soapy water, he surmised Holmgren had been doing dishes. When did a bachelor do his dishes?

He yawned and crossed his arms. Ever since Elie's morning visit to the office something had been nagging him. Until now there had not been time to try to figure out what it was. It had to do with papers she managed to see on his desk. She asked him something and shouted at him. . . . Damn the woman and her questions anyway. She had entirely too many of them. Holmgren was a worry, but the doctor would call if there was a change . . . Carl would return soon . . . His eyelids closed. His breathing deepened. He snored.

The sky was a velvety midnight blue and the stars resembled tiny chips of ice, or maybe those were diamonds winking and sparkling up there. Whatever they were, they looked as cold as Elie felt. Bundled up in coat, scarf, toque, and gloves she wheeled the bike out of the garage and set off for the airport and her appointment.

She rode steadily, afraid that she would be late. There had been little time to prepare. Just time enough for a quick shower, a change of clothes, and a note to the boys. When she got to the road running behind the row of hangars she was a little out of breath. She stopped to check her watch and discovered she had made very good time. Since she did not want to look overly anxious by arriving too early, she pushed the bike and walked the rest of the way, her feet crunching gravel with every step.

She wondered what Curly would say if he knew she was walking alone on a poorly lit and empty road, not locked safely inside her house. Probably give her a lively lecture about people who refused good advice. It was not advice but information she wanted, information about this new manager, Phil Mala . . . Phil Miller . . . no. Phil Mylanski. That was it. She wished Norm had told her more about him. She trudged along trying to remember what he had said. A pilot, that was positive. Norm seemed to approve of him, that was promising. Not much to go on.

She turned down the drive to the hangar just as most of the parking lot lights went out. Now the only source of light was from a lamp placed high on a neighbouring hangar. It was not much. She stopped in her tracks. What was going on? Was the place shut down because of Lars? That had to be it. They thought he was dead.

When her eyes had adjusted she began to walk again. Still, the roadway was so dark she tripped on a rough place. She turned into the smaller parking lot, passed a barely visible single car parked nose to fence, and located the bike rack in the far corner. She locked the bike, then sorted her keys by feel. It was easier to enter by the same south door she had used the other night than walk all the way around, but the lamp over the door was not lit, which made it difficult to fit the key.

When she finally got the door open she was surprised

to find the short hallway dark and the entire hangar lit by only a single light at lowest power. Nobody was around. At this time of night the place was usually a den of activity, but then, she reminded herself, everybody had probably been given time off because of Lars.

In the quiet gloom she wound her way through the maze of parked planes, exiting into the darkened corridor and crossing the hall to the women's locker-room. She still had plenty of time. She hung up her coat, ran a comb through her hair, dusted off her good leather boots, and plucked burrs off her slacks. Walking had not been such a great idea after all.

It was years since she had been interviewed for a job and she was apprehensive. What would he ask? She checked her appearance in the full—length mirror on the back of the door, trying to see what he would see. Did she appear competent and self-assured? She retrieved her log book from her purse. Surely, if nothing else, her many thousands of hours would speak for themselves. She combed her hair again and touched up her lipstick. Anything stuck to her teeth? She took a deep breath, squared her shoulders and opened the door. Show time.

Along the dim corridor light spilled from the dispatch office. She was tempted to visit Norm, but there was no time for any last minute words of wisdom. She went on through to the flight school. It was a perfect night for flying but the place was deserted. Only a few security lights were on to light her way.

She stood in the gloomy corridor and at exactly 7:00 she quietly knocked at the door of Joe's old office. That was the way she still thought of it, Joe's office. In reply she heard the ticks and creaks of the big, old building. She had never noticed it before, but some of the noises sounded almost like footsteps. She knocked again and waited, not sure what to do. Maybe Mr. Mylanski was waiting for her somewhere else. But where else would he be? Again she knocked, more loudly this time. She tried the knob. "Excuse me, Mr Mylanski. . . ." The door was locked. This was embarrassing. Did she have the time wrong? Or the day?

Griffeth opened his eyes and blinked for a moment, straightened, and stretched. He did not feel refreshed exactly but he did feel better. Except for his mouth. His mouth tasted terrible. He fetched himself some coffee, opened a file, and got back to work. When Carl returned he was smiling. "Keep your coat on. Let's go get us a killer."

Carl looked blank. "I don't get you. You talk to Holmgren?"

"Not yet. When Elie was in this morning I found her looking at a file. She was particularly interested in a list of terminations. Campbell had put marks against the names of everyone who had received notice. There were eight of them, but Elie's count was seven. The eighth is the dispatcher, Norm Driscoll. If he was fired, how come he's still working? We should have a little chat with him, don't you think?"

The phone was ringing in the dispatch office, echoing down the empty corridor when she left the flight school. Thank God Norm was working late. How could she have got it wrong? She was sure he had said seven tonight. From the door it was clear he was not in his office, but every light in the place was lit and the radios were on. He would be back in a minute. She went in and helped herself to coffee.

"Flannigan's flight forty-seven on the frequency." The voice jumped at her from the scanner. "We're fifty back and ahead of schedule, estimating at 19:35 local. Require four taxis."

She walked to the window and looked out into the darkened parking lot. Was that Norm out there? What was he doing? From the light spilling from the window she could just make him out standing beside a car, peering into it. He straightened, walked to the centre of the lot and looked around. He took his time about it. Then, flapping his arms against the cold, he walked toward the staff entrance. She heard the door open and bang shut and his quick footsteps in the corridor. Almost immediately she heard another door squeak and knew he had gone into the men's locker-room.

"Courier three on company frequency."

Why was looking at a car more important than tending his radios? It was very unusual for someone who took his job so seriously.

"Flannigan's dispatch, courier three on the frequency. Require refuelling for a quick turn around. Get the bowser to meet us on ramp four."

Where was he? Something was not right, not by a long shot.

"Flannigan's dispatch, courier three on the frequency. Five, four, three, two, one; how do you read?"

"Dispatch, flight forty-seven. Make that five taxis."

With sudden certainty she knew she had to get out of there. She left the office in a rush and, leather heels loud on the tiles, ran to the women's locker room for her coat. She pulled, pushed, and banged, but the door would not open. With her heart in her throat, she rushed across the hall and through the door into the dark hangar to thread her way between shadowy planes. She was midway across when the door she had just come through opened and banged shut. Her skin prickled and her heart beat wildly. She dropped to her hands and knees, ducked beneath the wing of a twin-engine aircraft and out the other side, banging her head in the process. She had to get to the door, she had to get out. Staying low she kept moving, working her way as fast, as quietly, as invisibly as possible toward the south door.

Who was back there? Was anyone there? She could see in the dark fairly well now. With an old Cessna 172 for cover she cautiously peeked through its windows. A man inched along the far wall. Her breath caught. He held something in his right hand and looked steadily in her direction. She froze. He could not see her, she knew he could not see her, common sense said he could not see her in the dark.

His free hand stretched for something on the wall. It was the switch box. He was turning on the lights! Overhead the bulbs began to hum as, one by one, current reached them and the filaments began to glow. She inched away from the 172, treading carefully, keeping low. The short hallway was close behind, but she had run out of cover. She had to move now. . . .

The plexiglas of the Cessna exploded, shards and splinters striking her head and back like hundreds of ferocious stinging bees as she ran. She moved fast in the growing brightness, but it seemed to take forever to cover the short distance. As she entered the hallway something pinged against the wall beside her head. Breathing hard she ran down the hall and slammed full tilt against the emergency bar. The door burst open and she stumbled outside into the blessed enveloping dark where she could hide.

On the quiet residential street Carl slammed on the brakes. "You're right. Her car's gone. . . ." He watched the lights in his rear-view mirror grow brighter. "Wait, that's her car—" but Griffeth was already out of the cruiser and running.

Even before the car had stopped in the drive he grasped the door handle and yanked it open. "Elie?" Grant gaped at him from the driver's seat.

"Where's your mother?"

"Inside, I guess. Why? What's the matter?"

"Come on." Griffeth trotted ahead and impatiently rang the doorbell while Grant fitted his key in the lock.

Inside, Brad flipped light switches on his way to the kitchen, which smelled of raw onion. On the refrigerator door an apple magnet held a note.

"What's the problem, Sergeant? Sounds like she's gone to get her job back."

"Sounds like she's gone to get herself killed. "

"What? That's not much of a joke!"

"I agree. Stay put. Move it, Carl."

Brad pounded after them bellowing, "What's wrong? What's going on?"

Elie tried to ignore the cold. Cold was much better than dead. Her blazer was little protection against the freezing temperatures and nothing at all against the wind. She turned up the collar, clutched the front together, and shivered as she ran. The parking lot was full of ruts and depressions and in the almost total darkness she had to lift her feet high to keep from tripping.

She had to get as far from the hangar as possible, get to the road if she could. The bike was useless, locked to the rack, the keys in the pocket of her coat. As fast as she dared she moved toward the lone car, its outline faintly visible, a marker, darker than anything else. If it was open she could get out of the wind, or at the very least, she could hide behind it, maybe under it if she had to.

Nobody had followed her out the door. She would have heard it, would have seen the light. She reached the car and tried the doors. It was locked. She paused beside it, listening, watching the shadows.

God, she was cold. Every muscle was taut and trembling. Her fingers were stiff and becoming numb. She moved into deepest shadow between the car and the fence and stopped. Was that movement? She thought she sensed movement. Had someone come round the corner of the building from the west? She was pretty sure. It would not be good to be caught in such a tiny space. She ducked down and moved back to the driver's side and crouched beside the front tire. No sense taking chances.

Her full attention was focused on hearing the least sound, her eyes strained for the slightest movement. All was quiet for a long while. Just when she thought she had been mistaken and was about to move, she heard a scuff come from near the building. A misstep? She stayed where she was, barely breathing. Someone was there. Then footsteps on gravel, just two, and endless moments of silence. Then more steps, coming closer, stopping.

"Elie. Don't be afraid, Elie. I'll protect you." The familiar voice was quiet, almost soothing. Even as he spoke she was moving away from the car into deeper shadow.

He stepped closer to the car and called out again, his voice a horrible, surreal mixture of reassurance and menace. Again she moved, turning to face his voice. She could see his silhouette faintly outlined against the meagre light from the west. He was behind the car, watching it, his gun pointing at it. Slowly she crouched, her fingertips against the cold ground for balance. She grit her teeth and shifted slightly to stop her freezing legs from cramping.

"Elie?" The rear and front car windows shattered, tiny pieces tinkling as they hit the hood. Before the sound stopped ringing in her ears she was further away. From the car she had travelled in an arc, now she was ten feet behind him. She wanted to run and keep running until she was home and safe, but if she ran, if she made a single sound, he would know where she was.

His voice was angry now. "Elie! Where the hell are you?" He fired again, the ping and rattle suggesting he had hit the fence. She tried to remember how many times he had fired, but even if she could it would not do her any good. She did not know what kind of gun it was.

"Dammit, Elie, I don't want to do this. . . . Elie? Please, Elie. Come to me, Elie."

He began to turn, searching the shadows that hid her. If he kept turning he would find her for sure. He was so close even a random shot would likely hit her. To have a chance of escape the gun had to go. She had no choice. None at all. She stayed low and drove hard, her arms circling just above his knees, bringing him down hard against the rear of the car. His gun flew and bounced off the trunk. She heard it hit the ground.

The blow stunned him. It stunned her, too, but now she was on her feet and running as fast as she could toward the light and the road. She heard footsteps close behind her and knew she had not been quick enough. His hand stretched out. She felt it brush her shoulder and in that instant her toe caught and she went down, gravel burning into her hands and knees. He fell over her, his weight and momentum knocking the wind out of her. She lay face down gasping for breath. She heard him scramble up and his footsteps circling. She heard a snap and raised her head in time to see the wink of a knife blade. Then he was coming at her.

She rolled just in time and he halted and backed off. She was sitting now, facing him. He began to circle again, talking softly as if to himself. She turned with him. Suddenly he rushed, the knife held in front of him ready to slash. Her only protection were her feet. She rocked onto her back, her legs lashing out. Again he stopped, again he circled. She turned, propelling herself with hands, elbows and feet, stones cutting and bruising, keeping her feet between them.

"Bitch!" It was a snarl. "You found the will, didn't you. That's how Lars knew Flannigan's was up for sale. Damn you both to hell. You're traitors!" He ran first in one direction then the other looking for a way to get at her, talking constantly. "You betrayed Joe, betrayed Flannigan's, you betrayed me!" He dodged back and forth and she had to scramble, holding her head up to keep him in view. Her neck muscles screamed and she rested her head briefly on the ground. It was the moment he was waiting for and he lunged. She saw him come and drew her knees to her chest, straightening her legs to propel him over her head to land in a heap. In one motion she rolled to her hands and knees and launched herself across his back. He had lost the knife. She saw it just a body-length away, too far away for her to reach. He struggled and twisted, trying to inch forward toward it. She clung like a barnacle, but her weight was not enough to keep him down. He bucked and kicked and tried to roll over. She dug her toes into the gravel and shifted her weight to push against his rising shoulder. He bucked again and she felt a stabbing pain as her knee hit the ground. She brought it up and kneed him as hard as she could in the ribs and in return got an elbow in the breast. The elbow struck again, painfully hard, making her gasp, and loosen her grip. He felt her weaken and renewed his efforts to dislodge her, twisting, bucking, his elbow jabbing repeatedly as she did her best to hang on.

Each blow caused waves of blinding pain, tears stung her eyes. She knew she could not hang on much longer. She swung a leg over to straddle his back and, in a rage, grabbed fistfuls of his hair and banged his face on the ground once, twice, as hard as she could, again and again, yelling over and over, "How could you? How could you? Why, John, why?"

15. Near Midnight, October 18

The emergency department of University Hospital was doing a booming business. Each of the curtained-off cubicles was filled. To Elie, who occupied one of them, it sounded like yet another ambulance was on its way. Maybe there was a full moon. Maybe the local knife-and-gun club was holding its semimonthly meeting. Maybe the knife-and-gun club was inducting new punks into its membership by the light of the moon. She grinned at the stain on the ceiling tile and pulled the blankets up to her chin. She felt a little silly and her muscles felt all rubbery. That was okay. It was the influence of a syringe full of Valium. She had been awake—and absurdly happy—while they dug gravel out of her hands, knees, and elbows, cleaned her cuts and scrapes, and stitched up her head. The wounds while plentiful were superficial, thank God. In spite of that, the doctor warned her she would be stiff, sore, and had better not look in the mirror for a while. It would be just like the time when she took a tumble while learning to ride a bike that was far too big for her. Talk about your second childhoods.

She shifted under the blankets, being careful not to roll off the narrow stretcher. Even such a small movement hurt. Cautiously she moved her hands over her body and found bandages everywhere. She touched her face and then her head. Lordy! They had used enough gauze and thread to make a Hallowe'en costume. The way she must look she could go out trick-or-treating and really clean up. She giggled at the thought.

A nurse pulled aside the curtain and came in to check on her. She took her temperature and wound a blood pressure cuff around her arm. "How are you feeling?"

"Like I fell off the back of a truck."

"Good. Shows that everything's working. Your boys are here. Want to see them?"

The nurse scrawled something on a paper clipped to a board and left. A moment later Grant pushed the curtain aside, his face a picture of concern. "How're you doing, Mom?"

She smiled up at him. "A bit sore, but I'm fine. You don't need to worry."

Brad manœuvred himself and three cups through the curtains after his brother. "Here you go. Tea. It's from the machine but it's got loads of milk and sugar just like the doctor ordered. You'll be warm in no time."

She sat up and took a cup in gauze-swaddled hands, trying not to spill on the blanket. The hot sweet tea tasted wonderful. She hurt all over now and she still felt cold, but at least she had stopped shivering.

"Tell me what happened after they carted me off."

"We don't know much. For a while there they seemed to think Brad and I were part of the problem."

"That's ridiculous!"

"Tell us about it! We got there in time to see them hustle you into the cruiser and race away. We started back to where we'd left the car so we could follow, but we saw two cops with guns drawn sneaking up on it. It sort of seemed like a good idea to stay out of their way. Anyway, Brad here had to pee and that's how we found Norm. He was trussed up in the shower with the water running. We thought he was dead until he moaned when we pulled him out."

Brad said, "I got to work on the wet strips of cloth binding him while Grant, our noble track star, took off at the speed of light to get help."

"Yeah. That was a mistake. They thought I was a bad guy trying to escape. The best I could do was to lead them back to the locker room. Then the place was crawling with winded cops. They evidently weren't amused by the chase because they grabbed both of us, wrestled us down, and held us to the floor even though we weren't resisting. We kept trying to explain but everybody was shouting and nobody was listening. Then they dragged us out—literally—took our shoes, cuffed us, and left us sitting in the hall. It took a while for Sergeant Griffeth to hear about us and come turn us loose. He was pissed off that we'd followed him but, hey, what did he expect? He said he thought you'd gone to get killed! We weren't about to just sit on our hands, for crissakes!"

"I love you guys, you know that? But are you sure you're both all right? Have you been checked?"

"The sergeant made them give us a once-over. It was a waste of time. We've got a few bruises but that's about it."

"How is Norm?"

Grant said, "I don't know. They stuffed him into the ambulance dripping wet. I don't even know which hospital they took him to."

"I hate to even ask about John."

Brad said, "Yeah, well that bastard oughta die and save everybody a lot of trouble. I saw his face, Mom. You did a real job on him. I'm going to nominate you for mascot of the wrestling team."

"We're real proud of you, Mom. Just promise you'll never get that mad at *us*, okay?"

Curly appeared inside the curtain with a cup of coffee and a large grin. "A toast to the only forty-something woman I know with a tackle worthy of the Saskatchewan Roughriders and a brain almost as keen as my own. A toast to health, long life, and beauty!"

"Modest, as always, and very funny. In spite of that, thank you."

"I wasn't being funny." He sounded aggrieved. "I hate

to admit it but if you hadn't looked at my files. . . ."

"I was talking about that crack about beauty."

"Not to worry. That little cut on your cheek looks fetching. It'll heal in no time and the stitches on your head won't show at all once your hair grows back. As for your hands, knees, and elbows, the doctor said he hadn't seen anything like that on anybody since his eight-year-old slid into first base last spring. He was impressed."

"How reassuring. Are you going to meet Don's plane and explain why his wife is black and blue and stitched together?"

"No."

"Coward. Grant, did that doctor say when I could go home?"

"As soon as you're warm enough. Hypothermia is nothing to mess with."

"I'm warm, I'm warm. . . ."

As soon as they walked in the back door, Grant said, "Mom, it's almost midnight, go on up to bed. I'll get you an extra blanket. You'll feel better in the morning."

She smiled and wondered if he realized he had spoken almost the exact words he had heard so often from her. She wanted to say how proud she was of them both but a lump had formed in her throat. Instead, she put her arms around Grant the quiet and Brad the boisterous and hugged them both fiercely.

Finally she said, "You know, I'm not the least bit sleepy. How does cocoa sound?" So they sat in front of the fire that Grant had stoked to white heat, drank cocoa, and talked. At about one in the morning somebody rapped on the back door.

"I knew you'd all still be up. How about some of that cocoa for me and Carl?"

"It's in the kitchen, help yourselves. Curly, how did you know it was John?"

"Elie, can't you ever stop with the questions? Carl, get us some cocoa." He took off his coat and warmed his hands in front of the hearth. "The truth, if you must know, is that I thought it was Norm. Remember, you always talked about seven people who were fired but that memo said eight. I should have twigged to the discrepancy sooner, but I didn't. Norm was odd man out and Carl and I went to his house to have a little chat. He wasn't there. I called Flannigan's but got no answer. I called you. You didn't answer and you were supposed to be home. It worried me. We came over to make sure Driscoll wasn't causing you problems and found your message. When we got to Flannigan's we could tell right away where you were because you were yelling something awful. Then, thanks to your boys, we found Norm. He was awake and able to talk before the ambulance arrived."

"Will he be all right?"

"He has a concussion and a few stitches, a lot of bruising and a dislocated shoulder, but nothing broken. The doctor says he'll be fine, but they're keeping him overnight. I just talked to him and more than anything, he was worried about you. He said he noticed a car pull in and park about six forty-five and shortly after that the lights shorted out. At least that's what he thought. Time passed and when seven o'clock came and went and he hadn't seen or heard you he got worried. He went out and checked the car. It was John's. He said he couldn't figure out why it was there. Then he thought that maybe he had come to clean out his locker, but he thought it was kind of strange for him not to have stuck his head in his office to say hello. He said he thought he better check. He went in to the locker room and surprised John getting into his overalls. John surprised him with a fist in the face. Norm went down hitting his head. John jumped on him and hit him again. Incidentally, Driscoll said to thank you for banging around in the hall like you did. He's convinced that it saved his life. He said he was half out of it so he wasn't sure about everything that happened, but the one thing he is sure about is that when John heard your ruckus in the hall he quit banging on him and dragged him into the shower. John tore a strip from a towel to tie Norm's arms behind him and plugged the drain with the rest. He turned on the water and went after you. Driscoll says he figures he was left to drown but the shock of the cold water revived him enough so that he managed to clear the drain before he finally passed out. He said the next thing he knew he was soaking wet and your kids were bending over him."

"Thank God he's all right. You know, I wondered about those lights. They went out just as I arrived."

"John turned them off. He also locked the ladies locker so you couldn't get your stuff. It never occurred to him that you'd go out without your coat."

"Curly, what about Campbell? Did John . . . ?"

"Yes, afraid so. He confessed before they took him into surgery. He seemed to want to get it off his chest. In case you're wondering, you reshaped his nose for him. He lost a lot of blood in the process and he's not exactly pretty. They're still working on him. You did a good job."

"But how, Curly?"

"After he found his notice Wednesday night he left Flannigan's all right, but he didn't go home. He drove around for a while. He spotted Campbell's Mazda outside a restaurant and waited for him to come out. Before long he did, yelling and swearing and chasing after a girl. You'll love this, Elie. It was Fiona. He said it was easy to make it look like he was keeping a drunk from driving home. He took Campbell's keys away from him, got him into the Mazda, and drove to the university lot overlooking the river bank. He forced him out and down to the path where he returned the keys because, he said, he just wanted to reason with him. He should have known better. Campbell wasn't about to listen to anything. He started yelling that he was being kidnapped and John lost it. They were near a big bush and he said he took a socket wrench out of his coveralls, hit Campbell a couple of times as hard as he could and pushed him under the branches. Then he just walked up to the hospital and got a cab back to the restaurant. He picked up his own car and drove home. Simple."

"Horrible!"

"Sergeant?" Carl had a question. "Who attacked Holmgren? It couldn't have been Gardner, he was still in hospital."

Elie said, "Not necessarily. Unfortunately, I think John could have done it. I talked to him this afternoon and, now that I think of it, the conversation was pretty strange. For one thing, he was trying to be funny, which isn't like him. For another, he sounded pretty keyed up, but I thought he was just anxious to be released. He also talked about the lunch he said had just been served, but it was after one o'clock and hospital lunch is over by then. He uses a cellular so he could have been anywhere. On Saturday night he said he thought he might be discharged on Monday but he could as easily have been released on Sunday."

"Thanks for that. It's easy to check and if he is as talkative tomorrow as he was tonight, he should readily admit to it. Why would he want to go after Holmgren? That's what I want to know."

"He blamed Lars for getting Campbell hired, thought he'd written a letter of recommendation for him."

Griffeth had pulled his notebook out and was scratching away. "That answers a big question. We found a copy of the letter in Campbell's office, a credit card receipt of Holmgren's, and some practice signatures in his desk. It looks like Campbell might have forged it. Pretty careless of him to leave it around. He should have destroyed it, but

216 *PLANE DEATH*

then he didn't expect anyone to rummage around in his desk. He undoubtedly didn't expect to die, either. That type never does.

"We found something else in Campbell's office that might interest you, Elie. Offers for the company. There were two contenders. One was a regional airline with what looked like a fair price. The other was a small outfit from outside the province that was offering much less. For a sizeable up-front consideration Campbell was acting as agent for the second company. He was also promised he would stay on as manager if they were successful."

"Question, Sergeant?"

"Shoot, Grant."

"Why did John try to hurt Mom? It doesn't make sense. They'd been friends for years."

"Good question. Elie?"

"More of the same is all I can think of. Friday night he thought I might be trying to defend Lars. He actually said as much. Tonight he called me a traitor and said something about us betraying everybody. I guess he meant Lars and me. He was friendly enough on the phone today, though. I told him about seeing Campbell's hit list in your office and said I was trying to get a copy."

"Ahh. That could be why he went after you. He told me that after he found his notice he went to tell Norm about it, but found him on the phone. He saw the same kind of envelope sitting on the end of the counter and simply took it. Norm never knew he'd been fired too. Strange as it seems, Elie, John was trying to look after Flannigan's and his friends. You were a friend, but you were also a threat. You saw that list and wanted a copy. You also ask questions and that made him nervous. Sooner or later you might have put the pieces together."

"I'm not so sure about that. My great ideas about Fiona didn't amount to much. In fact, I was pretty hard on her. I feel kind of sorry for her. The poor kid is really having problems."

Curly burst out laughing. "Just like you, El. Don't forget that she has a streak of dishonesty that got her into this in the first place. A lot of her problems are her own fault."

"I guess. But. . . ."

"El, you were just trying to protect your kids. It's the mother tiger syndrome. Forget it."

Stiffly she shifted her position on the couch and grimaced with the effort. "Curly, tonight John was going on about my having seen the will. I haven't, but the other day, when I was visiting Walter he suggested that Joe might have hidden it somewhere in that old logo that hung in his office. Is there any way you can check it out?"

"Funny you should mention that. That's exactly where we found it—or rather Carl found it—when we searched Campbell's office. Stop yawning and tell them about it, Constable."

"Well. . . ." Carl, turned a lovely shade of pink as he put his cocoa cup on the coffee table and fumbled in his pocket for his notebook.

"For heaven sake just tell them, Carl. You aren't testifying in court."

"Yessir. Well, it was kind of an accident really. I went to move that big logo thing out of the closet to make sure there was nothing else in there. It was heavier than I imagined and it kind of got away from me. But not to worry, you can hardly notice the dent at all. Well, I decided to just leave it leaning against the wall and that's when I noticed the envelope stuck in the back of the frame. It was one of those oversized, heavy, dark-coloured ones that're made to look like leather and close with a string in the back. It said Last Will and Testament in big fancy script."

"Carl brought it to my attention right away."

"I knew there had to be a will. Joe was such a great planner."

"But he couldn't plan when he would die, Elie. His illness felled him in a hurry. That envelope contained his original will made long ago and a handwritten codicil dated ten days before he died—which was the last day he was in the office. There was also a letter explaining what he'd done and why. He knew he was dying. The lawyer he always used had retired to Phoenix, and the new one he consulted wanted to follow the prescribed route of many meetings to assess the wishes and mental state of his new client before actually making out a fresh will. Joe knew there wasn't time for that which is why he hand-wrote the codicil. Judging from the look of the writing, he was exhausted when he finished. Maybe he planned to put it into his bank safety deposit vault the next day and so tucked it into the logo for overnight safe-keeping. Or, maybe he realized-as the dying frequently do-that he had run out of time and put the will in the logo hoping someone like you or Norm would twig to its location."

"Did you read the will? What did it say?"

"The letter explained it all. Joe wanted the company broken up and sold. According to the files we found, he'd been receiving pretty good offers over the last year or so for the scheduled service. He figured that selling was better than being forced out of business, which is what would eventually have happened. You can't fight the big boys forever. He wanted the proceeds of the sale to be distributed among the staff along with the suggestion that they use the money to purchase the charter business and the flight school."

"Really?!"

"Really. John knew what Joe intended, you know. He told me Joe told him last summer when he knew he was ill."

"So why would he be upset? I don't understand, Curly."

"Because he didn't want the will found. He wanted the company to stay the way it had always been. He thought if nobody could find the will, it would. Simple as that. His whole life was Flannigan's and selling the company was, to him, like losing his family. He's a damn fine engineer, you can't find a better one, but he's always been single-minded, and very intense and high-strung. With all the stress, I'm afraid he went over the edge."

"It's our fault—my fault—for not insisting he slow down and take a holiday."

"Don't kid yourself. He never would have listened. He thought the place depended on him being there every minute."

"You're probably right. It's sad. What about Mr. Mylanski?"

"He didn't know a thing about any appointment with you. John phoned a secretary at quitting time saying that he was Mylanski. He told her to arrange the interview and she turned it over to Norm."

"What I want to know is who broke into our apartment back in September?"

Griffeth turned his somewhat bloodshot gaze on Brad, who sat heavy-lidded but determined on the floor beside his mother. "We may never know for sure, but I think it had to be the great Professor Essen himself. It appears that he started putting his plan together as soon as he saw those rocks Fiona swiped from you last spring. After she came back from Hacker Lake with maps and fresh samples he tried to get her to write a paper with him so he could legally get his hands on her material. She didn't go for that so he moved to plan B. He had to have samples of his own to show Ev-Met in the early stages so he broke in and took yours."

"How about when the power was out?"

"That was Campbell. He was trying to get into Fiona's place and got the wrong door in the dark."

"And Campbell really did kill Essen?"

"The beach ball bully himself. He knew what Fiona was on to and he intended to profit from it one way or another. From what she had told him he was afraid that the professor intended to get his hands on the diamonds that he had plans for himself. Then Essen's plane unexpectedly went in for that lengthy repair. Campbell saw his chance and he took it. He knew Essen was headed for his cabin, and what better place to have an accident than in the bush? With a little luck he might never be found. Campbell put his plan together in a hurry and used what he could find: beach balls. Whatever else, you have to give him credit for improvisation."

"I hate to give him credit for anything. Everybody, it's really late. Curly, please give my regards to Martha. I'm afraid that if you don't get home before long she won't even remember who you are."

"You're tossing me out?"

"On your ear, my friend. On your ear."

16. Thursday, October 21

"You're sure we'll be in time, Elie?" Walter was a nervous traveller who, given his head, would arrive at an airport the day before a flight to make sure he didn't miss it.

"Positive. You have tons of time. Relax."

She pulled into the airport parking lot and unloaded his luggage from the hatchback. He was off for his latest one man show. Days before his paintings had been lovingly and carefully crated and air shipped to Vancouver.

"When does Don's plane arrive?"

"Not long after yours takes off. Perfect timing." It was not really. Don's plane did not land for another two hours. But the wait was nothing; she was anxious to see him. Besides, for the time being, she had nothing else to do.

They joined the check-in queue. "Are you going to tell him everything?"

"Of course. In the first place, he's bound to notice my scrapes and bruises. To explain that I'll have to start at the beginning. He'll probably be upset, but he should know what happened. Anyway, we don't keep secrets."

"And everything's back to normal, your job and all. That should help some."

"A great deal. I go back to work the first of November. It also looks like the new manager is settling in well. Did I tell you that Sergeant Griffeth found Joe's will where you said it would be? Flannigan's scheduled service will be sold to that regional airline, the proceeds will go to staff, and we're buying the charter business and flight school. Until the sale is approved, it's business as usual."

It did not hurt any that she was a part owner in a

potential diamond mine, either. Their little group now had another member. When Elie had pointed out that it was Fiona who had recognized that Brad's rocks were kimberlite, and she who had done the mapping, Maurice changed the claim name to G.F. Berm.

Walter stepped up to the ticket clerk and reluctantly surrendered his luggage. He was always convinced he would never see it again. When he rejoined Elie he was clutching his boarding pass as if it were a life preserver.

"Do you want a book or magazine?"

"No thanks." He thrust the pass at her. "Is this a window seat? I forgot to ask."

"It's a window seat over the wing. It should be smooth."

"Where is the emergency exit?"

"Walter, that's why they have those little safety feature cards in the seat back pockets. There should be an exit near you. . . ."

"Good. Now tell me about that fellow in hospital? Is he going to be all right?"

"Lars? I don't know. I saw him for a few minutes this morning. He's still in pretty rough shape and it's going to take a long time for him to recover. He's afraid that it might be the end of his flying career. He's pretty depressed. You know, he's a very big man and I couldn't understand how John was able to hurt him so badly. When I asked him about it, he told me that John had just dropped by on Sunday evening. It surprised him because he thought John was still in hospital. Naturally, he invited him in and, he said, as soon as John was through the door he started asking questions. Among other things, he wanted to know if Lars had written that letter of recommendation for Campbell. Since Lars thought John was a friend he told him what he wanted to know. He told him that he'd met Campbell in Mufti's over the summer and had groused to him about how badly behind in his alimony he was. When Joe died Campbell learned that a manager would be appointed and he immediately went to Lars and asked him to help him get the job. He needed a letter of reference and promised Lars a hefty raise if he became manager. Of course the raise never materialized and Campbell held the letter over his head. It explains a great deal."

"So he did write it?"

"Yes, unfortunately he did. He must really have been desperate, but all the same, I'm surprised and disappointed that he fell for it. Anyway, that's why Lars wanted into that office so badly, he wanted to find the letter and destroy it. He never did find it, but he succeeded in planting a VISA receipt and some signatures in a drawer in the hope that, if the letter were ever discovered, it might look like a forgery. That's what Griffeth believes it is."

"And, knowing you, you aren't going to tell him either. Right?"

"What good would it do? Anyway, Lars has enough trouble as it is."

"You still haven't told me how he was hurt so badly."

"When Lars went to the kitchen to make coffee John followed him. Lars said it seemed a natural thing to do since they were talking. He had been doing dishes and generally cleaning up. There were dishes, utensils, and knives on the drainboard. He said he was reaching to the top of the cabinet for the coffee can when he felt something hit him hard in the side of his chest. He said he could hardly breath and saw blood on his shirt. He didn't know what had happened, but he remembers hearing John shouting at him, calling him a traitor and telling him to die. He didn't know why. He said he was very dizzy and just stood there hanging on to the counter, trying not to fall down. He realized he needed help and tried to make it to the phone beside the couch. He never got there. That's all he remembers."

"That's awful!"

"You're right, it is. What's worse is that Griffeth says that John believes that what he did was perfectly justified. It's scary."

A small child ran away from a harried parent, tumbled over a suitcase and started to howl. Walter looked disgusted and said, "I hope that child isn't on my plane!"

His flight was called. Elie walked him to the security gate and waved as he disappeared. Then, with so much time to kill she bought a magazine and sat down to wait for her husband's flight to arrive. It would be so nice to have him home again. She had missed him. She was also anxious to learn how his trip had gone. It meant so much.

She roamed around, unable to sit. At the front of the terminal she looked out the window at the cabs and cars disgorging passengers, unloading baggage and tearing off again. She walked past travellers, single or in groups, each a unit self-enclosed and separate from all others. She looked through the clear spot in a frosted security door at the taxiways and runways, at the planes maneuvering on the apron. Her path returned her to the central corridor where she turned into the airport shop. She looked at everything, going up one aisle and down the next, ending at the newspapers and magazines, one of which she bought. The arrivals monitor overhead said there was still time to waste so she bought a cup of coffee she really did not want.

As she passed the florist's display case she caught sight of her reflection in the glass and smoothed the jacket of the smart, new, red pant suit she had purchased to replace the one that had been shredded. It was a very becoming outfit that had the added benefit of covering the worst of her bruises and scrapes. She had also carefully applied the makeup that she rarely wore, and her favourite gold earrings. She wanted to look her very best and, judging from the appreciative glances she got from a passing Air

Canada first officer, she did.

Sipping coffee and thumbing through the pages of a magazine to check what was passing for fashion this season killed some time. Finally, Don's plane drew up to the gate. No matter where he sat on a plane he was always one of the last to appear. When she spotted him she felt a little thrill of excitement, like the beating of wings. The California sun had tanned his broad face and lightened his dark brown hair. He even had a new and different hair cut. Oh, he looked good! Elie smoothed the jacket of her new pantsuit, put a hand to her short chestnut hair, and hoped all her lipstick was not on that styrofoam coffee cup she had just thrown away. Don saw her, smiled, and held up a small gold box with a large silver bow. It was a sure sign his trip had gone well. She smiled happily. Never mind the stitches, bruises, and scrapes. This was going to be a very good night.